# THE FALL OF THE KING

# THE
# FALL
## OF THE
# KING

*JOHANNES V. JENSEN*

TRANSLATED BY *ALAN G. BOWER*

UNIVERSITY OF MINNESOTA PRESS

MINNEAPOLIS

LONDON

Originally published in Danish as *Kongens Fald* (in three volumes) in 1900–1901 by Det Nordiske Forlag, Copenhagen.

First published in the United States in 1992 by Mermaid Press

First University of Minnesota Press edition, 2012

Published by the University of Minnesota Press
111 Third Avenue South, Suite 290
Minneapolis, MN 55401-2520
http://www.upress.umn.edu

LIBRARY OF CONGRESS CATALOGING-IN-PUBLICATION DATA
Jensen, Johannes V. (Johannes Vilhelm), 1873–1950, author.
The fall of the king / Johannes V. Jensen ; translated by Alan G. Bower.
— First University of Minnesota Press edition.
ISBN 978-0-8166-7754-2 (pb : alk. paper)
1. Denmark—History—1448–1660—Fiction. I. Bower, Alan G., 1931– translator.
II. Jensen, Johannes V. (Johannes Vilhelm), 1873–1950. *Kongens fald*. English (Bower). III. Title.
PT8175.J5K6213 2011
839.8'1372—dc23                                        2011037297

# Contents

# THE DEATH OF SPRING

# 1. Mikkel

The road bore to the left over a bridge, then in through the village of Serritslev. The roadsides were covered with dark grass and yellow wild flowers, and the fields were touched here and there with white, a mist of flowers in the dusk. The sun had set and the air was cool and clear, cloudless but without stars.

A load of hay came rolling in from the countryside to the village of Serritslev, slow and swaying on the poor road. Creeping along in the twilight through the narrow village street, it looked like a big animal, shaggy and short-legged, trundling off deep in thought, sniffing the ground.

The wagon stopped outside Serritslev Inn and the sweaty horses turned their heads to the side and chomped the bit. They were glad enough to stop for a while. The driver eased himself down onto the doubletree, stretched his legs over to the ground, and fastened the reins. Turning to the porch, he shouted in, and then he blew his nose with his thumb.

"Anyone around, eh?"

At once the windows were glowing—had they lit a lamp in there? A girl appeared immediately in the doorway. The driver wanted to wet his whistle. While he waited for his drink there was a stirring up in the load of hay. A pair of long legs stretched down carefully, feeling for the doubletree while their owner lay on his stomach, grunting heavily. But down he came, and then he stood shaking himself, a tall, bony fellow with a cowl over his head.

"Skål," he said as the driver tossed the reddish schnapps down and coughed properly. Maybe the driver would like to stay

3

a bit longer? They could always go in and have another one for the road, you know.

But when they came into the light the driver stopped short at the door, awestruck, and his companion faltered too. In the middle of the room at the table sat four fine mercenaries from the Saxon Guard, which had recently come to Copenhagen. They sported great finery, with slashed red sleeves, plumes, and beards that struck the eye like a festive bonfire. Leaning up against the table and benches were swords and spears, excellent weapons. Anyone could see that the fall of the leather straps spoke of skillful use. All four turned their heads, but then they looked quickly at each other again and talked on.

The girl brought two mugs of beer over to the door and set a candle on the little table there. She had hardly gone when one of the soldiers in the middle of the room straightened up on the bench and burst out laughing.

"Just look at him over there, the one with the cowl. That beer's good for what ails him!" He was speaking German.

The others looked over good-naturedly, but they couldn't help laughing either. The lanky fellow was just drinking. Standing there with knees bent and a big pointed nose sticking out of his cowl over the beer, he did indeed present a comical picture. When he was finished drinking he sat down leisurely. The light fell on his eyes and he squinted over at the table, half affronted, half scornful, like a man with a philosophical bent.

Then one of the soldiers stood up. He took a few steps across the room and began to speak politely in German.

"We didn't mean anything by our laughter. Would you do us the honor of joining us for a glass of wine?"

"Thank you," said the tall young man in German, going over to the table with much bowing and scraping. Before he stepped over the bench and sat down, he nodded to each and gave his

4

name: "Mikkel Thøgersen, university student." Then he fell to running his fingers through his hair and rubbing his palms over his rough cheeks. He heard four names mentioned, one of which sounded Danish, and he saw a glass of blood-red wine glowing before him. And then their toast, "Prosit!"

"To your health, gentlemen!" said Mikkel Thøgersen in German, drinking with careful dignity and straightening his gaunt frame as the wine ran down into him. He glanced quickly across the table, then stared at one of the soldiers, the youngest, who was sitting with his head resting on his hand. It was a firm, white hand, with no veins or bony knuckles to be seen. The fingers buried themselves in his light brown hair. The expression on his face was sad, and it made Mikkel suddenly think of a tightrope walker that he had once seen at a fair. The young acrobat had been sitting alone in a corner, doing nothing. Sick, probably.

And now Mikkel remembered that suffering young face. The one across the table had exactly the same eyes. Furthermore, it seemed to Mikkel that he had seen him before. Who was it? Where had it been? He looked like a nobleman.

Once again the glass stood full in front of Mikkel Thøgersen. He drank deeply and with elaborate courtesy, but he was distracted with the effort to remember and confused by the face on the other side of the table. There was something mysterious about that brown head. And now the young man was turning and facing him. His arms were set at a remarkable distance from each other—he was unusually well built. Why was he sad then? Gaiety would seem more in keeping with his appearance.

The talk ran on. The four German soldiers treated Mikkel courteously and inspired complete confidence in him. After all, they could not know that he was called "Stork" in town. Mikkel spoke a broken, eager German, but he became flustered again

5

and again because he couldn't help thinking about his nickname. But on the other hand, neither were these Germans aware that he was known in an exclusive circle as a composer of Latin odes and couplets. . . . Why didn't that young man there say anything?

Otte Iversen, that was the name! So that was who it was! And in a flash Mikkel saw a gray, dilapidated portal, a wall, and a turret—back home in Jutland. He felt himself standing outside, insignificant and wretched. He had been there several times, a long time ago, but only once had he seen him. . . . So it really was the same Otte Iversen, the young son at the manor. He had caught sight of him in the courtyard, a slender boy that he had thought of ever since. He was standing there in the middle of a pack of dogs, with a ruffled falcon on his thumb. And now he was sitting here, fully grown, slim as a girl.

The soldiers chuckled. Mikkel Thøgersen pulled himself together and drank again.

The driver appeared in the doorway. "I'm leaving now," he said, setting a bag and a little straw basket full of eggs on the floor just inside and shutting the door behind him. It was Mikkel's things, the fruit of his tramp through the countryside. So there was his ignominy, laid bare down by the door. He turned his back on it, embarrassed.

But the German soldiers laughed and came up with an idea. Nothing at all wrong with eggs! And so, humiliated and happy at the same time, Mikkel passed the eggs around and they were all sucked, just as they were. Otte Iversen didn't want any, and he still didn't say anything.

Then Mikkel Thøgersen sat down on the bench, ardent and awkward and amiable. The marvelous wine eased his heaviness, and yet he felt hopelessly discouraged. His heart reached out eagerly to these carefree soldiers, but at the same time he was

6

afraid of falling under their sway—and his whole spirit began to float, to ebb and flow. He stole a glance at Otte Iversen, loving, mistrusting, fawning. . . . Could it be that he didn't recognize him? No, just as well if he didn't.

One of the German mercenaries had a cleft in his upper lip, only poorly covered by his moustache. He couldn't speak clearly, and Mikkel Thøgersen, listening to his sloppy speech, was sadly amused. Now he was warmed by everything he saw and heard. But even as the wine and the feeling of well-being mellowed him, he was growing hard deeper down. He felt a raw coldness rising up, but he held it down and got a grip on himself.

The three Germans crowded together over at the counter, leaving Mikkel Thøgersen and Otte Iversen alone at the table. Neither of them said anything, and Mikkel tried to draw into himself. He looked down into the darkness between the table and the bench and felt a bitter loneliness. And then he tried to resign himself, sighing and drawing his lath-like legs in under him, drying the sweat off his forehead and pulling himself together. Otte Iversen sat turning his cup, still looking as if he were sick.

When the soldiers came back, now with all sorts of newly discovered drinks, Mikkel Thøgersen was more composed, drinking sensibly and quietly. They were all guzzling now and thinking of nothing else. Otte Iversen emptied his cup as often as it was filled, and this changed him not a bit. Clas, the one with the cleft lip, livened things up with a song, which sounded curious to say the least.

Mikkel Thøgersen picked up one of the great two-handed swords, testing it in his hand, and they showed him different grips. Each time the sharp tip was pointed at him, a pang went down his backbone like an ice-cold wind—which surprised him, since he was usually not afraid of a blade.

7

And Clas sang …

> First the battle's thunder,
> Then the pikes and spears,
> And then he's six feet under—
> Tell me what he hears.

> Chances are he'd rather
> Hear a smart tattoo
> Than any parson's blather—
> Tell me, wouldn't you?

Half of the words leaked out in his beard. And then they treated each other to war stories, tales of skirmishes one place and another—swish! swish!—tales of victory and mortal danger and . . .

"Heinrich, do you remember that blonde Lenore?" shouted Clas exuberantly. Yes, Heinrich remembered Lenore. The story poured out of his mouth at once and Clas and Samuel writhed in laughter.

But Mikkel Thøgersen remained silent, wincing under this flood of bawdry. He stole a glance at Otte Iversen—and he was the only one to see a smile on the haughty young face, an imperceptible curve of the lips, as if he had caught a disgusting smell.

Mikkel could hardly breathe, and he passed his hand again and again over his face.

But Heinrich went on with gusto. Otte Iversen turned in his place at the table and threw one leg over the other. When the story finally came to an end it was dead still, as though his gloominess had been noticed. Feeling perhaps that he was the cause of the lull, Otte Iversen turned back to the table as if to stand by his opinion, seeking out the narrator's eye with a cold stare.

Heinrich seemed taken aback, but then Samuel stepped in with another story. He was not young so it was not one about love. He told instead of a certain mad slaughter he had once taken part in, one where they had stomped the guts out of people with their boot heels and choked them in their own filth. This tale seemed to make the air in the room sharper and fresher to breathe, and Clas's eager questions were those of a connoisseur. Suddenly convulsed by Clas's odd speech defect, Mikkel Thøgersen lifted his nose and guffawed. Then Otte Iversen looked up reluctantly and twisted his lips wryly, as if by compulsion. Finally he too threw his head back and laughed, but his laughter was more like a loud clatter, breaking off sharply. Then he just sat there, withdrawn as before.

A little later they left in order to slip back into Copenhagen before the gates were closed. When they came outside Mikkel Thøgersen felt once again the distance between himself and the soldiers. He hung back, and he left them as soon as they came in through Northgate. The mercenaries went on toward the center of town. Mikkel stood looking after them for a moment before he turned left and headed home.

## 2. Nighttime in Copenhagen

Mikkel Thøgersen lived in a house just across from the palisades out toward Pustervig, and there he shared a loft room with another student, Ove Gabriel. When Mikkel came in Ove was still up, studying by the light of a tallow candle as usual. He glanced up from his papers, and then he went on reading. Mikkel dumped down at the other end of the table and pulled over some of his notebooks. This was the scene when he had left in the morning—nothing had changed since then.

Mikkel breathed heavily. Ove Gabriel looked up at him and slowly waved a cupped hand past his face.

"You've been drinking," he said. He was just making an observation: Mikkel had been out carousing. And he could keep on staring unblinkingly with wide, moralizing eyes, and they wouldn't even water. Mikkel Thøgersen had had this staunch and praiseworthy face in front of him for three years, with Ove Gabriel's eloquent silence sitting in judgment over him at every moment. Now Ove Gabriel's blameless eyes would follow him and skewer him with disapproval, with real malice, until he wilted on his chair. In a moment Ove Gabriel would remark, "Remember now, it's my candle we're reading with."

Mikkel Thøgersen got up and opened the roof hatch. He was so tall that his whole torso stuck up through the hatch. This was his way of escaping Ove Gabriel's scrutiny.

Oh, the air was cool and the stars were shining high overhead! On both sides the thatched roofs arched their backs, like animals sleeping with their heads hidden. Down in the street the watchman was making his rounds, shining his light up on closed doors. On the other side of the palisades the water shimmered and a star was reflected between the rushes in the moat. The countryside lay silent out in the mossy green darkness, and far out from the lakes there came the dense, insistent music of frogs. The town had fallen asleep. The water lapped gently at the piles in the moat. Somewhere on a roof far away a love-sick cat was agonizing.

Mikkel Thøgersen turned in the narrow space and, leaning sharply backward, he looked up at the chimney and the stars. He felt dizzy, and it was as if he were sliding out on his two bare feet over a sheaf of knives. But it made no difference, for he could bear his torment no longer. It would be better to dangle from a rope right up in the middle of the sky—this would perhaps be more in accord with the giddiness he felt in his heart. Mikkel turned and leaned his arms on the cold roof.

Susanna! he thought. Susanna. And then he felt such tenderness that all mute and lifeless things around him seemed to be infused with spirit and given a heart. The hushed houses remained silent but radiated sheer goodness. The stars glimmered passionately. The soft silence pulsed, and the surface of the bay was ruffled by the wind. The dark air itself seemed to shudder, like a creature musing over its secrets and its fate.

But just because Mikkel had secretly spoken the name, he felt deep sadness—and then meanness. He shook himself and collected his thoughts.

Listen! Voices could be heard down in the town. With the shouts came a vision of lighted rooms and things happening.

Mikkel Thøgersen lowered himself down into the room again. Ove Gabriel was standing naked on the floor, ready to go to bed. His eyes spoke of accomplishment and he glowed like a wax candle burning serenely.

"You're pretty gaunt. It's funny that your soul stays in you," said Mikkel, chuckling in a badgering way. He looked up and down Ove Gabriel's body, which hung together like the carcass of a poor, worn-out cow. Ove Gabriel pushed himself under the fur blanket, and when he had settled down he folded his hands and fired off a verse at his roommate. *"Et nunc extingue lucem!"* he added smugly.

Blow out the candle, blow out the candle! thought Mikkel. It wouldn't take much of a puff. He bent over and blew the little dip out. Then he took his spiked stick and groped his way down the steps. Above him he heard Ove Gabriel's self-satisfied voice as he said his prayers.

It was past the time when it was permitted to be on the streets, but Mikkel Thøgersen went out anyway. He took a sharp right down Pile Street, but after going a short way he began to hang back, and he finally stopped. There was not a soul to be seen. All the houses were dark, and the trees in the gardens stood close, resting their leafy crowns against each other. On all sides there was the fragrance of trees bursting into leaf, warm and sharp like after a rain.

Mikkel went on slowly. When he passed the corner he could hear them singing vigil in the Cloister of St. Clara. The voices, muffled by the walls but easily heard, were entreating, as if they were coming from prisoners down under the ground. And Mikkel could imagine the crucifix, looming there, red and blue in the half-light.

He stopped outside a garden between two fairly tall houses, with a picket fence on the street side, and here he stood for a few minutes. Now and then the leaves rustled quietly, as if they were falling into a pile. The dew-covered edge of the gable glistened in the starlight. . . . Then he moved on hesitantly.

Down around the central square there was still life and light. It was the foreign mercenaries, who couldn't stay in their quarters—but there were also many townspeople among them.

12

Mikkel Thøgersen was going to turn down Købmager Street and go home, but then he ran into a group of soldiers swarming down on him in very high spirits.

"Why, it's our learned friend again!" shouted one of them, and there was no mistaking his twisted speech. It was the four he had met out in Serritslev, together with a few others. Clas took him by the arm, urging him to come with them, and Mikkel couldn't refuse. So they roamed about, out of one merchant's shop and into another, having a drink in each one. Mikkel wanted to cut loose like the others, but he couldn't because he saw that Otte Iversen was still somber and dejected. He also knew of course that the men had only taken up with him because they found him amusing.

They passed through Højbro Square, and here they were joined by a thin, yellow-hosed fellow who told them something that seemed to make a great impression on them. They sped up the street and the whole party swept around the corner to Hysken Street. Mikkel Thøgersen, forgotten by the others, stood for a moment and looked around. The castle lay dark and silent, and the only thing that moved was a yawl, which lay rocking in the moat by the bridge struts. The tower in the distance stretched leisurely upward, gazing out through apertures that looked like puckered little eyes. Mikkel mumbled to himself a few verses from Vergil—about the eternal night and the one who holds watch.

Should he go home now and lie listening to Ove Gabriel's snoring? No. Mikkel lowered his head and followed the others. The fact that they had left him standing there didn't necessarily mean that they no longer wanted his company.

At several places on Hysken Street there was light. Mikkel slipped past the closed gates, noticing the special odor that he remembered here, the odor of bast mats and muscat. He had vague images of caravans from India, camel dung, drought.

13

Voices could be heard from Conrad Vincens' shop, and the door stood open. Mikkel Thøgersen moved up cautiously and looked in. All the men were standing around the room, and it was clear that something unusual was going on. Mikkel couldn't bring himself to go in, but he crept over to where he could see without being noticed. And then he made out a figure there beside the great set of scales. He recognized the young nobleman, the king's sixteen-year-old son Christian. Mikkel started and flushed, stepping back a pace, uneasy and upset. The image of Prince Christian at that moment never left him. He was standing with his legs slightly apart, wearing greenish-white hose and red poulaines, half facing Mikkel. Over his shoulders and down onto his chest hung a golden chain. In his left hand he held a bunch of expensive grapes, and from time to time he would pluck one off with his right hand and eat it. Mikkel could clearly see his fine, smooth face, with a delicate shadow about the chin, just the beginnings of a dark beard. But Mikkel was especially surprised by the eyes. They were small and tilted slightly upward toward the temples, and they shone brightly. The back of the prince's head was large and his throat was full. Now he was turning his head and nodding to an ecstatically fawning Conrad Vincens. His hair was of a rich, dark red color.

Oh, but I have red hair too, thought Mikkel.

Such seriousness in the face of that maturing youth—no, now he was laughing and his eyes were full of merriment. Such composure! Amazing! That was how a real human being should look.

Mikkel stared and his eyes grew misty. Unwittingly, he sighed aloud as he gave himself over to adoration. He noted carefully what was happening now. All the men were moving about the prince with elegant bearing or standing in graceful postures. One came forward and with a flourish swept the feathers of his barret backward on the floor, and then another spoke

14

with a broad smile and bowed. Beakers were raised and drained to the prince's health, while he nodded in the same way to everyone, with his chin in against his chest. Conrad Vincens tripped about in a pure fever and with a halo around his head.

But there was one who moved about at his ease, a hunchbacked little fellow in gaudy clothing. When someone spoke to him he jerked one leg out to the side and answered saucily, like a pug standing on its hind legs, yapping. Mikkel could see that he always thrust his right cheek out with his tongue when he had said something. At one time they all laughed—even the prince smiled—and the dwarf thrust his tongue violently into his cheek. At that point Mikkel also laughed—he too could appreciate this. How refined and restrained those voices! Two large ambergris candles were burning. In the very back of the shop Otte Iversen was standing, alone, yet apparently in a good mood. Mikkel didn't have much interest in him at the moment, however.

For a long time Mikkel Thøgersen stood absorbed, taking his fill of the colors in the shop and the picture of the carefree men. He felt that a little ray of favor also fell on him outside. When all the men began to mill about, preparing to come out, Mikkel drew back quickly. He watched the entire party swarm gaily out onto the street and directly over into wealthy Martin Gälze's shop, and at this point Mikkel could observe Prince Christian's manner of walking.

Mikkel wandered around town for a couple of hours more. Long past midnight he saw his German friends again, just as they were turning into a notorious back alley down by the shore. They did not notice him, and it could be heard from their voices that they were far gone now. Otte Iversen was no longer with them.

The next day all the townspeople of Copenhagen saw a wagon mounted on a tall house just opposite the central square, all four wheels astride the roof ridge. In the night someone had taken it to pieces, lugged the parts up on the roof, and put them together there. Before noon the whole town knew that it was Prince Christian who had masterminded the escapade.

# 3. The Dreamer

It was very late in the day when Mikkel Thøgersen woke, and he lay for a time before he was fully awake. He had had such a strange dream, but now he couldn't remember it.

The light fell from the roof hatch right down into the miserable room. Ove Gabriel had left for lectures much earlier, but he could still smell him. He wrinkled his nose in disgust.

Could anything happen today? Was it worthwhile to get up and offer himself to Fate out in town among the people? Mikkel pondered. Actually, nothing decisive had happened yesterday, and yet he felt those experiences so strongly. He had been given a wrench somehow. All values had sunk even lower. He felt that he could no longer bear his situation in life.

Mikkel lay up against the wall and thought, his eyes fixed directly ahead. A moment later, beginning to think of Susanna, he bent his head back and closed his eyes. At once he became aware of a great gnawing hunger, and he got up and reached for his clothes.

Mikkel had nothing. He lived like the sparrows, scraping through each day by the grace of God and man. While he was putting on the red leather trousers that he hated, he considered where he should go begging today. He decided to try his luck in the countryside, where students and other riffraff from town had not taken advantage of people so much.

It was a fine day in May. Mikkel went out briskly through Northgate, but when the fields stretched out before his eyes he felt bewildered by the delight of it all, and almost shyly he looked up in the sky. The green rye was already well up and the earth gave off a springlike fragrance. What was it now this reminded him of? There was a blessed warmth from the sun.

Mikkel strode along the road, looking around on all sides. Surely it was his lucky day, and he felt buoyant and at ease.

Yes, it was his lucky day, and Mikkel lost no time in using it. Soon he was sitting comfortably at a farm out by the lakes, a cheerful place, where they set out hearty food for him without any folderol and without any hangdog piety. The farmer poured foaming beer into a mug for him, enlivened by his visit. Learned folk probably didn't come this way with their devout greetings every day. Mikkel made a mental note of this. When he had eaten and drunk royally, this was sufficient unto the day, as it were, and Mikkel walked back to town at peace with himself. He sucked his teeth and squinted up at the clouds, following a bird with wonder in his eyes and speaking Latin with his immortal soul.

Suddenly Mikkel stopped and began to think. Was this the day to do it, the thing he had been planning for so long? Give it a try with Jens Andersen? Mikkel was counting on success, since the great academician came from the same part of the country he did. Yes, it had to be today—now he'd have a go at it.

But just when Mikkel had made the decision and pushed himself into action, he lost heart and hung his head. Full of doubt, he came to the street where he knew Jens Andersen lived. When he was standing outside the door all his courage had evaporated, but he was underway now and he wanted to see it through.

Mikkel Thøgersen came into a large room where he caught a glimpse of folios against the walls. And there was Jens Andersen, getting up from a table and coming quickly over to him. Jens Andersen, a short, thickset man with a mighty forehead, wearing a fur tunic. Mikkel was looking at his long, clean-shaven jowls just as Jens Andersen began to speak to him. His voice was low and flat, and Mikkel sensed that he was speaking more quietly just because it was someone of his ilk that he was talking with. What was his purpose? What was his name? Jens Andersen was busy.

Mikkel Thøgersen came right out with it. Could he perhaps ask for some advice, since he would like to go abroad and study? But as always Mikkel became distracted, made dizzy by the things around him. He saw a long, thin crucifix of plain iron hanging on the wall, and he couldn't help wondering if Jens Andersen didn't use it sometimes to keep his dogs under control. Furthermore, he was used to people showing a bit of surprise when they met him, "Stork." Jens Andersen didn't do this—that's the kind of man he was then. But at the moment Mikkel could have wished for such a reaction, even though he usually found it so painful. And while he was talking about traveling abroad he faltered helplessly, faint with the thought of Rome and everything so far away in the south. He was, after all, the son of a blacksmith from up by the Limfjord. . . . Yes, that's where his roots were.

Hmm! Jens Andersen rapped on the floor, his head tilted sideways. He was as blunt and terse as a shopkeeper. Mikkel looked up with a frown and saw the thick neck of a bull, the short-clipped, almost white hair at the nape. And now Jens Andersen was boring through him again with his lusterless eyes. The look was polite and noncommittal, but it held a power that was dreadful. In need of rescue, Mikkel lowered his eyes to the man's large, beardless jaw. The skin was colorless and smooth, without a single wrinkle. Black teeth—it was easy to see he was from Jutland. Mikkel couldn't bear his scrutiny any longer. As if spellbound, he looked over at the bookshelves, and they swam before his eyes.

Fifteen minutes later Mikkel Thøgersen was standing down on the street. Now how was it that it had ended? Oh, yes, Jens Andersen had hemmed and hawed and talked about one thing and another. And then finally he had graciously given Mikkel an *examination!* Mikkel had answered in a stupor, but somehow he managed to display his knowledge. Nevertheless, he scanned a verse of Horace wrong, and then Jens Andersen had chopped in the air with his hairy hand—"Like this, da da da da!"

Mikkel Thøgersen slunk away, wet and cringing, like a cur that has been kicked out.

When he once again ventured to poke his humiliated beak out of his cowl in order to look around, he found himself down on Højbro Square. As always there was a great deal of bustle here. Mikkel stood at the corner of a gateway, his face screwed up as if he were engaged in weighty deliberations. The truth is, he was half unconscious. Shame and disappointment weighed heavily on him, and his monumental inner pride was stirring like a dangerous animal. Even though he was quiet as a mouse with his burden of thought, he was watching everything around him. Indeed, the bright colors burst into his vision with painful clarity. An old crone was hawking her herring. Mikkel stood there flayed—flayed and quivering like freshly slaughtered meat in the evil air.

Listen! Trumpets were sounding over at the castle. It made the scalp creep!

Mikkel shook himself and went on, completely crushed. The drawbridge was lowered from the castle portal and immediately a body of horsemen thundered out onto the planks, all men of high rank. They roared out into the street and rounded the corner to Højbro Square at a fast trot, both horses and riders leaning into the turn. How merrily they bounced in their saddles. Swords danced crazily in their straps—click, click!—and the colored capes waved gaily in the air.

Mikkel went on into town. Soldiers everywhere, and the noise of horses. Junker Slentz himself came riding through the streets in full armor, his esquire behind him. This magnificent iron man turned his helmet to the right and the left with the dignity of an emperor. The visor was raised and his terrible moustaches gleamed in the sun. The horse snorted under its caparison—it wasn't just any horse.

Mikkel wandered around the town, up one street and down another, recovering his composure. Sooner or later all streets ended at the ramparts. He was imprisoned in this impoverished, squalid town, which was filthy with fish slime and herring scales and befouled by monks and pigs in every alley. He looked up at the sky so that he could feel the freedom of the heavens. The air was humid and clouds were drifting up there. Mikkel's thoughts turned to the open sea, and he went down to the shore again.

The wind was freshening and the waves running brisk and choppy. Out on the troubled blue sound, restless yawls were pushing forward laboriously, standing on end.

And suddenly it was as if a fog raised from Mikkel's eyes. He remembered his dream. He had been sailing on far-off seas, and there he had seen a strange sight. Out on the horizon shone a brilliant white pillar, no larger than a finger, but he knew how enormously high it must reach, since it was so incredibly far away. It stood shining against the sky like a snow-white pinnacle of silver. And a quarter of the way around in the firmament, a low, glass-blue dome could be seen. It must have extended for miles if you came close to it. While Mikkel was gazing at this vision from the surface of the empty, roving sea, it seemed to him that a great river must stretch from the sea into the city. For it was a city, and it lay on the other side of the earth.

Mikkel Thøgersen set out for home. He was tired of living, for this day at least. He didn't go by way of Pile Street—he didn't want to pass the picket fence and gawk at Susanna today.

He lay down on his bed when he got home. Ove Gabriel wasn't there. Probably out singing on doorsteps, rolling his blameless eyes. Mikkel lay on his back for a couple of hours, his thoughts drifting. Toward evening Ove Gabriel came home with a full sack. Mikkel got up without a word and left.

When darkness had fallen Mikkel Thøgersen found himself out on the road beyond Westgate. He heard a horseman riding out of town at a full gallop. He had barely turned to see who it was before the rider reached him. It was Otte Iversen. In a flash he was past, bent forward in the saddle, tearing off into the country. Mikkel stared after him, and from the horse's muzzle he could hear the heavy sounds of the furious ride. Dirt and stones sprayed from its hooves.

On all sides there was the fragrance of unripe grain, and the evening was completely still. The frogs sang and sang in their unending dreams.

An hour later, when Mikkel was walking back toward Northgate, he heard the wild hoofbeats behind him again. He stepped aside and saw Otte Iversen thundering past once more, pounding on toward town.

A few days later Mikkel Thøgersen, also known as "Stork," was summarily and without warning expelled from the University of Copenhagen. It didn't come to him as a complete surprise, however, because he had neglected the required church attendance for some time. And that same day Ove Gabriel looked on Mikkel as just another man on the street.

But in spite of suffering in secret from a bad conscience, Mikkel felt liberated. The first thing he did was to let his beard grow. And although in the coming time he was overwhelmed by misfortune—want, delusion, fear—he actually grew a fox-red moustache too, a pair of exuberant thatches, one at each corner of his mouth, stubbornly growing straight down.

# 4. The Throes of Spring

All Mikkel Thøgersen knew about Susanna was that she was a member of the household of an old Jew named Mendel Speyer. Perhaps she was his daughter. He had known her name long before he caught sight of her there in the garden. Time and again it was chalked up on the corner of the house, together with lewd drawings. The name and the drawings would be rubbed out, then they would reappear—and be rubbed out just as quickly again. One day Mikkel saw the old Jew coming home, and before going in the door he let his eyes run over the corner of the house. But this time there was nothing.

Her name was Susanna. Mikkel had only seen her clearly twice. Since then he didn't dare loiter outside the house anymore. He would go down the street like a person with a reason to be there, and then, when he was beside the picket fence, he would look in, as if by chance. Sometimes he would catch a glimpse of Susanna, who was usually out walking on the overgrown paths at noontime and in the evening.

The garden was full of weeds, tall chervil, and wild horse-radish. The ancient apple trees stood with their trunks leaning in all directions. In the corner out by the street there was a mighty elder, dense as a thatched roof. Mikkel had the feeling that it formed an arbor on the garden side, and that Susanna sometimes sat there. He had heard rustling there behind the leaves. Maybe Susanna was sitting there hidden, looking out. Mikkel didn't really like that tree, and yet he felt drawn to it because he imagined she was there.

23

In the evening when Mikkel was walking by, he would see light in a little window up in the gable over the garden. At night the light was out when Mikkel passed and looked up.

Across from Mendel Speyer's house and a short distance away lay the Cloister of St. Clara, and here there was a dark corner where Mikkel liked to stand motionless in the evening and at nighttime. He could see the window from there.

He was standing here late in the evening on Pentecost, after calm had fallen over the town. For things had really been throbbing, with festivities beginning at sunrise and the whole town celebrating Pentecost with music and dance, drink and din. Out in the gardens north of town the maypoles stood thick as a forest. Every blessed soul was drawn out there, and there was prodigious eating and drinking. The German soldiers had given themselves over to uninhibited pleasure—quickening their animal spirits probably, before going off to war.

Mikkel Thøgersen had ventured out into the happy swarm, but he had immediately collected crowds roaring with laughter. The boys recognized him, and besides, he had now put aside his gown and cowl, so his red legs were visible in all their fabulous length. Young people made a veritable cult symbol of him, dancing around him and singing ditties. Mikkel floundered away and then hid himself in the churchyard of St. Nicholas. Here he lay most of the day in a verdant, overgrown nook between the graves, letting the sun shine in on him. It was peaceful here, with the birds chirping and the flies buzzing about. A kite launched itself from an outlook hole high up in the tower and flew off into the countryside. Mikkel lay flopped down on his back, sinking deep in the grass and weeds. He broke some stalks off a plant growing by his head and saw there was yellow juice in them. He stuck tender shoots in his mouth and chewed on them, then he rolled up blades of grass with his fingers. Time passed, and around him the town was alive. From time to time screams of delight could be heard in the distance.

When it finally grew dark Mikkel slipped out of town and wangled a meal at a humble farm. Every bite he swallowed reminded him of his deceit, since he no longer was a student.

And now he was standing here in the cool, quiet night. The town had fallen asleep, but Mikkel was awake, like the hushed hum that hangs in the ear when all sound is stilled. The night was full of fragrance from the dewy gardens. It was very light—the moon was rising and it was bright in the east above the gardens.

Someone was coming farther up the street. Mikkel heard the steps drawing near. At first he thought it was the watchman, but soon he made out the clink of spurs. Mikkel didn't want to be seen so close to Mendel's house, so he stepped out of the shadows and sauntered down the street. As he approached Øster Street the person behind him was catching up. Suddenly the steps fell faster and Mikkel felt a clap on his shoulder. He turned and saw to his astonishment that it was Otte Iversen. So he recognized him after all. But what now?

"Good evening," said Otte Iversen, softly and in a familiar tone, like a friend. "Isn't it Mikkel Thøgersen?"

Yes, it was him.

"We were together out in Serritslev recently. And I've also seen you since then. You're out for an evening walk now, aren't you? Such fine weather! I don't know whether . . ."

His voice was husky and strangely gentle, as if he had been alone for a long time. He stood quietly, his head bent slightly in embarrassment. The feeble nocturnal light touched the knob at the top of his dagger.

"Yes, the weather is almost too good to waste with sleeping," said Mikkel.

25

"You might . . . since you're already out walking . . . shall we go on together?"

Mikkel had no objection to this, so they walked along Øster Street in through the town.

"I don't know anyone else here in town," continued Otte Iversen, "that is, no Danes."

"Oh, no." Mikkel thought this was quite likely. He fell silent, and they walked all the way up to the Church of Our Lady without saying anything.

"Ahem." Otte Iversen was clearing his throat. "Would you like to come back to my billet for a cup of wine?" He was speaking with another tone now, colder, and he sounded dispirited.

Mikkel saw no reason to refuse, and they went to the place on Vester Street where Otte Iversen was quartered. The house was closed.

"We can't get in without waking them so they can open up," said Otte Iversen to himself. "But I have a jug of mead out where my horse is."

They went over the moonlit courtyard and came to a big shed with a lean-to roof. Otte Iversen pushed the door open. "It's me," he said when a stable boy sprang up from his straw bed. "Light a candle for us."

When he had lit the candle the boy looked at Mikkel out of the corner of his eye. It was a large stable but there was only a single horse, standing in one of the stalls. Otte Iversen went over and patted it and busied himself with it a bit.

"Better go back to bed," he said to the stable boy. Then he reached into a corner and took out a tall wooden tankard. He opened the lid and looked in.

"As a matter of fact, I spend most of the time out here with my horse. . . . Can't we just sit here on the trough? There's a tot left—it's the wide end of the jug we've come to. Here you go!"

26

Mikkel drank, and the taste of the strong mead was enticing. It ran down in him and he was warmed instantly. After him, Otte Iversen took a long pull on the jug. Then they sat there side by side on the trough. The stable boy, who had thrown himself onto the straw again, was already fast asleep. The horse nibbled from the rack and then chewed quietly. The candle stump burned in its clamp on the wall, and it was dead quiet all around. Outside the door the courtyard was bathed in moonlight, white as new-fallen snow. It was past midnight.

Mikkel stole a glance at Otte Iversen. He was feeling more and more strange in his presence. But nothing could be seen on his face other than strained brooding. He was pressing his lips together as he sat with downcast eyes.

Finally Otte Iversen jumped up, saying, "It's stifling here. Shall we go back outside? But let's finish the mead first."

They emptied the tankard and then went out. Otte Iversen pushed the door shut. A few minutes later they were out by the town walls. They turned right and walked along the walls for a time without speaking.

But Otte Iversen couldn't remain silent. "Ah, yes!" he burst out in a joking tone, and Mikkel saw him raise his smiling face to the moonlight. "Here we are, walking along in beautiful May weather. In fourteen days maybe it'll all be finished—the moonlight and everything else."

Astonished, Mikkel looked at the young soldier, who had stopped short as if a chill had fallen on him.

"Do you think I'm afraid of going to war and fighting?" Otte Iversen asked, walking on again. "Surely you can't believe that. But tell me . . . well, are you married perhaps? Or are you betrothed?"

"Ah . . . no," said Mikkel, shaking his head as fear rose up in him.

"Could you imagine being betrothed and having to go to war? I am, and I've left the girl behind. Before I went she promised to wait for me, even if it was for a very long time."

Mikkel didn't even dare to move, so uncomfortable had he become because of Otte Iversen's embarrassment and the strain he seemed to be suffering.

Her name is Ane Mette," said Otte Iversen after a pause, very quietly.

They went on in silence. But when Otte Iversen spoke again, his voice was ardent and faint. It was because he had brought himself to say her name.

"I'm from up in Jutland, from a small manor by the Limfjord." He coughed nervously and waited until his voice was steady again. "My father died many years ago, so my mother has the manor." He hesitated, clearly considering whether he should continue.

Mikkel felt he should reveal who he was. But why should he, really? He had spared Otte Iversen embarrassment earlier by not doing it. He remained silent.

They went past Northgate. The watchman, strutting back and forth with his halberd on his arm, stopped and eyed the two night owls suspiciously.

"I have known . . . we have known each other for more than five years," said Otte Iversen, "ever since I was a boy. My mother wasn't aware of it at all. It happened so strangely. I used to like very much to sail in the stream in a small boat I had, and in this way I would come all the way out to the shore of the fjord. Her father is a fisherman and they live in a house down by the fjord. It was there I first saw her. She was fourteen years old and practically grown up. And then I saw her many times later. One time we were fishing out where the stream flows into the fjord. When I came down there it was easy to get her to go out in the boat with me."

28

Otte Iversen was quiet for a moment, breathing deeply. Mikkel knew the fisherman very well. Jens Sivertsen was his name. He had seen Ane Mette almost every day—that is, when she was a little girl. She had blond hair then and was red and white like all small children. . . . But what was the meaning of all of this?

"And then suddenly when we looked around, we saw that we had drifted away from shore!" Otte Iversen continued with great emotion. "We lay looking down into the water. I guess I'd noticed that it was getting deep but I hadn't really thought about it. We had drifted out from the shore. I grabbed the pole in the boat and tried to pole us in—but I couldn't reach bottom!"

Otte was nodding nervously.

"There was an offshore wind, and we couldn't see anyone. Jens Sivertsen, the fisherman, lived farther up the shore, and he wasn't home anyway. What should we do? At first we were so frightened that we couldn't say a word, couldn't even shout for help. But when I saw that the boat kept on drifting and we were far out from land, I screamed as long as I could. Then we both broke down and cried. The boat was rocking and taking in water because we were jumping around in our despair. It's a miracle that we didn't capsize and end up in the water. I couldn't swim at that time. My father died when I was a child, so I've been late in learning everything. Well, we finally got tired of screaming ourselves hoarse. The truth is that we really weren't very clear-headed at that age. We each sat down on a thwart and sobbed and sobbed. From time to time we looked up and saw the shore growing smaller, and then we would start screaming again until we were out of breath and exhausted. It was frightfully dangerous. I guess we fell asleep in the boat a couple of times because we had cried so much. At any rate, we kept on drifting out. Finally, however, we came over to Salling on the other side."

Otte Iversen let out his breath.

"That same day a fisherman rowed us back over. And then four years passed before we were betrothed. That was just this past spring. But we've both been grown up for a long time now."

He fell silent. They had come to an open, moonlit place by the wall. Otte Iversen pointed to a stone. "Shall we sit down for a few minutes?"

They sat down. Otte Iversen, buried in thought, had more on his mind. Mikkel didn't know what to say. He saw how uneasily the young nobleman sat there, fingering one of the slashes at the knee of his clothing. There's no difference between him and me, thought Mikkel. Bless me, we're in the same situation. It's the same with both of us.

"But I can't have her," said Otte after a few moments. In his voice there was heartbreak, pensiveness, obstinacy. "My mother is against it because Ane Mette is beneath me. I won't inherit the manor if I go through with it. But then I heard that the king was preparing for war. And if I should start from the very bottom, that would be a way out."

Otte Iversen had now said everything he *could* say. All that was left—the poor soul's consuming yearning for the girl whose name he could scarcely utter, his sickness of heart—these things Mikkel sensed through sympathy.

"Who knows what Fortune has in store for him?" said Otte Iversen wearily. He leaned forward with his hands pressed together between his knees.

"The manor is old and run down," he went on huskily. "Everything is falling to pieces." He shuddered, and then he yawned mightily. "Let's go."

They went. The moon had paled in the sky and the sun was brightening the horizon, while a thin, rose-colored haze was spreading over the town before dawn. Mikkel sensed that Otte

Iversen now regretted his confidences. Soon he said good-bye and went away.

Mikkel had no place to go. He lay down in the nook in the churchyard, where it was light enough now. Just as the sun was breaking over the town, he fell asleep.

# 5. Mikkel Sinks

At midday the sexton came up to the churchyard and saw the tall, motionless figure lying in the weeds. He went over, thinking it was a dead person, but the man was only sleeping, his eyelids quivering against the sun.

Mikkel dreamed that he was climbing a great, precipitous mountain, floundering and nearly buried in the loose snow. When he had almost reached the top he sat down, exhausted. High above him the path sloped down to the left. Just to get this much higher up he would have to climb a long way, clear around the mountain. He had given up, and now he was sitting with both legs planted firmly in the snow. Everything was finished. The path above him was a maelstrom of shimmering whiteness, with the whole of the mountain's powdery snow being churned up from the ground. Down the path came a long file of young girls in black cloaks, and while they fought their way with grim hilarity through the swirling clouds of snow, their cloaks blew aside from time to time, revealing bodies that were raw and red from the cold. They kept coming down the mountain in an endless file, some smiling, others laughing. They all looked like Susanna—but none of them was her.

When Mikkel woke late in the afternoon, he remembered the dream clearly and was troubled by it. He had a premonition that he would never come nearer Susanna, even though he felt that she was his destiny. Things will surely turn out badly for me, he thought, full of foreboding. Misfortune hung over him, even though he had foreseen greater happiness for himself than for most others. And suddenly he was stricken with a dim and desolate vision of death by his own hand.

Not far from Hanging Hill outside Westgate lay the knacker's pit. Now in the months of summer it was filled with haze most of the time, so the carrion in it couldn't be seen. At the edge nearest the road the knacker had raised a pole topped by the skull of a horse, to keep people from falling in. Mikkel passed it often— he preferred to keep to the churchyard or to the place where executions were carried out. Here he could avoid people.

Gradually Mikkel developed a curious affection for the horse head there on the pole. It was as if he shared something with the dead and defenseless cranium. The skull's mighty gape seemed to emit a sustained, inaudible whinny from hell, the eye sockets glowered, the bared teeth conjured up Satan's eternal hellfire. In its stubborn malevolence it even seemed eager to jab with its muzzle. But deep down, Mikkel had a fraternal feeling for it.

One evening Mikkel found the knacker flaying a jade that had died of natural causes. He began to talk to him, but for a long time Jerck paid no heed to him. He was a man of few words, Jerck was. A short distance away lay his shack. That evening, however, Mikkel was eating horse flesh at the knacker's table. After that he joined him a time or two on the job. The offal collector's nature was marked by a sort of reserved levelheadedness, and Mikkel looked on him as a friend.

One day when they were flaying a horse, Mikkel sat for a long time with the knife in his hand, deep in thought.

He had started thinking about the time back home when Anders Graa's horse got sick and was dying. Anders Graa gave himself the pleasure of doing away with it. The instant he shot it between the eyes with an arrow from his crossbow, it bit the snow.

33

The earth took the head first, and then the carcass sank down as the tension went out of the hocks. Yes . . . yes, the earth knows all, even though it remains silent. We have our way for a time, and the more lighthearted we are the more we dance about on it. But all flesh is created in defiance of nature, in opposition to the law of gravity. Humans have even lifted their forequarters up from the earth, cheating gravity out of a couple of limbs. God fattens up living things so that they will fall even harder to the earth, for God and Satan are one and the same person. But the earth . . .

Mikkel sees a helpless infant lying at his feet on the earth, and the image is vivid. It is lying on its back like a fetus, with its arms and legs folded. But now it is growing before his very eyes, so fast that he can't follow all the details at once. First there is a pair of wide open, alert eyes looking up at him, with delicate white arms lying at the sides of the body. See how long the legs have grown! The face is clouded by sorrow, then a smile flits over the features—and then joyful cruelty, fear, indecision. The hands are already large and brown. Just as he looks from the toes up to the head, a beard spreads across the jaws like a dark cloud, the brow arches in anguish. It is a grown man now, lying still for a moment, preoccupied with his inner world. And then he is already old. His beard is turning gray, his hair is disappearing, and his sharp knees stick up in the air. He is all wrinkles now, for his flesh has wasted away under his skin. And suddenly the piteousness of age is framed in black. There is a glimpse of yellowed legs, and then the coffin lid fuses shut as the earth rains down on it.

Yes, the earth reclaims its own. It flings them down and stretches them out on its crust. Just get a hole in you somewhere and your ribs will slap the earth. You will smack the ground like a post whose base has rotted away.

34

. . . When Anders Graa had shot the horse, the knacker had his turn at it. He cut it up out in the snow while Mikkel stood watching.

It took place in the moonlight early one morning with heavy frost. The snow stretched for miles under the feeble, spectral candlelight from the western sky. It lay with a bluish cast far out over the meadows and arched over the hills in nebulous whiteness. It was impossible to distinguish between the pallid gleam and the snow-banked earth. It was so cold that the snow crunched loudly underfoot, and fingers tingled as if touched by dripping acid. But through the frozen death of the meadow crept the brook, black and open and incurably alive.

The knacker threw Anders Graa's horse over on its back and began to cut it open. The blood lay in a big brown puddle, melting down into the snow, and the pinkish froth turned quickly to ice. With every stroke of the knife color welled up out of the steaming carcass, with marvelous shades of blue and red gleaming from the flesh. Shreds were still twitching, jerking, quivering in the frosty air. The severed muscles writhed like worms licked by flames. The long windpipe was laid bare, the back teeth exposed like four rows of mystic characters. A delicate pink membrane appeared, patterned with a myriad of blue veins, like a countryside scored by many rivers and seen from a great height. When the thorax was opened it was like a cave, with great whitish-blue membranes hanging down, brown and black blood coming out of small holes in the veined walls, and yellow fat stretching from top to bottom in elongated, dripping masses. The liver was more vividly brown than any other brown thing in the world. The spleen appeared, blue and dappled like the night and the Milky Way. And there were many other bright colors—entrails of blue and green, bits and pieces that were brick-red and ocher-yellow.

All of the luxuriant, garish colors of the East—the gold of the sands of Egypt, the turquoise of the skies over the Tigris and Euphrates—all the rampant colors of India and the Orient blossomed there in the snow under the knacker's filthy knife.

## 6. Otte Iversen's Fall

People throng into Copenhagen as the weather gets warmer. Noblemen have come with their retainers and are quartered everywhere. The peasants who have been called up come to town in droves every day. The town is pulsing with preparations for war. Without plan, and quite as a matter of course, the beginning of each summer is marked by bustle and outfitting of troops. About the time when the rye flowers each year, the stone steps of Copenhagen teem with peasants, each man sitting distrustfully on his haversack. Great meal-cakes from the area around Ringsted or from Himmelbjerget are brought out, misshapen from their long confinement. Salt flounder from Blaavandshuk are devoured in company with smoked hams from the western heaths. Horsemen, Germans, young noblemen—all swarm in the streets from dawn to dusk. It is June, the time when men mass and ships lie in readiness. The king conquers Sweden at this time every year.

It was nightfall of the day before the army would depart. Mikkel Thøgersen bent down to pick up a bacon rind that had been thrown on the street, and farther along he found the skin of a blood-sausage. He was going into town for a special purpose. At his chest was an inscription that he had written that morning.

Just as Mikkel was walking past a house entrance, a stick whistled down on his neck. There was a well-dressed man standing up on the steps by the door, out for a breath of evening air, and Mikkel had passed too close to him. His blow was accompanied by some angry words. Mikkel shook himself. The blow had fallen on the most tender part of his backbone. He walked

37

on a few steps, an omen perhaps of his intentions. Suddenly he wheeled around, grabbed the man above by the foot, and wrenched him over so that he was left hanging astraddle one of the spikes of the banister. The man gave a loud scream and fainted. Mikkel hied himself around the corner.

"Hey, look there!" someone shouted from the other side of the street. "After him!" The hot pursuit was punctuated by loud shouts, and Mikkel's wild flight ended only after a leap brought him over the stone dike around the churchyard. Breathless, he slumped down between the graves.

It wasn't very dark yet, and for the moment Mikkel could only think about the sausage skin he had found. He took it out and savored it. Until now Mikkel had not been in the churchyard after dark. His sleeping there he had done in the daytime. As the darkness deepened he became alert, looking left and right, and soon he started to tremble with anxiety. He lay down quickly and hid his head in the tall grass.

When he had lain there for a time he heard a crackling sound. That would be the Devil, standing over him, bending down and laughing! Mikkel looked up wildly. There was nothing there.

The church loomed up, black and ominous against the sky, an obscure blob of intense gloom. Mikkel sat up, trembling in horror. An invocation of the Evil One burst from his lips and he cursed madly in the name of red-hot hell! The graves just lay there, silent and emanating malignancy, the crosses and gravestones grinning with crass familiarity in the darkness. An invisible malevolence, gloating from its hiding place, floated nearby and mocked him. He trembled, he glowered belligerently, and in a pure fever he breathed the name of Satan.

Mikkel forced his eyes into a fixed stare straight ahead for several minutes, his agony tempting him to expose himself and give the Devil free play from behind. When he turned, a loathsome ape would rear up silently from the earth. He swung around in mortal terror, but there was nothing there. His teeth chattered. But it would come, and he would be lying under the beast, vainly attempting to shield himself. No explanations, not a word, just the beast raising hits hairy hand over Mikkel's head, spreading two fingers, aiming. . . . Mikkel just has time to wonder if there isn't some way to foil this hateful force, these two fingers aimed at his eyes. Oh, no! No! The Evil One thrusts the two rigid fingers into his eyes! Oh! Again! Mikkel kneels impotently, his head erect. The Evil One is burying both fingers in his eyes!

For a long time Mikkel challenged the dastardly powers. Come on! And he was more frightened than a desperate sparrow defending its chicks from the jaws of a dog. But the evil around him meant to slay him by its silence. All the crosses stood indolent and soundless, like assets of terror and damnation put out at compound interest. The darkness itself enveloped him in its burden of venomous mockery. The murk closed behind him and stung him. Nothing revealed itself, and the vicious silence would not deal him the deathblow.

Yes, yes, by the skin and bones of the Devil! Mikkel lay down and swore in order to calm himself. He felt at his chest to see if the paper was there. However, doubt had already gained the upper hand. Mikkel was by nature a heathen. For centuries the only thing he and his kin had actually grasped of religion was the oaths. Did the whole thing really have any meaning?

But he was afraid, cowed and trembling. In the hours up to midnight he lay there, feverish with dread. A cold sweat sprang out and the drops fell from hair to hair on his chest. Terror ate at his entrails, so he was forced to yield to nature's demands on the spot.

Time crept on and it got darker and darker. The silence deepened. Everything was changing, imperceptibly and irrevocably, as it does for one who is dying. The air congealed at the slightest sound. Horror hung in the air and stuck forth its stony face with mouth agape.

When it finally struck twelve up in the tower Mikkel was so sick that he could hardly rise. He had given up the whole idea. It was impossible, and there was no sense in doing it. But he would do it anyway, even though he no longer believed in it. He moved stealthily over to the church door, holding in his hand the strip of parchment on which he had written his pact. He bent down to the keyhole . . . and jumped back as a cold blast struck him beneath the eye. Then he hurriedly blew through the keyhole and rapped three times with his knuckle on the door, uttering all the appellations and honorifics of the Devil.

Satan was on his guard. He didn't come.

Mikkel sighed deeply with shame and took to his heels.

At noon that day Otte Iversen had been walking on Pile Street, and there he had caught sight of Mendel Speyer's daughter. He was lost in his thoughts because he was to be sent out the next day. Ane Mette! How was it going with her? Ane Mette with the beloved golden hair! Then he saw Susanna, but he went on without taking any particular notice of her.

That evening Otte Iversen was sitting out in the stable with his horse. All his gear was in order, everything was ready. So what should he do now? His heart was bursting and he was wrought by homesickness and yearning. It was late, but the flame within him was not to be quenched.

He went out and stalked the streets. While walking along Pile Street, he passed the garden where he had glimpsed a black-haired young girl. Roughly he wrenched two slats out of the fence and forced his way in, plunging like a stag headlong through the bushes and onto the pathway. There was a little scream at his left

40

and he heard the rustling of a dress as someone ran off. Then, bounding forward over the grass and weeds, sensing more than seeing, springing round a tree . . . Otte caught her.

He let her go at once and lowered his arms. They stood facing each other for a moment. He couldn't see her clearly but he heard her breathing heavily. A branch that had been bent down sprang back, stroking his face with cool, downy leaves.

Suddenly she made a quick movement, as if to escape.

"No." Otte's voice was hesitant and painfully pleading. He quickly stretched out both arms, one on each side of her.

"What . . . what . . . ?" she whispered thickly, trembling and swaying forward. Otte looked at her but he was unable to make out her features in the darkness under the tree. Then with his right hand he touched her hair, cool with dew. He sighed longingly, then drew his hand back and asked gently, "What is your name?"

"Susanna," she answered in a breathless whisper. Then she jumped to the side, tumbled against the tree, swung around it, and was gone. The bushes swished together behind her and then continued to bob up and down. Finally everything was still again.

Otte Iversen looked up. The summer sky arched over the garden with its pristine stars sparkling. The dark triangles of the gables hung on both sides. She was gone! With stifling heaviness of heart Otte walked slowly back toward the street. Each time he moved the deep grass with his foot a cool smell of herbs and earth wafted up. No, Otte could not leave the garden yet. He walked behind the bushes along the path and came to an elder which formed a bower that opened into the garden.

She had hidden herself there. Otte found her as he felt his way forward with outstretched arms. His hands touched her hair. Without a sound she hunched her shoulders, quivering. Otte kneeled, wanting to embrace her, but she pressed resolutely back into the entwining branches. Still kneeling, Otte moved forward, bumping against the edge of a table that was there.

"Susanna!" he whispered, "Susanna!" Calmed now, he repeated the name. She tried to spring away from him, but he held her fast with both arms around her dress and knees.

"Who are *you?*" she asked, trembling.

Instead of answering he laughed quietly, lost in her, feeling the warmth of her body. Her dress was coarse and uneven to the touch, but this only filled his hands with joy. In his delight he reached up around her waist and pulled her to her knees before him. He caressed her hair and burning cheeks and tried to turn her face to him. And he did succeed in this, but then she craftily twisted her face the other way. Again Otte forced the round, unwilling head about—and with a sudden yielding she managed once again to hide her face on the opposite side.

"No! No!" whispered Otte ecstatically. He felt that his passion lent justice to his deed. He pulled her roughly to him, but she resisted with knees and elbows. He stretched his head forward and managed to kiss her before she was aware of what he was doing. He kissed her again, getting nothing in return but a taste of tightly pressed lips. But then she let her body sink slowly in under his, and he held her in his arms, slender and pliant and full of fervent submission. Otte kissed her again, and her mouth blossomed like a rose with many waxing petals. His throat tightened and he drew back self-consciously. Once gain he kissed Susanna, feeling her ardor. Then his courage left him and he leaned back against the cool leaves of the elder, sick at heart. But Susanna nestled her head high on his chest.

They sat like this for a long time. It was quiet in the town. The stillness was broken by the deep, resonant pealing of the bells ringing midnight.

"We leave tomorrow," said Otte. There was no unhappiness

in his voice, and this could not be why he was lifting Susanna's head with deep sighs.

"Do you have some reason for sorrow?" asked Susanna.

"What?" The word rang out. Then after several moments he answered dully, "Yes."

Susanna bit and kissed his knuckles.

Otte heard steps in the street and listened intently for a moment. Then they stopped and he forgot them.

But it was Mikkel Thøgersen, now standing outside the elder. He had come by and seen the hole in the fence, and he remained standing there until he heard the church bell ring one o'clock out over the sleeping town. Then the two emerged from the bower, and Mikkel recognized Otte Iversen. He saw them glide between the bushes of the deserted garden, where ancient trunks stood askew in a fragrant tangle, primeval and hoary creatures, thrusting branches forth in all directions as if they did not know where to point in their gnarled wisdom.

With Susanna leading him by the hand, Otte climbed up the steps to her little room. Here the full light of the summer night fell in through the roof hatch and Otte saw how lovely she was—dusky and yet fair, like the night and the day, a child of the sun from a world he did not know. Her skin was lucent, but tinged with golden brown, as if she had been deeply tanned by the sun before she grew up and turned fair. Her blood was also like the night and the day, both wild and chaste. Otte yielded, dazzled by her radiance, although he was secretly afraid and thinking of Ane Mette. But as his distress deepened Susanna glowed more and more with understanding, joy, and concern. She was enraptured by his timorous suffering. She loved him because of his silence and because his eyes were full of strange despair. Three times she enticed him, in a radiance of tenderness, with her hidden, golden breast, and three times he resisted as if it meant his death. Then finally, with a broken heart and hidden sobs, he embraced her.

The watchman was singing down in the street: "Four o'clock and all's well!" Far away a trumpet was heard in the quiet paleness of the morning. Then Otte Iversen stumbled out of the garden—and right into the arms of the watchman, who gave him a few sharp and testy words of advice. Otte hurried away into the hazy morning. Horse hooves could be heard pawing the cobblestones in closed courtyards. Everyone was making ready for departure.

Here and there a bit of light slipped out through half-open doors and the soft clinking of weapons could be heard. Men were standing in the middle of the floor, putting on their armor by candlelight. . . . Otte Iversen cut across town to get to his billet. He only wanted to come to the end of the earth at once and cast himself straight into pandemonium and battle. He had to sweat out of his heart what he had done—forget! forget! While he was running he screwed up his eyes instinctively because he kept seeing the one who had opened herself to him with such consuming passion. He could still feel her hands in his hair. How she had pressed his head so tightly, so tightly to her breast, while he cried secretly at her heart! Struck by this thought like a bullet, Otte cleared the ground in a great leap, then rushed on wildly through streets wrapped in the morning mist.

In his blind flight Otte lost his way and came into a narrow alley. He moved more slowly now, and soon he was easing his aching throat with open sobs. Then he felt stifled by his anguish and started running again. Suddenly he saw a sickly light in the mist, shining from a windowpane in a poor little house. And just as a child takes to picking flakes off a whitewashed wall when he is overwhelmed by grief and heartache, Otte Iversen went over to the pane and looked in through a tiny triangular hole at the edge.

He saw a low-ceilinged, untidy room. Just in front of him a man was standing with his back to the window, leaning over a chair. In the chair was a young woman, with only her pink sleeves and her hands visible. The two figures blocked the light of the candle standing on the table. Just at the instant Otte happened to look through the small hole he saw the man lift his right arm in a sinister gesture, and he seemed to lay his left hand on the forehead of the woman sitting in front of him on the chair. Lord Jesus! With a great sweep he slit the woman's throat! There was a smothered, gurgling croak, and the man turned the knife in his hand and planted it in his victim's breast. He let the knife sit, and with a thrust of his knee against the back of the chair he rolled it and the murdered woman over against the table. The candle went out.

Clutching his head, Otte Iversen turned and stared out toward the street like a madman. Then he dashed off, running bareheaded and with his hair streaming behind him until he got back to his billet. In complete despair, he threw himself into the stable where his horse was.

## 7. Stones Are Borne Out of Town

The next day the army was gone, King Hans with his men, mercenaries and peasants, banners and spurs, guns and food bags—the town was purged. The streets echoed their emptiness from one end to the other. Yesterday the air had been filled with clank and swagger. Now these were replaced by a penitential stillness. With less danger now of casual kicks, dogs and pigs came forth boldly from all sides, nosing the offal left behind by the army. For the most part the town could see to its own affairs now. That very noon the gallows outside Westgate was adorned with two moth-eaten miscreants, a big one and a little one. A number of crimes committed during the night were set under investigation, including the murder of Hamburg-Lotte, found in her house with her throat slit. All sorts of strange things had happened that night, as could be imagined, with many hearts moved in strange ways by the thought of imminent departure. As for the perpetrators—not here, not hanged.

Toward the end of the afternoon a small crowd had gathered before the Town Hall. Two people were sitting in the stocks there, a man for thievery and a woman for whoredom. The woman was very young and very lovely. It was Mendel Speyer's daughter, Susanna. The watchman had caught her early in the morning, just as her customer was running away. Alerted by the blunt inscriptions people had written on the corner of her house, he had had his eye on her for a long time—his only eye, in fact. A rogue had stuck him in the other during a fracas one night. . . . Now if Mendel Speyer's daughter had been a Dane, so that one could have been sure that her industry would lend support to the town's economy, the watchman could easily have turned his blind

46

eye to the present episode. He was accustomed to adjusting justice. But Susanna was dark and a foreigner, so now she was being exposed in the stocks, and when people had spit on her she would bear stones out of town.

People stood tightly around the stocks, with more coming all the time. The thief sat with wary, darting eyes, and if someone came too close he snarled through a froth of saliva, snapping at the air with bared teeth like a mad dog. Even his feet, sticking out of the holes in the block, trembled with rage. Then he quieted down a bit and his features relaxed into an expression of sorrow. But when he saw a distinguished, elderly man moving up to him with a joke on his lips—arrgh! the prisoner lunged out with such a vicious bite that the man jumped back in fright. This gave the people a good laugh. But the distinguished face hardened, and with a malicious twist of the lips the man looked to see if the armed guard was watching before he aimed a kick at the nose and mouth of the man in the stocks. And then, with a leer that said, "Just look at that trash!" he turned on his heel and walked away. After blinking three or four times, the thief fixed his steely eyes on the retreating figure and gritted his teeth, but he did not cry out. A dead-white spot appeared on each side of his nose.

At the respectable distance of four holes from the thief sat Susanna, her naked feet sticking through the stocks. More than one person felt tempted to tickle the soles of these dainty feet. She was wearing a green dress, but over her shoulders they had laid a piece of coarse sackcloth that concealed her arms. She sat completely motionless, with her face bent to her breast. Her luxriant dark brown hair was covered with spittle.

Off to the side stood old Mendel Speyer, stooped and wearing a black caftan. His beard hung down under his elongated and troubled features. As he stood there he was talking with a swarthy young man that no one knew. He had a mass of curly hair and the reddish-black eyes of a rat, and he was gaunt as a knife. He was a merchant in Helsingør, sent for by Mendel Speyer that morning.

In the meantime the knacker, Jerck, had arrived, and he had bound two big stones together. No further ceremony was necessary. But before they released Susanna from the stocks, her father approached her, hesitant and uncertain. With lifeless eyes he looked first up at the guard, then at a pair of small shoes he held in his hand, and finally down at his daughter's bare feet— and then he repeated this round. The guard leaned on his halberd. His ferocious moustache moved not a fraction of an inch. So he had not said no—but did that mean yes? Faltering and ready to retreat at any moment, Mendel Speyer lost no time in binding the shoes clumsily onto Susanna's poor feet. He gave her a hand up, but then he had to stand back.

Not a muscle twitched in Jerck's hard yellow face as he laid the rope over Susanna's shoulders. There were in fact some who thought that the stones he had chosen were really rather small.

The procession got underway. At the front were Jerck and Susanna. On the other side of Susanna tottered Mendel Speyer, with the dark young man he had talked with a little behind. Then came the whole happy horde of decent and respectable townspeople: shoemakers and fishermen, students, matrons and maids. Down Vimmelskaftet they went, ever so slowly since Susanna was staggering under her burden. Each time she stumbled Mendel Speer thrust forth his bony brown hand in order to support her, and his face contorted with pain, as if from a whiplash.

Today there was merriment in full measure. Look, "Stork" was also out and about. The red scarecrow had shown up at the corner of the Church of the Holy Spirit. The young people were delighted to see him, but this time he drove them away, striking out with his spiked stick. The boys scattered with angry cries, letting him pass unmolested. "Stork" was sporting a moustache now, the people observed with chuckles. Just see what a hurry he was in to move up and have a look at the girl!

When the procession reached the square it drew even greater attention, with people appearing in doors and windows. A young fellow darted out from one of the shops in the highest humor. He roared with mock outrage, grabbed Susanna's dress and whirled it up, baring her body to the waist. But even though folk found this a great joke, it was improper and could not be allowed. Jerck lowered his eyelids in warning to the merrymaker and stepped closer to Susanna to protect her from pranks. As Jerck glanced around he noticed Mikkel Thøgersen, but he gave no sign of recognition.

Susanna could hardly carry the stones any farther. She was trembling with exhaustion and her cheeks were deeply flushed with her exertions. When they were moving along Øster Street she opened her large and lustrous eyes for the first time, burst into tears, and stopped. Without a word Jerck lifted the stones and set them on the ground. Then he leaned on his staff and waited. Mendel Speyer whispered some words hurriedly to his daughter. The corners of his mouth trembled with sobs, but in speaking he found courage. Susanna lowered her head and cried no more.

Then once again Jerck gave her the stones to carry and they made their way out through the town gate. Here the bailiff read a summary declaration to the effect that Susanna was now free of further chastisement, but if she ever ventured inside the city gates again the law would deal with her harshly. A short distance away a cart was waiting. Father and daughter climbed in, together with the Jewish stranger, and they drove off.

Mikkel Thøgersen followed after.

It was hardly a smart departure the miserable cart made. The driver, a little peasant with sun-bleached hair on the lower part of his head, urged his nag into action with energetic prods and a prodigious "Giddy-up!" and the cart did indeed roll down the hill a way, raising dust on the road. Then it creaked wildly in pride over its accomplishment. A moment later it was barely inching along.

It was a dry July day, and the great bushes of golden goose grass growing on the roadside spread their honey-like fragrance over the road. In the fields the rye was ripening in the warm wind. The dark blue sound stretched away in the distance, and the woods, below them on the left, billowed in the opalescent summer haze. But the sun was dipping toward the west and evening was not far away.

Mikkel followed the cart for several miles, but those in it did not look back even once.

Before reaching Helsingør they stopped at an inn to rest. Darkness had fallen. Half a mile inland a poor church bell was sending its peals toward the glow in the western sky—lamenting, reproaching, meowing inconsolably, like a cat wandering among the sheds in a farmyard, shaking the dewdrops from its paws, searching—searching for its dead kittens.

Mikkel Thøgersen had nothing to go into the inn for. He sat over on the beggar's bench under the big linden tree. A bit later lights were lit in the taproom and he got up and went over by the open door, just looking inside.

Susanna was sitting at the table and the other two were standing, talking to her in an animated fashion. It seemed that Old Mendel wanted to sustain and comfort her with his life's wisdom. He was consoling her, and his bearing expressed all the tenderness and longing to help that a father can show his child. The young Jew, with the mass of curls and the cold eyes, joined in with broad and confirmatory gestures. Wasn't this right? Wasn't this true? But Susanna was surely listening to nothing they were saying.

She sat with her hands clasped above the back of her chair, her tired head resting on them. Her face was turned to the door, but she saw nothing. Mouth slightly open, a faint shadow above the lips, the strange, unquiet nostrils—yes, all so characteristic of Susanna. How soft these features were in grief, inexpressibly beautiful and sorrowful, with the eyes strangely limpid and looking inward. . . . Ah, but she was not grieving over what they thought. The lines of suffering at the mouth might also be a mysterious smile. Those weary, weary eyes mirrored not only pain. That expression in the tearful eyes was half sorrow, half sweetness.

Mikkel drew back and then moved off, walking hurriedly along the road to Helsingør, up and down over the hills. Only when he saw the lights of the town did he slacken his pace and then sit down beside the road. He was worn out. He had experienced so much inhumanity since yesterday, but this was the most bitter of all, seeing Otte Iversen in Susanna's grief-shrouded eyes. From this moment forth she would mean nothing to Mikkel. He remembered the sordid pictures on the corner of Mendel Speyer's house (which he had once found secretly exciting), and then he became wildly aroused. . . . No, enough of her!

And while Mikkel sat there beside the road his ardor burned for a moment in isolation. He threw himself down in the ditch and moaned with dread. But he was young, and his yearning could not yet remain adrift—it craved an object. And so all of his passion turned to hatred, hatred of Otte Iversen. With the thought of destroying Otte Iversen came liberation. He fell quiet immediately, and in his imagination he began to torture and kill. This is how Otte Iversen would shrink from the knife! This is how he would see him crushed in misery, broken joint by joint!

Mikkel was awakened from his burning dreams of revenge by the far-off sound of the cart, with its wheels creaking in the quiet evening. Now they had reached the top of the hill and Mikkel heard the driver urging the horse on. He got up and walked into the town as fast as he could. That same night he took passage with a skipper to the town of Grenaa in Jutland. When the boat was becalmed off Sweden under the promontory of Kullen, Mikkel lay in the front of the boat, sleeping as if he would never wake again.

It was still dead clam when the sun came up. The boat had drifted a certain distance north, and Kullen now appeared as a low cloud crest to the south. The skipper and his two men put out a couple of oars, but this did not help much.

In his impatience the skipper brought a keg of beer up from the hold and woke Mikkel. Mikkel rubbed his eyes and looked around, dazed by the mirror-like surface of the water. They cleared a place on the deck and began to drink. Famished and suffering as he was, Mikkel was tipsy before he was fully awake. He swung his mug and drank himself roaring drunk. Finally the others were silent and Mikkel raved on all alone.

"Long ago I was delivered up to damnation!" he shouted, slobbering and gasping. "I'm such a miserable soul that not even Satan will have me! But that's all right—there can even be a celebration. I'll just give up the whole show when I'm tired of it. No problem at all—I'll simply clear out. Hurrah! Come to the celebration with me, all who are dead, all who are lame, burned at the stake, bashed on the head. Hi, ho! The table is set. Find your places, everyone! Don't change clothes—your shrouds are fine. There's room here for those with cheeks hanging in shreds and fingers bedecked with pebbles. Come, corpses from the sea! Come, paupers from the wheel! I'm one of you, and I'll soon return your visit. Why should I be concerned about my neck?

No longer do I have bonds with any living being. I stand completely alone. What do I care now if there might be a bird they call an ostrich? Why should I worry when a fool is ascending the throne in France? I'm breathing my last now. My eyes can no longer see. Farewell, farewell!"

The boat lay completely dead in the sea under the sun. There was no sound other than the whispering of the water. The skipper and his men were having great fun. For a long time Mikkel drank, sobbed, and swaggered, now in Danish, now in Latin. Finally he slid down onto the deck and slept once more.

# 8. Homecoming

It was during the hay harvest that Mikkel Thøgersen came home to the valley where he was from, up by the Limfjord.

The nights were still bright, and the heat had moderated only enough to allow the meadows and the stream to be wrapped in fog when the soft twilight fell. Hay was being stacked in the meadows, and the young people from three surrounding villages stayed out there at nighttime. Late every evening those from Kourum could be heard shouting, "Bedtime!" The call was passed from haystack to haystack. Soon the warm voice of a girl answered far away from the Graabølle haystacks: "Bedtime!" This sound was mimicked by its echo up in the hills, like a stammering troll. And then from an infinite distance and shattered into gossamer fragments: " -time!" This was from the folk at the Thorrild haystacks at the far end of the valley.

From the bluffs came the song of birds as the fog thickened over the stream. The night lay in godlike repose, and the heavens shrouded the chaste silence.

From the fjord the valley stretched deep into the countryside. At the far end lay Moholm Manor. Iver Ottesen's widow owned the manor now, as well as the valley and the villages.

A short distance from the fjord was the house and the little water mill of Thøger the Smith. Thøger had lived there for more than thirty years. Besides Mikkel, who had now been away at the university for eight years, Thøger had a son called Niels. Niels was following his father's trade.

Mikkel's visit to his home filled Thøger with joy. He took his place up on the chest and fell to talking. Mikkel saw that his father's legs were bowed sharply inward with rheumatism. The strong, broad face revealed pitilessly its age, precisely because the old man was secretly moved by this reunion.

"You're certainly a fine dresser," said Thøger cheerfully, eyeing Mikkel's red leather breeches. Mikkel lowered his eyes, unwilling to accept admiration.

"Oh, yes, anyone can see that you are well situated," declared Thøger. "But it looks like you've gotten a bit peaked with all that reading. And yes, that nose you've certainly inherited from no one but me," he added with warm humor. Thøger's nose was unusually long, bent twice like the snout of a wild boar and with a many-faceted tip, giving him an inordinately shrewd look, just like his son. But Thøger was indeed a very capable man—wise too about many things, and with a natural aptitude for everything in the world. In his younger days he practiced a magical art which he himself had called "cooking." When he was a child Mikkel had sometimes seen him melting strange things in a little pot: wool, lead, red pebbles, mouse teeth. But Thøger didn't "cook" anymore. His passion for alchemy had simply cooled with age.

"It was gold I was trying to make, you know," joked Old Thøger. This confidence went straight to his son's heart because it was a memento of times irretrievably lost. "But I never found gold. And then the last time I tried—let's see, when was it? A long time ago anyway—well, I hit on an idea! All of a sudden— ha, ha! If I just threw in the recipe for the whole thing, then it had to work. I'd bought it from an armorer in Stettin—oh, such a long time ago! I never let anyone see it. He also taught me how to interpret it. So, you see, I melted the recipe in the pot, together with lots of other things with power and punch. . . . And I got no gold. No, Mikkel, my boy. And so afterwards the matter simply took care of itself."

Thøger the Smith had grown old. His bald and furrowed pate had now begun to sprout a second growth of hair, and the full beard—long at the ears as with all old men—was white. His face was covered with pale blotches and the mighty hands had also lost their color.

Sometimes Thøger worked at one thing or another in the smithy, but otherwise he watched over the mill, and Niels stood at the bellows, grimy and covered with soot. At the forge Thøger would work dispassionately and with formidable skill. Standing at the anvil, he drew his head far back because he was farsighted now. Yet he could do justice to a piece of hot iron—but only for half an hour at the most. Then, acting as if he had come to think of other matters, he would cease working abruptly and go into the house. There he would sit down, gasping and trying to conceal his treacherous shortness of breath.

"Look what I've got," the old fellow exclaimed one day, rummaging vigorously in a little wooden box among old shell buttons and pieces of metal. "Where is it? It's an old coin, if I can only find it. I've been keeping it for many years, waiting for you to come home. I couldn't read what's on it, of course, even if my eyes were good enough—it's probably Latin. Here it is. I found it in the ground once. Well, Mikkel, what's written on it?"

With glistening eyes Mikkel bent over the coin and translated its patina-covered inscription.

"And now it's yours," said Thøger, deeply pleased with his son's erudition. "It's pure silver."

"Thank you." Mikkel took the coin and put it away carefully. From this time on he was never without it.

In the first days after his son's return Thøger sent many a thoughtful look his way.

"Things can turn out strangely," he said. "No one ever knows where ability may be hidden. Just look at the cobbler's son from Brøndum. How far up has he gone? I've heard tell he's highly placed among the king's men."

"Yes, he is," answered Mikkel uncomfortably. His visit at Jens Andersen's he remembered vividly and with great distress. "But of course he was so fortunate as to be able to study in Rome and Paris."

"Yes, there you are," mumbled Thøger, and his venerable countenance grew slack at the thought of the wide, wide world. He had been outside himself, but no farther than to the northern part of Germany

"Yes, there you are," he repeated, twiddling his thumbs. "Have you ever run into the young master from down at the manor? Sir Otte they call him."

The question came so unexpectedly that Mikkel started as he sat on the bench. "Who? Where?"

"Our own young nobleman. Maybe you haven't seen him. He went to Copenhagen last spring. Yes, it was really quite a curious story."

Mikkel shook his head and looked away, as if the story would hardly amuse him.

"Well, it was perhaps unlikely that you would see him," Thøger continued. "Young gentlemen like him and other learned folk like you probably move in different circles. Yes, he went to Copenhagen in April, of his own accord and after a falling out with his mother. He didn't have to, though. Since his mother's a widow he wasn't called into the king's service. He just wanted to get away. And they say it was because of Ane Mette. You remember her, don't you?"

Yes, Mikkel did.

"She has grown very beautiful, that Ane Mette," said Old Thøger, his voice filled with simple wonderment and his eyes opened wide. "I guess I've never seen such a lovely girl. She takes after her mother. You'll get to see her. Her mother was the daughter of Sturdy Knud, who was killed in the Peasants' War.

There were a lot killed then. Well, Jens Sivertsen had the most beautiful wife in these parts. We were both of us up in years before we took a wife, you know, though I'm afraid his wife and your mother were never especially close—no, they weren't. . . . At any rate, both of them are dead and gone now. Yes. Ah, yes. . . .

"  . . . You ask what Jens said to the whole thing? Well, what could he say? He could hardly take a cudgel and drive the young nobleman from his door. And a strange thing it was, how devoted he was to her. Now she's down at her father's, pining for him. He's probably promised to come home with the world's riches so they can have each other. Who knows? The lady of the manor is not happy with the situation You bet she isn't."

"Shall we go down and have a chat with Jens Sivertsen?" suggested Thøger the next day. "He'd be glad to see you. And I can probably hobble up to his place when we've rowed down to the mouth of the stream."

Getting ready for the trip, Thøger put a woolen scarf around his neck. Mikkel rowed the pram, and then when they had tied up where the stream flowed into the fjord, they walked the rest of the way to Jens Sivertsen's house.

So Mikkel got to see Ane Mette. Until he was standing before her he had been unable to visualize her as anything but a blonde little girl with a fair complexion. And now, as if by a miracle, he saw her transformed into consummate womanhood. Her hair shone in the quiet room, and she was still as innocent and tender as a child. Her lips were red and her eyes light blue and pure. The goddess Freja must have looked like this.

Ane Mette gave her hand to Mikkel. He looked at her until she lowered her eyes. She was lovely. Mikkel felt as if his palm was burning. Otte Iversen, now you'll pay the price! he thought.

58

It was Thøger who did the talking while they were there. All sorts of things came up, also quite personal matters, but the situation with Ane Mette and the young nobleman was not touched on. Neither was there anything to be seen in her demeanor. Like all girls, she was modest and gentle. But she seemed like a mortal raised by good fortune above all other mortals. She had the openness of an eighteen-year-old in her inborn fine features, but at the same time they glowed with the inner harmony of youth. Yes, Mikkel could understand that Otte Iversen would move heaven and earth in order to have her. All the better the chance to make him miserable! And this resolution tightened like a girth around Mikkel's heart.

"Ane Mette should have been yours," said Old Thøger on the way home, half in jest. "You two would have hit it off well. But I guess I shouldn't say that. And when it comes right down to it, Jens Sivertsen is not exactly generous. I haven't been able to provide you with very much. So whether you and Ane Mette would have been able to go to Rome together, as you mentioned . . . But anyway, it's not so few smoked eel that Jens Sivertsen has docked in town with over the years."

Since it appeared that Mikkel was not enjoying the joke, Thøger stopped. Nevertheless, he added a final touch to his dream a little later with these observations: "She's still of worth, Ane Mette is. They say, of course, that they *love* each other. What this means you're maybe not old enough to understand. But then, as anyone can plainly see, they didn't go too far with things. . . . Yes, yes, Mikkel my boy. Let's get on home."

# 9. Longing

Mikkel had come back to the place he came from. Once again he was sleeping in his father's house. Once again he could wake up in the night and see the same three big stars over the smoke hole in the roof and hear the rafters groaning as beetles and woodworms gnawed in the moldering timbers. Outside the night wind moved in small and intimate gusts. Mikkel remembered this good sound. Otherwise it was so quiet everywhere, in the sky and on the earth, that Mikkel was tormented by the clamor in his ears. There was a ringing, a rushing and crashing in his ears. When he was a child sleeping here, he would wake and hear the stillness seething. He would imagine someone outside, passing endlessly by, sledge runners sliding quietly through eternal snow, and from time to time a slight, delicate sound, as if from distant bells. Later it was as if he were listening to swans on the fjord—this after hearing one winter their fragile music, brittle as the frost itself, from out by the holes in the ice.

Now Mikkel heard the stillness again, but this time it was very different, so intense and poignant, so full of muffled rumbling that it frightened him. Eight years of life as a homeless wanderer, eight years of absolute nothingness—these were the canticles of memory that resounded in his ears and would not cease.

One night a horribly oppressive certainty overcame him. He was convinced that this crescendo of emptiness would haunt him until the time when it would suddenly swell and explode, a single, terrifying blast that would split his head and blow him into damnation.

Mikkel yearned to go away.

"It seems to me you're looking a little out of sorts," said Thøger. "Why don't you go fishing? That's a peaceful way to spend time. Go out with Jens, or if you want to, take the rowboat and get old Børre to go with you. Maybe he's not so bright, but he's not a bad fisherman."

So Mikkel went fishing with Børre, who was simpleminded and peculiar, a fixture in the area from time immemorial. But Børre was all right. They would lie out on the open fjord all day without speaking a word, or they would wade in the shallows with the push net. Børre was sensible enough, and he was given only to tame antics. For example, he would hide his face deep in a corner between two sheds and stand there for hours in fine feather, giggling to himself. Most of the time you only saw Børre's back, and it was always shaking with laughter in his secret merriment. Even as they were moving chest deep in the water with the push net, Børre would turn to the open fjord and laugh with such delight that the water quivered and rings spread out from his body.

Mikkel also went out with Jens Sivertsen, and he often saw Ane Mette. A glossy little spot had appeared at the corner of her mouth, just a token of youth and health.

How long and unchanging the summer was that year! The valley and the meadows bore such grass and flowers as never seen before. The course of the sun was unhurried, and all living things took their time. A bird flew through the air, up and down, up and down, as if it were flying over hill and dale, and when it was gone it left behind the memory of its carefree chirping. Bumblebees lazed out over the waterlogged moors, and water bugs traced the mirror over the black depths in the stream.

It was the Valley of Immortality. The heather-clad hills joined their brows around it on both sides, the stream crept luxuriantly through it, with white clouds floating above, trailing weblike vapors.

The water in the stream hurried laughing over the stone beds and burrowed down silent at the bends. The fish rose, holding their breath and snapping at flies and mosquitoes. A specter shimmered in the air over the shining water, merely a colorless reflection. A muffled laughter sounded in the distance and then echoed ephemerally up among the bluffs.

The hot stillness of noon was as absolute as the stony hardness of midnight, for the sun brooded in silence over every living thing. Under the brightness of the sky was an imposed muteness, far more fraught with foreboding than the darkness of night. Happiness wafted in the luminous air, not to be experienced by anyone before it is dead . . . dead . . .

When twilight finally fell, a pregnant sonority covered the whole land. The hoopoe flung itself up into the giddy heights and its harsh cawing filled the misty darkness. Out from the island in the marshes came the delicate, sharp little whines of the fox cubs. And suddenly there were waves of frightfully wild laughter up on the bluffs. Then it was quiet—until the fox cubs resumed their impudence.

The night fell. The waters in the deep bend of the stream were cleft as the troll below raised his muck-covered shoulder into the air. Over the marshes the spirits from the Land of the Dead hovered, like black terns hanging in the air, probing the depths.

Mikkel stood in the door of the house one evening, looking out over the meadow. There was a light moving out there, far away in the darkness—surely foolish fire, a will-o'-the-wisp. The time when someone might be out was long past. The harvesters were not spending the night in the meadows any longer—the hay had been brought in. It was the month of August.

All was solitude and stillness. The birds and animals were quiet. On such an evening when he was a child, Mikkel had not even dared look out of the door over to the marshes for fear of seeing a will-o'-the-wisp. And even now he stood gripped by uncontrollable fright. He felt painfully exposed to the cold, as if he had been placed naked and defenseless out in a biting wind. But although he was gnawed by fear in his very marrow, Mikkel *had* to go out and encounter whatever it was in the baleful night. It was as if he could not live without dread. Fear within had to be tested against terror without.

Mikkel delivered himself up to the powers of the night. He went out in the marshes. It was as if he were walking in the midst of licking flames, with the horror lifting before him and settling behind. The foolish fire in front of him vanished. Toward midnight Mikkel stopped, and at that very moment bewitching laughter rang out, flying over the hills, echoing and reechoing. He fell down on his hands and knees and bored his head into his arm. He crept away hurriedly, maneuvered awkwardly around, and crawled off headlong toward home. Only long after it had become quiet did he stand up and begin walking.

"I don't want you out walking at night," said Thøger the Smith to his son the next day while they were eating.

Mikkel sat in astonished silence, almost relieved with this summary resolution.

Later in the day Thøger spoke of these matters. He didn't believe in any of it. He had never seen anything, nor had he ever been at close quarters with anything. But it was unhealthy to be out and about at night. You should never take chances.

Mikkel assured him that he didn't believe in such things either. It was just a habit of his to walk outside at night when he couldn't sleep. And by the way, what was that laughter from up on the bluffs? Had anyone heard it?

63

Thøger raised his brow scornfully. "Oh, it's probably just some animal bawling. Or maybe it's the Beast."

"The Beast?"

"Yes." Thøger laughed uncomfortably. "I can't tell you anything about it. I've never seen a Beast, by God! But you must know all about it, since you're educated."

With this Thøger stood up and went out and pounded hot iron so that the sparks flew about him.

Mikkel went fishing. Jens Sivertsen was in his boat a short distance from the mouth of the stream. As soon as he saw Mikkel, Jens stood up and hailed him. Mikkel rowed over to him.

"We've heard some war news," said Jens. "There's been a peddler at the manor and we've heard it from the folks there. It's going mighty well. The king has luck on his side all the time."

Jens Sivertsen was clearly excited. He didn't speak about Otte Iversen, but Mikkel could see that they had also heard good news about him. Not wanting to ask about it, he rowed off.

"Well, shall I tell you about the Beast?" Thøger asked pleasantly that evening. . . . "There've been many Beasts, if you should believe what people say. But if there's one now, then that's what's possessed Børre. Yes, you're staring at me, but that's what folks would have us believe. Not really him, you know, but his wits— which have left him. Børre's been touched in the head for many years. He's a lot older than folks think. I can just barely remember it. He went foolish one spring, and it was lost love that muddled his brains. But since that time everyone's been talking about a Beast up in the hills. I've heard it many times. Long ago, when I was burning salt, I often heard it at night when I was watching the cauldrons down at the beach. Børre was with me many a time, and he heard it himself. No one has seen it. No one ever sees a Beast and lives to tell about it. You die if you look at one."

64

# 10. The Thunderstorm

One night Mikkel awoke to a heavy rumbling in the air, and he was instantly blinded by a flash of blue lightning. His father was sitting on the chest, fully clothed.

"We'll be getting some thunder," said Thøger quietly. "I didn't know whether I should wake you."

Mikkel put on his clothes. Then Niels woke up and dressed too. The thunder was still a long way off, but its rumbling was almost unbroken. It sounded like it was coming closer and closer, by fits and starts, but inexorably. One flash of lightning followed closely on the other, irregularly, like a flickering flame.

"It will be a bad one," said Thøger, turning his face to the small window. There was a flash of lightning and Mikkel saw the solemn look on his father's face.

"Can you go out and take the sluice gate up," Thøger said after a pause. "Then when it comes, the water won't spew out over the whole place. And fasten the water wheel tight."

Niels and Mikkel went out. It was not especially dark, but in the east the murk loomed like a wall. The sky billowed, threatening and black, and out of it sprang flashes of lightning that lit up even the pebbles on the ground. The brightness was cast all the way up to the heights of heaven, where the purest blue of night could be seen. Niels secured the water wheel in silence, and when this was done Mikkel opened the sluice gate and the water gushed down over the immobilized paddles. Then they went in and sat down quietly over on the bench.

The storm was approaching quickly. From time to time a wild white streak would stand out from the constant flashing, and each time the crash would be closer than before, its violent reverberation blending with the foreboding rumbling in the distance.

A gust blew up outside, raising dust against the outer wall. Then a great raindrop splashed against the windowpane . . . then several more, and the wind plucked at the heather-clad roof. Thøger closed the smoke hole. A violent flash of lightning made the room as bright as day. Mikkel saw his father's clear but aging eyes. At that instant there was a wild and brutal crashing all around them, two appalling claps and a long, sharp clattering, like the sound of a rock slide, followed by hollow thundering.

"Watch out for your eyes," said Thøger.

And when the next flash came Niels was sitting with his cap in front of his face so that he wouldn't be looking at the sky and be blinded. A moment later he lay down on his bed without a word. Flashes of yellow and green fire were now lighting up the room. Niels pulled the fur blankets up over his head, and they saw him lying there with his knees drawn up to his chin like a child in his mother's womb. And then crash!, a dreadful, paralyzing blast, as if the heavens had come tumbling down.

Was it ordained that such a thunderclap should be the final sound that Mikkel would hear?

Now the flashes followed each other so closely that there was constant light in the room, and the thunder was shaking heaven and earth from all sides. The rain lashed the roof, splashing down on the stones at the door and rushing off to the stream.

Suddenly there was a roar out in the smithy, as if a pile of iron had collapsed. "Merciful Name of Jesus!" cried Thøger, lifting his white head in an aura of fire just as the bolt struck the smithy. They heard a great sucking sound, with clamor and creaking. Then they sat for a moment in a tomb-like blackness filled with the smell of sulphur. Mikkel gasped for air.

66

Thøger struck a light, working feverishly with the tinder-box until it caught. He opened the door to the smithy and looked in. The anvil had been thrown from its mount and the coals blown from the forge, but nothing had been set on fire.

Soon the storm began to die down and the last angry drops of rain were wrung from the sky. Thøger and Mikkel went out.

The thunder-filled cloud was hanging over the fjord, blue-black and heavy. Lightning cleft the waters and turned them to foam. In the east the sky was clear and cleansed, and the stars were shining again. The stream was swollen, dark, and restless. Everything was soaking wet and there was a scorched smell in the air. But when they came up on the hill across from the house they saw a dreadful sight. The countryside was burning, burning a dozen different places, with great blazes lifting their flames violently into the sky.

"Oh!" cried Old Thøger in dismay.

He took stock of the situation quickly. "It's burning in both Graabølle and Kourum," he said with great heaviness of heart. Suddenly he turned. "No!" he exclaimed with great relief. Mikkel looked the same way. Jens Sivertsen's house lay completely untouched down by the beach. He thought of Ane Mette and was deeply moved, for she was more a part of him than he realized.

"There goes the roof," mumbled Thøger, who had now turned back to the countryside and seen a place where the flames leaped up, towering and throbbing in the sky.

The storm was now over Salling. With each flash of light-ning they could make out houses there and fields like checker-boards. It was so bright that they could see the sheaves of grain set in shocks up on the slopes and the foam on the waves at the edge of the shore. It wasn't long before fires were blazing up over there. Lightening was streaking down. Thøger groaned with the pain of it all.

"It's a hard night for some folks," he said, shaking his head. "Let's have a look at the mill."

Everything was all right. The mill pond had risen high but the dam was holding. The water wheel stood in the middle of the stream, almost covered by the water. Thøger sighed and went back into the house, but Mikkel moved up onto the hill, drawn in awe by the mighty spectacle.

The storm cloud had now dropped very low. The thunder boomed, as if from a great distance, and the lightning was not of such blinding power. Like glaring red pyres the fires shone around the countryside.

Mikkel turned toward the south, and there he saw a high, misty cloud looming like a wall. It was bright at the highest edge and there was a strangely animated unrest in its center. Marked by a latticework of minute flashes of lightning, it had a red luster, as if flames were rising behind it. Suddenly a silent specter sprang into the shining vault of heaven, a horseman. The horse leaped with all four legs extended and its tail straight out, and the horseman's feet jutted into the air. Behind him nebulous waves of horses and men ascended into the sky. A thousand lances turned as one, and new horses and lances sprang into the air, flowing out along the celestial ways, hurling themselves up and down, pulsing tremulously through the sky without a single sound. At giddy heights they kept coming with lances raised, only horsemen and all at full gallop, driving forward and lowering their lances like grain bending in the wind. They were riding at top speed and there was far to go. The armies would fade and then become clearer, as if by some inner undulation. And there! Myriads of soldiers were flowing out into the sky, spreading and then rejoining. Stouthearted men-at-arms in ornate uniforms and with harquebuses on their shoulders marched off into the lucent air. Commandants in armor rode forth with their batons resting imperiously on their hips. Cannons and carts full of cannonballs were drawn at full speed. Terns flew about erratically, fat young women moved off with their skirts bound up. Sniffing dogs, marauders, priests, and clouds of ravens! And then soldiers again, richly ornamented, in velvet and with plumes and fancy shoes, all with their noses in the air. Young flag bearers, comely as shepherd boys, held their curly heads high, while lean gray-beards glared, greedy as vultures. The cavalcade passed off into the stars . . . all the soldiers of fortune, all the voracious stormers of heaven, and they vanished like mist in the endless firmament.

# 11. Revenge

One day in September Mikkel Thøgersen was out fishing, there where the stream opened into the fjord. He saw Ane Mette coming, and he rowed in to the shore and waited for her. When she was only a few steps away she stopped and smiled. She had a dark kerchief over her hair. Mikkel said hello, then both of them were silent for a moment. Flocks of birds were on the gray fields. The air was wondrously luminous and clear, with everything green seeming to fade in its strange brilliance. It was as if the weather had caused both Mikkel and Ane Mette to fall silent. Ane Mette was the first to recover and speak.

"If I met you I should ask if you'd check my father's fishing lines tonight, the ones off Gull Island. He's sailed in to town. But it would make no difference if I didn't see you."

"I'd be glad to," said Mikkel, looking steadily at Ane Mette. He was thinking of other things than Jens Sivertsen's lines. Ane Mette turned to go, but then she hesitated, apparently feeling that she should make a show of even greater casualness.

"Would you . . . wouldn't you like to go for a row in the boat?" said Mikkel, trying to smile.

Ane Mette stood quietly, and her expression was friendly.

"It's such a pleasant evening, with the sun still up," Mikkel continued. He was looking directly at Ane Mette. She gazed out over the mouth of the stream, and Mikkel sensed a fleeting animation in her blue eyes. Yes, it was a memory—the memory of another time. . . .

"That would be nice." Her voice was strangely hushed. She was still looking out over the water, lost in her thoughts.

"Well, come on then," said Mikkel impatiently. She did not respond to the hard edge in his voice, but only stretched her foot out to the rail of the boat. Mikkel had no chance to help her as she sprang in lightly and sat down quickly on the rear thwart. Mikkel rowed out into the current.

For a long time they were silent. Ane Mette looked out over the water. The sun touched the horizon and flamed, coloring the fjord with its glow. It was so quiet that the chirping of the birds could be heard clearly from land. Ane Mette ventured a bit of small talk, but Mikkel had little to say. The boat drifted out with the final faint current where the stream joined the fjord. Ane Mette fell silent again.

And the sun set.

In a few minutes the offshore wind rose in the twilight, rippling the water.

"We'd better go back now," said Ane Mette, sighing as if to chase her thoughts away. Mikkel did not answer. She looked up at him, catching the hardness in his eyes at the very moment his hands shot out, shoving the oars away from the boat. She sprang up, and this movement caused the boat to tip dangerously. She turned toward the land but they were already far out, out over the deep water. She wanted to scream, but then the thought left her as she was paralyzed by a memory that welled up. She made a small choking sound and sank down on the thwart again.

Mikkel's arms, empty now, were crossed.

Then Ane Mette leaped up and tears and screams burst from her. "What on earth, Mikkel! What are you doing! The oars . . . !"

"Let them float away," said Mikkel with uncontrolled rage in his voice. "I'm going to take you away from Otte Iversen."

"Oh, no, Mikkel! Mikkel! No!" she begged in terror. She pleaded and she wept, dragging herself forward in the pram and raising her clenched hands imploringly to him.

"Sit down," said Mikkel harshly. Meekly she sat down, buried her head deep in her arms, and cried.

Night fell and the water grew dark. The beach could hardly be seen in the gathering mist, and the green depths of the western sky seemed infinite. The boat drifted on quietly, the wind quickened, and the water lapped gently.

Mikkel figured that they would land in the northern part of Salling in four or five hours.

Time dragged on. Mikkel looked at Ane Mette, who still sat weeping with her head bent down toward her lap. Suddenly she took her hands from her face and looked at him.

"I thought you were a good man, Mikkel," she cried plaintively in a voice exhausted with sobbing.

"I am," answered Mikkel, deeply shaken. He controlled himself only with great effort.

"You are in my heart, Ane Mette," he said after a few moments. His voice was broken and full of pain. This was all he could say. He was not conscious of anything else, and he was unable to understand how things fit together. He felt only injury and heartache weighing on him, committing him to misery.

The boat drifted tranquilly over the dark fjord. Land could not be seen anywhere now.

# 12. Retribution

It was a mist-shrouded morning in October when a big ship tied up at the wharf in Copenhagen, coming from Sweden. When the gangplank was in place several men went ashore. They were in a jovial and elated mood, and they immediately went on into town.

After heartfelt good-byes with the others, one remained behind. It was Otte Iversen. He was waiting for his horse, which was still on board. The war in Sweden had ended favorably and he had won honor and fortune. Then he had mustered out, and now he could only think of going home. Home!

He stood waiting for his horse and looking around in wonderment over having come this far. There were all the houses and everything else, just like three months earlier. He noticed an old man clad in a black caftan who approached the ship humbly and spoke with the shipmaster. Then he saw the head of his horse as two men came with it and tried to coax it out onto the gangplank. It shied, tossing its head in the air. When Otte Iversen turned, the old man had come up to him and was standing before him, bowing politely.

"Would you be Herr Otte Iversen?" he asked, speaking in German. When he received confirmation of this, the servile expression vanished from his face. He pressed close and continued quietly: "It was three months ago that someone named Otte Iversen broke into my garden and defiled my daughter. Yes—you're the one. I can see it."

He stretched his head forward and stared Otte Iversen in the eye. With twisted lips and a guttural voice cawing like a bird, his words were now distorted. "May you be accursed on this earth, do you hear! Without rest and without sleep! May your cup flow with yearning and your bread be as stone in your mouth! May you rot—yes, rot!—and your pride putrefy between your legs! May you see your father and your mother die of shame! Ugh! Misfortune on you! May you shrivel up like a mangy dog and your corpse ooze from the holes in your coffin! Calamity on you!"

The old man's eyes rolled and he lifted his thin brown fists in execration.

Otte Iversen had drawn back. Behind him he saw his saddled horse and he turned on his heel and seized the reins. The horse began to trot with Otte at its side. He leaped twice on one leg, came up in the stirrup, and rolled into the saddle. A few minutes later he was galloping out through Westgate.

As he set up the speed he blotted out all awareness, not admitting to himself that he had heard anything. His body tensed, his legs tightened around the horse, and he surrendered himself to the tumult of the ride. The air thundered past his ears and he held the curse off, not letting it touch him at all. Fields and houses and yellow forests wheeled by him, and every time he thought of the old man he set in with reins and spurs, reaching ever greater speed. In this way he blotted out the onerous encounter. Racing through Roskilde in a billow of sweat and steam, he had nearly forgotten the incident. When evening found him in Sorø Forest, seared and scorched by the wild ride, he had forced it out of his consciousness. Only in Korsør did he dismount and seek lodging. It was now pitch-dark.

The next morning Otte Iversen awoke. Ane Mette! he said to himself and sprang out of bed. Half an hour later he was crossing Storebælt in high humor—impatient though, with longing for his home burning in his limbs like a fever.

It was as if Otte discovered his horse only while crossing the island of Fyn. He hadn't been aware of it before. His own brown horse had been shot from under him in the attack on Stockholm and it had been replaced with a sorrel—a long-legged stallion and a hell of a horse for covering terrain, but as hard as a tree trunk for riding. No chance that this horse would choose a smooth course down the road! So it was a matter of whip and spur the whole time. No indeed, this one was not Otte's own horse, which had been so gentle, always ready to push itself to the limit. It was lying dead in Sweden now. . . . "Hi-yaahh!" Under Otte's hand the bit sawed away at the mouth of the long-legged sorrel. However, he was developing a certain respect for the beast, which was racing and laboring and sweating unceasingly.

On the other side of Odense a storm struck, bringing driving rain from the north. Otte lowered his head and set up the speed. And soon he flew into a rage again—do you think this clumsy jade would exert itself in the least? Otte had to lean out to the side, bracing himself against the storm, screaming at the horse and raising five or six welts on its neck until it reached top speed. The storm was growing and Otte forced the horse wildly on. But then it stopped short and shook prodigiously, taking no heed of its rider. Otte Iversen roared in fury. He was not going to rest before it was absolutely necessary. He wanted to get home.

At every inn where Otte Iversen was forced to stop, the stable hands eyed the horse with solemn critical appraisal. The verdict of their silent wisdom: horse today, hack tomorrow.

Ane Mette! thought Otte Iversen on Lillebælt. "Ane Mette!" he even said aloud at one time, riding through the woods near Vejle. For two days he fought and wrangled with the horse, up and down across the rolling countryside, through forest and over ford, past peasant hamlets, huts, and heifers, past village

75

churches and peddlers. First it rained, then the sun shone. Migratory birds whirred in flocks above the yellow woods. It was night when he got to Randers and the gates were closed, but he went around the town, letting his horse swim the stream. Then he rode on.

Coming down a steep hill at dawn, Otte Iversen suddenly felt the horse's back arching under him. Then its forelegs collapsed and it crashed headlong into the dirt. Otte leaped from the saddle and got the horses's head up, but its eyes were already glazed. Its long hairy hanks jerked a couple of times and then it died, just as uncomplaining as when it was galloping, struggling, and shying its way across most of Denmark. He took the saddle and bridle off the dead animal and walked to the nearest town.

It was after noon when Otte Iversen reached home on a new horse. He rode at full speed down over the hills, crossed the valley in a few minutes, and galloped up to Jens Sivertsen's house. He sprang out of the saddle and turned gasping toward the door. Jens Sivertsen opened it slowly and came out with his head uncovered.

"Ane Mette, where is she?" demanded Otte.

"Ane Mette is not at home," said Jens Sivertsen. His voice was low and his manner hesitant. "No longer," he added.

"What do you mean? Where is she then?"

Jens Sivertsen shrank into himself, as if from the cold wind. He was about to say something when he saw how the young nobleman's face suddenly paled and fell. Jens remained silent, aghast.

"Where is she?" repeated Otte in alarm.

"She's a servant in Salling," said Jens Sivertsen, and in his misery he stepped forward and began to stroke the mane of the horse, which nuzzled him as he stroked and smoothed its hair. Then Jens began to speak calmly of what had happened.

"Yes, she turned up missing a month ago. At the same time Thøger's son disappeared too—that fellow Mikkel, who'd come from Copenhagen. When I got home people told me he'd gone out fishing. So I thought they might have drifted over to Salling."

At this point Jens Sivertsen looked up uncertainly.

"For many days I searched and asked questions over there, but there was no one who had seen them or knew anything. It was only four days ago that I found her. She's a servant on a farm in the western part of Salling. But she was dead set against coming home, no matter what I offered her, and no matter how much I tried to persuade her."

Jens Sivertsen lowered his voice.

"Nothing seemed to be wrong with her, at least nothing that could be seen, but she was in very low spirits. She didn't even want to hear the name Mikkel. He was away and gone."

Jens Sivertsen looked up again, and the truth was written all over his sorrowful face.

"It was him who'd done it," he added, deeply upset but with conviction.

Then when Otte Iversen remained silent, Jens carefully straightened one more tuft of hair in the horse's mane and almost whispered: "Thøger the Smith is no happier with all this than I am. He has lost his son, with disgrace to boot. But he still has Niels. I'm completely alone now. A lot can happen to a man, even to an old man. You bet there can. I don't know what to say."

Jens laid his chin on the horse's neck and gazed in deep thought over the fjord, out where the water ran cold under the billowing clouds. Finally he turned and looked at Otte Iversen's face for a few moments. It was hardly a face at all. The features were erased, crushed in like a smoke-choked cat's.

Jens Sivertsen drew back from the horse with stifled words, a prayer cut short.

But Otte climbed into the saddle and then straightened his shoulders.

"Get up!" he said to the horse. And he rode home to Moholm with his horse at a walk. One step at a time.

# 13. Death

At noontime in midsummer, when the sun is at its highest and everything lies in a state of embroiled repose, flashes may be seen in the southern sky. Into the radiance of daylight come bursts of light even more radiant. Exactly half a year later, when the fjord is frozen over and the land buried in snow, the very same spirit taunts creation. At night cracks in the ice race from one end of the fjord to the other, resounding like gunshots or like the roaring of a mad demon.

The peasants dig tunnels from their door through the drifts over to the cow shed. Where are the trolls and the elves now, and where are the sounds of nature? Even the Beast may well be dead and forgotten. Life hangs in suspension—existence has shrunk to nothingness. Now it is only a question of survival. The fox thrashes around in a blizzard in the oak thicket and fights its way out, mortally terrified.

It is a time of stillness. Hoarfrost lies in an eternal shroud over the fjord. All day long a strange, sighing sound is heard from out on the ice. It is a fisherman, standing alone at his hole and spearing eel.

One night it snows again. The air is sheer snow and the wind a frigid blast. No living creature is stirring. Then a rider comes to the crossing at Hvalpsund. There is no difficulty in getting over—he does not even slacken his speed, riding at a brisk trot from the shore out onto the ice.

The hoofbeats thunder beneath him and the ice roars for miles around. He reaches the other side and rides on into the countryside. His horse is a mighty steed, not afraid to shake its shanks, and now it cleaves the storm with neck outstretched.

The blizzard blows the rider's ashen cape back, and he sits there naked, with his bare bones sticking out and the snow whistling about his ribs. It is Death, out riding. His crown sits jauntily on three hairs and his scythe points triumphantly backward.

Death has his whims. When he sees a light in the winter night he takes it into his head to dismount. He gives his horse a slap on the haunch and it leaps into the air and is gone. For the rest of the way Death walks like a carefree man, sauntering absent-mindedly along.

In the snow-streaked night a crow is sitting on a wayside branch. Its head is much too large for its body. Its beady eyes sparkle when it sees the wanderer's familiar face. It caws and laughs soundlessly, throwing its beak wide open and sticking its spear-like tongue far out. It seems almost ready to fall off the branch with its laughter, but it keeps on looking at Death with consuming merriment.

Death moves on with the wind. Suddenly he is standing beside a man. He raps the man on the back with his fingers and leaves him lying there.

There is a light. Death keeps his eye on the light and walks toward it. He moves into the shaft of light and labors his way over a plowed field, frozen hard now. But when he comes close enough to make out the house, a strange fervor grips him. Finally he has come home—yes, this has been his true home from the beginning. Thank goodness he has now found it again after so much difficulty.

He goes in, and a solitary old couple welcome him. They cannot know that he is anything more than a wayfaring trades-man, spent and sick. He lies down quickly on the bed without a word, and they can see that he is really far gone. He lies on his back while they move about the room with the candle and chat. He forgets them.

For a long time he lies there, quiet but awake. Then there are a few low moans, faltering and tentative. He begins to cry, and then quickly stops.

But now the moans continue, becoming louder, and then going over to tearless sobs. His body arches up, resting only on head and heels. He stares in anguish at the ceiling and screams, screams like a woman in labor. Finally he collapses, and his cries begin to subside. Little by little he falls silent and lies quiet.

## 14. Meeting Again

In the year 1500 Junker Slentz was on the march up through Holstein with his troops. He had been engaged by King Hans and Duke Frederik, who had their covetous eyes on the Ditmarshes.

Mikkel Thøgersen was on the right flank of a small detachment. Half a year earlier he had entered the service of the Junker. Mikkel cut a smart figure in the ranks. He was tall and lean as a bone, and his magnificent red moustache was most imposing. He looked like the thief on the cross—not the one who would be with the Nazarene, but the other one. His weapons were matchlock and broadsword, and he was clad in blue velvet breeches with tassels, leather tunic, and iron helmet. The whole outfit was taken from a corpse Mikkel had found on the road one morning. At Mikkel's side marched Clas, still alive.

The comrades-in-arms were singing lustily in German, and Mikkel joined in as best he could:

> Think, my friend, of that glorious fight,
> Remember the gore—what a marvelous sight;
> Their guts a morass, their heads in the dirt,
> Bells of hell, how their blood did spurt.
>
> So lop off an arm and stick out an eye,
> Don't think of the end and who's going to die;
> Run 'em through and hack off their head—
> When the sun goes down we'll all be dead.

Remember now your faithful wife,
Forget the sighs, the tears, the strife;
But why that chuckle, that knowing grin?
Are you thinking of whose bed she's in?

> So lop off an arm and stick out an eye,
> Don't think of the end and who's going to die;
> Run 'em through and hack off their head—
> When the sun goes down we'll all be dead.

Learn from the bird that flew the nest,
With dreams of glory in its little breast;
Now it's lost its taste for spear and spoil,
And the worms taste the same in foreign soil.

> So lop off an arm and stick out an eye,
> Don't think of the end and who's going to die;
> Run 'em through and hack off their head—
> When the sun goes down we'll all be dead.

Bells of hell, my loyal friend,
Forget pain's triumph and pleasure's end;
Remember what the raven sings:
Down here it's schnapps and then it's wings.

> So lop off an arm and stick out an eye,
> Don't think of the end and who's going to die;
> Run 'em through and hack off their head—
> When the sun goes down we'll all be dead.

The day wore on and most of the men fell silent. They had covered a lot of territory and there was more to come. In the middle of the night, when they finally neared the king's encampment, every man was tired as a mule. The moon was up and there was a thin blanket of snow on the ground. Mikkel walked along with eyes cast down. He was exhausted and had been dragging himself along for the past several hours. Then suddenly he became aware of the shadows slanting down on the snow, six restless shadows from the detachment he was with. He saw with wonderment that there was a great difference between the shadows. A couple of them were a shade lighter, while it seemed that his own was darker than the others. He pondered this, shivering with fear for a moment, forgetting it, coming back to it. . . . The march continued, with the great mass of men flowing along. Every single one was ready to drop with fatigue but they moved on together, and Mikkel moved on with them, shutting out the world once more.

They reached the encampment and rested. Mikkel slept in a barn with a hundred others. But not long after he had fallen asleep the tension of the long march brought a flash of fervor, and he jumped up gasping. About him was only the darkness of the barn, and yet he had seen an army pouring on and filling the whole horizon, with black banners far away to the fore against the lowering sky. And Mikkel had been part of it all, feeling the same dumb dismay that strikes every single toilworn soldier in an endless troop of men. Almost at the same moment Clas sprang up at his side. He too was gasping. With a chuckle he whispered to Mikkel, as between two comrades, that he had been dreaming that they were still on the march.

Mikkel leaped up several times that night, wracked by the pain of marching and the agonizing vision of troops. And each time he was awake, he heard someone in the rough barn sit up fitfully in the straw and groan.

It was in January that the troops joined King Hans's army. After two years Mikkel could talk with Danes again. One day he found out that Otte Iversen was with the king's army. He was an officer in the cavalry, a banner-bearer. Hate flamed in Mikkel and he was consumed by a wish to see him. Maybe Otte Iversen also loathed him. It would be good if he did. Mikkel was not so lucky as to see Otte Iversen, but Clas did by chance one day, and he told Mikkel about it. He reminded Mikkel of the evening in Copenhagen three years earlier. Clas found it all quite strange, really. Heinrich? He was dead, killed by stupid peasants. Class shook his head—he could never forget Heinrich.

And now the war unfolded. The aggressors, as everyone knows, began with enormous pomp and confidence, then ended in inconceivable misery and death by the sword. Yes, they played out impressive scenarios in the old days. Notice the comic antithesis in the plot: on the one side the noblemen, fully convinced of their military superiority, putting their armor on the ordnance vehicles and riding off proudly in the adornment of their gold chains, with the cruel Junker Slentz ready to gore the men of the Ditmarshes to death with his very moustaches—and on the other side fifteen thousand hearts with hot blood pounding. The nobles' buffoons, Duke Per of Meldorf and Count Poul of Hemmingstedt. And, as a final monstrous poetic license, the fifteen hundred wagons bringing up the rear, meant to carry off the booty. This vainglorious gala would not surprise anyone— that is, as long as they didn't know the outcome. The spectacle was purely a display of human nature. It is natural for a living man to boast of his immortality. The most convincing display of vigor and vitality lies in bluster and threat, and a man's finest moment is when he produces a crashing lie. When he is at the pinnacle of power, he must kill. Life kills.

And so, on to the second act: the slaughter. These proud heads were bashed by the peasants' cudgels against the backdrop of a magnificently staged storm, with snow, thaw, and rain from the northwest and tidal flooding from the raging sea.

Ten crude cannons were shot off and the cannon balls plowed into the compact ranks. Death chomped away like a boor in such luxuriance. They drowned, they were trampled down in the mire. The peasants of the Ditmarshes showed great prowess in turning on the streams of blood, which then spurted eagerly into the air. The old soldiers who were run through bled to death rather slowly, but the virile young fellows emptied their veins with almost a single splash. And that was exactly the point of the whole cynical drama. As mentioned earlier, the plot itself hung together by virtue of its inner disparity.

Mikkel Thøgersen saw Clas fall. Like a stroke of lightning a Ditmarch peasant was at his side, chopping a big slice off his head with an ax.

A little later Mikkel was forced out into a ditch and sank under the surface of the numbingly cold water. The current carried him back a way before he came up. When he had caught hold of something and got some air into his lungs, he saw that he had come all the way in to the king's cavalry. It was more a mush of men and horses than a battle formation, and it could neither advance nor retreat. Panic and butchery reigned . . . but Mikkel was looking for Otte Iversen. And he saw him. He was holding to the center of the impenetrable mass with the banner in his hand. His horse was wedged in beneath him so he was completely motionless, and his expression was almost one of indifference. His face was blue from the cold.

Mikkel looked carefully for some sign of the hurt he had inflicted on him. He stayed where he was until Otte Iversen caught sight of him. But Otte Iversen was frozen stiff and he did not react when he saw Mikkel. His hand was blue on the standard. The skin becomes extremely sensitive in the cold, and even a small tap on a frozen knuckle can bring tears to the eyes. The sense of smell is lost in the cold. Mikkel was himself sluggish from the cold and half dead. He let himself be pulled farther along by the strong current, in the midst of the slush and the bodies. He managed to come behind the army, and then he crawled up on the bank and escaped alive to Meldorf.

# THE GREAT SUMMER

## 15. Axel Rides Forth

Jens Andersen Beldenak was entertaining at his bishop's residence in Odense. The light fell on the street outside, the only place where there was light in the dark town.

A man had ridden up, and while he was looking for a ring where he could tie his horse he heard voices from the bishop's house, billowing like gusts of wind. Axel was the horseman's name, and he had been in the saddle a long time. He could hear the sounds growing louder and then quieter as doors opened and closed between the rooms. The portal where he was standing was open, and when the noise suddenly welled up and remained at a roar, like water gushing from an open sluice, he knew that the entrance door leading to the steps must be wide open. Hurriedly he tethered his horse the first place possible, while prolonged bursts of shouting and laughter came from the house. In the general uproar the laughter of one man stood out. It cut through like a rain of blows, faded away, then rose again with renewed strength. Axel's imagination formed a lusty picture of a man who would laugh like that, with guffaws spewing out of a deeply flushed throat atop an enormous wanton body. Axel sprang up the steps and burst into the banquet hall.

He came just in time to see four strapping servants march up to the table with a young woman on a big brass platter. She was sitting down, holding fast to the edge of the platter, adorned only in her black, flowing hair. Before anyone knew what was happening, the servants set the platter in the middle of the table among the other food dishes. Torches were burning on the plaster walls. Over a score of revelers were there, and they were the ones who were laughing—doubling over on their seat, then throwing their head back in laughter. Axel stopped short, clasping his hands, captivated by the scene—but he had already noted that the explosive laughter which dominated all the others was coming from the sturdy man at the end of the table. He didn't really seem to be enjoying himself as much as his laughter would suggest. It was the bishop himself.

Suddenly silence fell over the hall. When the laughter had died it was as if the jest had turned stale. The party stole embarrassed glances at each other with moist, red eyes, and then they wiped their brow and tried vainly to revive the laughter. The girl on the platter lowered her head slowly, and her black hair fell forward and hung straight down.

"Who's that? What does he want?" cried Jens Andersen, getting up from the table. His face turned quickly serious as he made straight for Axel, and when he stopped short a foot from his chest it looked as if he were going to strike him.

"What is it?"

Axel groped under his clothing for the letter he was to deliver. Jens Andersen understood what the movement meant.

"All right," he said. "We can talk about it later. Welcome. Take something to eat."

Jens Andersen turned back to the table, threw up his arms, and was in fine fettle again, growing even more merry as he shouted and was met by renewed hilarity from the party.

"Well, doesn't anyone want a bite?"

Finally Jens Andersen turned like a cat and looked Axel in the eye. Suddenly his face lit up with clear rakishness. He seized him by the shoulder and lowered his voice, speaking with authority, solicitude, and a certain benevolence.

"He who comes last comes famished. Leftovers are the tastiest! Take her!"

This incitement loosened the whole crowd up. They were laughing again and slapping their thighs madly. But then Axel bowed, cordially appreciative of the favor, squinting his eyes amiably and scrutinizing the girl, who shrank under his gaze and shook her hair.

"Thank you," said Axel. His forthright answer and his golden voice fell just at a lull in the merriment and brought forth a roof-raising cheer. Everyone looked for a moment at the young man standing there. He was well dressed, although a little damp and dirty from his ride. His color was up from the rain and his hair hung wet about his ears. He glanced around the table with an alert eye. The guests were in their cups again, and the girl was being carried out without a single eye following her. But at the doorway she turned and smiled wanly from her raised position. A draft caught her long hair and she shivered piteously. Then Axel nodded to her. She was a whore from the town, hired by the bishop.

"What's her name?" asked Axel later, after he had eaten. The carousers were still going strong, and Axel had fallen into conversation with one of the servants who had borne the *pièce de résistance* on the platter. He was a tall, red-bearded, forbidding fellow. It was Mikkel Thøgersen, now serving the bishop.

"Agnete," said Mikkel.

"She wasn't bad."

Mikkel was not talkative and Axel got precious few words out of him. Axel stood smoothing his hair. His clothing was almost dry now, and he was breathing heavily after his meal. When he saw he could get no more information from Mikkel, Axel turned his attention back to the boisterous guests, but he soon lost interest in them. There were a couple of shabby noblemen in riding boots, several fat burghers with signet rings on their thumbs, a Franciscan monk, a scribe, shipmasters from Lübeck. Most of them were drunk. Axel walked around in the hall with his big, star-formed iron spurs clinking.

The hall itself was dilapidated and cheerless. But then, Jens Andersen hadn't been in residence for long. Only recently had he come home after his hard altercation with the king and ensuing imprisonment. The bishop was no longer young, and he was still hollow-cheeked from that ordeal. But now he was already preparing to leave again, this time for Stockholm. The banquet he was holding was intended to mark both his return and his departure.

After midnight Jens Andersen beckoned to Axel. The bishop was aglow, flushed to the top of his bald pate like the aurora borealis in the northern sky, but he still walked with a firm step. They went into a room where two big growling dogs were prowling about in the darkness. The room was heavy with the smell of books.

Jens Andersen lit a candle and seated himself in the chair at the table. While he was reading the letter Axel sat with the head of one of the dogs in his lap. The room was awash with open boxes of letters, with books in sacks and disorderly piles on the floor.

"Yes!" said Jens Andersen, turning to Axel. Now his large gray head seemed transformed, his face full of deep furrows. His voice was harsh and distant, and only in his eyes was there a trace of lightheartedness. Axel was to ride on to the Bishop of Børglum and he was to take a man with him. It would probably be best if it were Mikkel Thøgersen. Tomorrow morning he was to come for letters and messages—the affair was urgent. But tonight was his own.

At this point the bishop stretched out his heavy hand and began to rummage among the writing materials on the table. He had drawn into himself now. Axel stood up and went out to the others. Mikkel Thøgersen was surprised and pleased when he heard that he was to accompany Axel to Børglum. He and

Axel agreed on how they would use the remaining time. They went to Agnete's and spent the night there. Now that they were going to be traveling together, both saw the advantage of establishing their new relationship, at least cursorily, by sharing a common weakness.

Agnete presented Axel with a lock of her hair.

It was eight o'clock the next morning when Axel and Mikkel rode away from Odense, and both had letters and instructions from the bishop. Axel carried letters for various noblemen along the way. Jens Andersen had many irons in the fire at the same time. Just as they were riding out of the city Axel had his only glimpse of the main street of Odense: a few gables and a flag showing the direction of the wind as it rippled languidly in the morning mist. He was thinking of Agnete, and at this moment a tenderness for Odense welled up in him as he embraced the town itself in his memory.

They rode the first few miles in silence. The morning was raw, and moisture gathered at the horses' nostrils when they began to stretch their necks. As the day brightened and Axel looked at his companion, he saw that he had slender wrists and thin, colorless hands. But Axel was familiar with such apparently weak forearms, where the muscles conceal themselves higher up in the sleeves. Every time Mikkel Thøgersen's horse broke into a gallop he noticed how he restrained it and made himself one with the horse, with distinctive and slight movements of his body. He was dressed like a mercenary in comfortable circumstances and he had good weapons. But the dash of his clothing contrasted sharply with the impoverishment of his countenance. To be sure, the red moustache gave his face a dire aspect, but this could not conceal the mouth's silent token of perpetual homelessness: the upper lip was swollen, as if from secret weeping.

Little by little they began to feel warmer. Mikkel coughed and began to look around. The horses were going uphill now.

"How were things in Copenhagen?" asked Mikkel.

"Plague and sickness," Axel answered briskly. "The last thing I saw when I was riding out of Westgate and looked back was flames."

"Hmm."

Axel continued talking, and soon he was telling about the winter war, where he had done service. It was still vivid in his memory. He told about the battle of Bogesund and the incredible hardships in the forests at Tiveden. It was so cold, Axel assured Mikkel, that your fingertips would freeze to your armor at the slightest touch. The snow was different from Danish snow, fine and sharp as pumice. It left its mark on you—once you got it on you it burned like fire. While you rode along, spines of snow fell down from the boughs of the pine trees, and if they hit your skin they sat fast like greedy leeches. The Swedish snow was purified or parched, as it were, by the frost—at any rate it *drank* away on the back of your hand like a real bloodsucker, devouring everything it came in contact with. It was the worst kind of snow, not lying lightly on your skin like gauze but growing like moss. The bodies of those who fell were overgrown instantly. Ah, yes, those were hard days indeed. When the sun was shining the air was full of tiny splinters, so that you winced in pain just drawing a breath. At night the horses stood huddled, groaning and coughing like old men. And when it came to the fighting things really got bad. No one could bear a wound. Those who were cut down screamed like pigs. Pine trees hit by cannon balls shattered like glass. Many men ended up hysterical or mad. But they had won a great victory of course. Now the army had reached Stockholm. . . .

From time to time the April sun broke through the clouds. They almost didn't make it over Lillebælt, where the current was

96

strong in the heavy weather. The horses took fright in the ferry and tried to jump overboard, so they had to throw ropes around them. When they came ashore and rode on, Axel raised his head and looked around eagerly.

"So this is Jutland," he said in wonderment. "I've never been over here."

Mikkel was silent. Axel felt that the tall, uncommunicative soldier's mind was still on other things. He looked over at him and studied the scars on his face as if he were reading ciphers.

"Here in Jutland there's buried a treasure that I can get hold of at any time," Axel shouted a bit later. They were riding at a gallop now, with the wind roaring about their ears. Mikkel turned his head and nodded absently in his direction.

"A great treasure . . ." began Axel again, and then, angry at Mikkel's lack of interest, he spurred his horse. They were riding side by side, at top speed. Axel rode with mouth agape, pitching up and down, while Mikkel sat low and firm in the saddle with his legs bent, looking as if he were hardly breathing.

The rain clouds moved in from the west, opening to reveal a pale sun that gave no warmth, then closing again. Crows clamored out on the wet fields. The wind whipped the leafless hedges. And far ahead a cloud set its foot on the earth and moved toward the two riders, who then rode into a swirling murk of merciless rain. The road was awash in the lashing rain and the horses galloped in a vapor, with the steam torn from their hide like storm-driven smoke from a heath fire.

Thus they rode the whole day long.

# 16. Home Once More

They were sitting in an inn in northern Jutland. It was late in the evening and they should have been asleep long since, but Axel was telling Mikkel about his treasure. And now Mikkel was listening carefully, with his elbows on the table and his chin cupped in his hands. The candle was burning directly in front of his face.

Axel bent forward and said: "It's supposed to be somewhere in mid-Jutland. But except for this I know nothing. I've never wanted to show anyone the paper. It's a great treasure and I think about it every day, but there's no hurry since I'm sure of getting it. When I'm good and ready I'll have the inscription deciphered. Here—look at this."

He reached in under his slashed tunic, felt around on his chest, and drew out a great fat horn capsule, hanging from a thong. He indicated with a fingernail how it could be opened and explained that it held a piece of folded parchment. Mikkel glanced from the capsule up at Axel's face, conscious of a callowness bordering on the foolhardy. The look in his blue eyes was hardly human. Missing was that calm expression associated with someone whose name is Ole or Josef, and who knows perfectly well who his is. He was handsome, with a dark beard and an innocent mouth. His skin was so fair that it seemed to merge with the air around it. But his hand was broad and covered lightly with hair. Not a hand to be misunderstood.

Axel put the capsule back and nodded several times, saying "Yes, yes," almost to himself.

Mikkel asked how old he was.

"Twenty-two." Axel looked up, quite composed now. He told what his plan was to keep from being cheated out of the treasure. He could't read the inscription himself because it was written in Hebrew.

Mikkel said that he could read Hebrew.

Aha! Axel's eyes were still shining as he bent forward and spoke in a low voice.

"I'll wait a while. I'll wait until I meet some educated man, maybe a priest, who's nearing the end of his life. I'll keep an eye on him, and when his last hour has come and he's just able to see and hear—then I'll have him read the inscription. That way I'll be sure. Even then there's really no great hurry. I can always come some day and poke around with my toe in the gravel at the foot of an old dike, or wherever it is the treasure is buried. Maybe in a hill, or a stone duct under the road. There I'll turn up a golden ring, a thick reddish neck ring, one made of antique gold, the kind with heft to it and a glow. As far as I know it's a lawful inheritance I'm getting. When I turned twenty there was some cash for me— quite a bit, as a matter of fact. I haven't even used it all yet. But the paper with the inscription I got when I was only eighteen. An old man came and gave it to me. I've taken good care of it and I won't let it get away from me. . . . On top there are all those golden rings, but deeper down there's an old leather apron wrapped around a coffer. The first time I dip into the treasure I'll only take one of the neck rings, and a finger ring for myself, one with a stone—it should be the largest of the diamonds. The rest of it I'll simply let lie there and go to seed. I like to imagine the precious jewels moving as the years pass by, creeping out into the naked soil, growing. Later I only need to stick my fingers down and pull them out. I'm not much interested in the gold coins—I won't hold onto them long at any rate. They'll roll freely when I travel, as I've already seen. I want to see Cologne and Pavia. . . . And there are also magnificent sword hilts and chains and clasps—for the time being they're doing fine right where they are."

Mikkel began to smile a little and look around the empty room. Wasn't it about bedtime?

Yes, Axel was all for this, so they stood up. But when they came in to the guest bed it turned out that the fur blankets were dank and rotting—it was completely impossible to crawl in between them. With curses they lay down on top, fully clothed, and Axel was asleep at once.

Mikkel lay there for a time, unable to sleep. Suddenly he laughed cheerfully to himself. Then he fell to thinking, not especially about the past or anything in particular. He felt keenly his humble position in life, the old, well-known anguish over his misfortune. He felt his loneliness. And as he was drifting into sleep that mass of noble gold rose up in his fantasy, lying just under the ground so that you only had to brush off the gravel and pebbles to see the dull, scored gold, creeping like a root under the earth. He would place both feet right on it. On the other side of the chasm he saw shining women, holding objects in their hands and sitting on stones in a circle, with the great woman in the center, looming up over them. Then he would release a dove. A little later he saw them all climbing down. An hour later they appeared one by one on his side of the chasm, hands and knees green and wet from the foliage they had crawled through. And he was standing proudly on the gold. In the distance, the king inclined his head to him.

The next day they rode on in clear, bright April weather, with the horses' hooves splattering the blue puddles on the road. Beyond the forests the land stretched out in a sheen of spring color, and they could see for miles in the tender air. Far away were round burial mounds, rising up boldly on the highest ridges, white with dew on the west side.

Throughout the splendid morning Mikkel Thøgersen had not said a word. He rode deep in thought. They were nearing the part of the country where he had grown up. More than twenty years had passed since he was here. He had been thinking of nothing but this since he heard that he was to go to Børglum. He was riding wrapped in reflection, but suddenly he sat bolt upright in the saddle.

"Isn't Moholm Manor in this area?" Axel had asked.

"Moholm? Yes."

"I have a letter for Moholm. Otte Iversen is the name of the nobleman."

Mikkel whistled to his horse. It stopped and looked back at him, but then he urged it on again. They said no more to each other until well into the afternoon, when they rode over the hills and saw the stream. It ran through the sallow meadows like an exposed vein of silver. To the west Mikkel could see the fjord, changeless and seeming to belong there. He saw the bluffs and the ridges he knew, stretching away under the chaste blue of the sky with the same constancy as the last time he was here.

They stopped at the inn in Graabølle. There Mikkel showed Axel how to get to the manor. He himself was going to ride down to the fjord where his brother lived. The next morning they could meet here at the inn.

Axel rode into the courtyard at Moholm just as it was getting dark. A dog barked wildly from where it was chained at the wall. A boy in red breeches was clearing up around the steps. Otherwise there seemed to be no one about. Just as Axel reined up across from the steps a man appeared at the door. It was the nobleman himself. When he heard why Axel had come he took him up into the main hall. Axel was given a seat at the table and Otte Iversen went over to the hearth and lit a brand, which he then stuck into a ring on the wall.

While Otte Iversen was reading the letter, Axel studied him. He was middle-aged and dour, his face half covered by a beard clipped short at the mouth. His joyless eyes moved quickly over the letter and his face did not reveal what was in it. Then he broke off reading, went to a door, and called out. An old servant brought a dish of meat in to the table and withdrew. After this no one entered the hall and not a sound of life was heard in the house.

When Otte Iversen had read the letter, he drew beer himself for the stranger from a barrel over in the corner, and then he sat down with him in order to hear news from the outside world. Axel told eagerly about the war in Sweden, about the battle at Bogesund and the king's victory, about Tiveden and the Swedish snow. . . . As he livened up with the food in his stomach, he began to extol the horrors of war. From time to time Otte Iversen cleared his throat, the sort of nervous habit a man can develop. He flicked at the brand with his finger when it burned poorly. There was a pause and Axel ate with gusto. Suddenly he looked up.

"This must be about the middle of Jutland, isn't it?"

"Yes, pretty close to it."

"Somewhere in this area there is a hidden treasure, and I have a paper telling where it is," said Axel between bites. "Maybe it's near here."

Otte Iversen did not answer immediately, and Axel pulled at his tankard, the sound telling how deeply he had come in it.

Finally Otte Iversen permitted himself just the shadow of a smile and asked Axel who he was.

Now it was Axel who hesitated before answering. Finally he said quietly, "My name is Axel. I've never had a family name. I guess it actually is Absalon, but on the farm where I was brought up they just called me Axel. My cradle was rocked on the island of Sjælland."

"It was, eh?"

"Yes. I'm in the service of King Christian as a cavalryman and dispatch rider now. . . . The day I turned eighteen an old man

102

came to me and gave me a piece of paper that I was supposed to keep carefully hidden. He told me this out on a field where we were walking, and with his name he vouched for the legitimacy of the inheritance. His name was Mendel Speyer, he said."

Axel then went on eating, but he was beginning to regret his talkativeness. He raised his eyes and Otte Iversen was staring at him. Axel laid his knife down, thinking that he was sick. But Otte Iversen stood up, cleared his throat, and flicked at the brand. He cleared his throat once again.

Ah, yes, Mendel Speyer. . . . Would Axel perhaps be of his family?

Not as far as he knew, said Axel, raising his face. At that instant Otte Iversen knew who he was. He was Susanna's son.

Susanna's son!

In a few moments Otte Iversen asked in an unsteady voice if he knew anyone in Helsingør.

Axel shook his head and set to again. When his hands came into view Otte Iversen recognized them, the short hands of the Iversen family. At this he was deeply shaken and great disquiet struck his heart. There sat his old sin, alive and voracious. Now the old curse was having its effect. What was all this talk of a treasure in Jutland? What paper was he talking about?

Otte Iversen took several steps forward in the room. He was paralyzed, just like a man who sees flames licking up over a roof and wants to rush to the rescue but is rooted to the spot, stumbling over his own legs. What was he to do?

Otte Iversen had been married for twenty years and he had eight children. A portrait of his wife hung in the banquet hall, with her thin hands lying crossed in her lap and her figure bent like an S, showing refined humility—a respectable woman with red-rimmed eyes. They had been fortunate with their children. Otte Iversen sold game from his forests and dealt in oxen. He was

103

well-to-do. And at this very moment—with this stranger, the son of Susanna, sitting here and crunching a bone between his teeth—his smallest children were lying asleep, and his sickly wife would bear another child in June. Was this wolf now to force his way into the nest and gobble their food to the last morsel? No! Otte Iversen's mother rested in a velvet casket under the floor of the church in Graabølle, and he was thinking about her now. It could surely not be God's intention to strike him.

Axel was not eating any longer and it was dead quiet in the manor. The walls of the hall were dripping with moisture, and the light from the brand revealed the cold stones of the floor. In the semidarkness the nobleman stood looking at Axel without a word. Axel was wondering how night lodgings would be at this miserable manor—surely a fraternal relationship with ear-wigs and baby mice. Then Otte Iversen came back to the table. He looked like one who has been meditating on catastrophe. His brow seemed discolored and his mouth was buried in his beard.

"Unfortunately we cannot offer you lodging for the night," said Otte Iversen very quietly, fingering the edge of the table and lowering his eyes. "There are several in the house who are sick, and we already have a guest. . . ." He looked up.

So Axel moved on at once, and hardly with a heavy heart. When he rode away from the courtyard he had put the miserly nobleman out of his mind for all eternity. An hour later he reined in before the smithy down by the fjord and Mikkel came out to receive him.

Their evening at the smithy was comfortable and cheerful. Niels Thøgersen was doing well. He had a wife and children but otherwise little had changed with him. He seemed just as gloomy and indestructible as ever, and he was still clad in his leather apron.

As fate would have it, Mikkel found his old father still alive. Thøger was nearly ninety. He sat in a corner by the hearth with his legs packed in in straw. He was almost deaf and his mind had dimmed, but otherwise he was in good health. His son Mikkel he had not recognized.

While they were eating Mikkel watched his father. Niels's wife saw to his needs with great care. Old Thøger's hands were now as white as mold, as if they had been boiled. They were covered with pale spots, but they were still quite steady. Niels told how eight years earlier their father had nearly died when the pit they used for storage of peat had collapsed over him. It happened that Niels was away, and the others didn't notice anything. Only the next morning did they realize where he might be. They found him lying there, his fists clutching his clothing and his eyes wide open. Luckily there was sufficient air around him so that he had not suffocated. But since the accident he had suffered occasional attacks of terror.

When they had eaten, Mikkel sat down with the old man. He tried to talk with him, but this gave no result. So he just sat there, looking at the great head, shaggy and helpless. He recognized his father's features, even though the face had nearly collapsed and the eyes were expressionless. Soft tumors and blisters had formed on the ears and on the desolate brow.

At length Mikkel took an old silver coin out of his pocket. He looked at it for a moment, then tried to put it in the old man's hand, but he could not hold on to it.

"Can you remember this coin?" he shouted in his father's ear, forgetting the others in the room.

"Ah ... ah ..."

"Can you remember the coin?" shouted Mikkel again. His voice was breaking. The others remained silent and did not enter in, and for a long time Mikkel sat before the old man's chair with his head buried in his hands. Soon afterward Old Thøger was asleep, his wasted mouth agape.

That night they all slept in the same room. They could hear Thøger babble, and then growl like a dog that is sleeping fitfully.

When Mikkel and Axel were mounted the next morning, ready to ride, and farewells had been said, Mikkel turned in the saddle and with great effort addressed his brother.

"And Ane Mette? How . . . ?"

"She's married and living in Salling and she has grown children," shouted Niels quickly, running a few steps after the moving horses. "Jens Sivertsen died at peace with the world. Yes, it's going well with her, Mikkel. That's what I was to tell you. . . ."

He shouted still more, but Mikkel spurred his horse into a gallop. Axel caught up with him only on the other side of the hills.

## 17. Consumatum Est

It was a Tuesday, and there were great festivities in Stockholm in celebration of King Christian's triumphal entry and coronation. Mikkel Thøgersen was standing in the guardroom of the castle with a message for Jens Andersen. He had been told that Jens Andersen was in the bath. But since it was an urgent matter it ended with Mikkel taking off his own clothing in order to carry out his mission.

He came into the stifling bath, and at first he could not see an inch in front of his face. The steam was thick in the room, like white batting, and he could hear the clanking of buckets and the great hissing splash of water against the oven stones. From the sweating fog came the sound of voices. Mikkel remained standing at the door, with the steam burning his chest and beginning to trickle down his legs.

Suddenly the steam seemed to take human form and come toward him. One more step and a man became fully visible. The heat had given him the color of burnished copper. It was King Christian. Mikkel took his eyes quickly from the King's face and fixed them on his brawny chest, covered with red hair. Then he heard the king's angry voice. What did he want? With head bowed Mikkel stated the reason for his presence.

"Jens Andersen!" the king cried harshly. "There's a man at the door here with a message for you." With this he retreated into the steam.

Mikkel raised his head, but his knees were still shaking. In a moment Jens Andersen came forward and Mikkel gave him the message that he had committed to memory. He himself did not know what the cryptic words signified, but they provoked great thoughtfulness on the part of the bishop, who said, "Wait here," and then disappeared.

In the seething vapor Mikkel heard the voices of both the king and Jens Andersen, as well as several others. Then the king shouted a few angry words and it became almost still in the bath as they stopped throwing water on the stones. The hatch at the top of the chamber was opened, and for a moment the steam became as compact and white as a wall. Then it began to clear. Immediately Mikkel could see everyone in the bath. He had thought they were ten times farther away, but they were actually all very close to him As well as the king, who was sitting on a bench, there were Didrik Slagheck, Jon Eriksen, and two more that Mikkel did not know. Jens Andersen was speaking with the king, quietly and seriously, while the others listened, but Mikkel paid no attention to what they were saying. He could not take his eyes off the king. Such a powerful chest and such strong upper arms he had never seen. The chest muscles lay hard and sharply defined against the skin, with the tendons twisting tightly in under the arms. In the steam a profusion of dark red hair lay about the king's head, like moss fluffing up in the rain. Water ran over his wet face and down into his beard. The king was in a vile mood, it seemed. He moved his steely eyes from one to another in a strangely calculating fashion. His entire bearing was ponderous and threatening.

Mikkel hardly noticed the others. Jon Eriksen was standing straight as an arrow, with a diffident and harrowed expression on his face. He was so frightfully thin that it looked like only skin and bone held him together His long, knobby feet were stuck into a pair of clogs, and his ankles were covered with scabs and snow-white scars from the fetters that he had worn until recently. Beside him could be seen Jens Andersen's welt-covered back. He was crouching slightly and his flexed, hairy thighs were those of a horseman. Didrik Slagheck was a well-built man, but unfortunately his entire body was disfigured by the purple, starlike marks of syphilis, as close to each other as the arrows in St. Sebastian's body. Didrik Slagheck had the head of an ape because the bridge of his nose had collapsed.

Suddenly Jens Andersen jerked his head in Mikkel's direction, as if to remind them that he was standing there. Mikkel had heard nothing, but the king looked up, enraged.

"Get that man out of here!" he exploded. Jens Andersen turned to Mikkel with an almost apologetic expression. Mikkel left quickly. "Throw on some water!" he heard the king shout. And while he was standing outside putting his clothes on and waiting, he heard water once again splashing and hissing in the bath. No voices could be heard.

Half an hour later the bishop came out, glowing from the heat and very short of breath. He was blowing drops of water from his lips and mopping his brow, and the ends of his fingers were corrugated from the hot water. Mikkel received an answering message for Archbishop Gustav Trolle, just two words in Latin. Mikkel couldn't suppress a smile when Jens Andersen had him repeat them three or four times like a child.

"All right, remember now! Remember!" shouted the bishop as Mikkel dashed out the door.

The archbishop was standing at his window with a goose quill in his hand. He turned quickly when Mikkel came in, and when he heard Mikkel's message he threw the quill on the floor and stalked from one end of the room to the other in great excitement. It was the last words of Our Lord Jesus Christ on the cross that Mikkel had brought to him from the king. The archbishop said them softly to himself several times. A portable altar stood open on the table. The archbishop nodded, and then he nodded again.

109

*Consumatum est.*

Mikkel waited for any possible new message, but Gustav Trolle seemed to move to a new thought. He returned and stood for a time, somewhat distracted, looking into Mikkel's face. A vague contraction passed over his bloodless lips, either a sympathetic smile or the harbinger of a sneeze. His voice strangely gentle and hesitant, he asked Mikkel if there was anything he wished.

Mikkel flushed. Twenty years of hard, futile soldiering—suddenly they seemed like only a day. He remembered the desires of his youth as if it were yesterday. Was there anything he wished! If he had imagined that anyone would ask this question he would have made mute answer: everything! Yes, that is what he desired—until now, when he was asked. Now there was nothing.

But he raised his eyes meekly. If only he could come into the personal service of the king . . . His voice was dull. He lowered his eyes again and fell to rubbing his hands warily, like a beggar standing at the door, waiting for a handout and then suddenly becoming aware of the cold.

Fine! Gustav Trolle nodded. He asked if Mikkel would like to be one of the scribes, since he knew Latin. But Mikkel shook his head. If he might just be a cavalryman in the king's personal guard . . .

Mikkel went down the street, stooped like an old man. For many years his greatest wish had been to enter the king's service, but now, even though he glowed with pleasure because he was nearing this goal, he was nevertheless crushed by a feeling of wretchedness.

In the evening of the same day a great ball was held at the castle for a large number of guests.

Mikkel Thøgersen was standing as guard of honor at the door of the great hall, resplendent in shining new armor. Jens Andersen had given generous assistance in the speedy promotion, rewarding Mikkel for his faithful service. When Mikkel was presented to him, the king did not remember him from the incident earlier in the day, and he received him with extraordinary graciousness. And yet, Mikkel was the very same man the king had been about to nail to the door of the bath with his eyes. Yes, things could be quite the opposite of what they should be, thought Mikkel, with nakedness concealing rather than revealing.

The previous evening the guests had been the dignitaries of the realm. Now tonight it was the turn of the king's officers and young soldiers, who had been invited, together with Stockholm's leading citizens and their ladies. It was an evening of great merriment. Standing at the door, Mikkel commanded respect with his statuesque presence, gleaming from top to toe in polished metal and mail, his beard bristling from the visor as he followed the dancers with his eyes.

And that nimble dancer over there, all bravura and dash—why, it was none other than Axel, his youthful traveling companion from last spring! Mikkel had been unable to understand the matchless ebullience of this fellow, who confided his secrets recklessly to all and sundry. See there how he was prancing, and as if that were his normal way of moving about! Even when he was motionless he seemed to glitter like a fragment of a mirror lying in the sun. His eye was constantly on the rove—even now, swinging about the floor with a young beauty in his arms, he was glancing flirtatiously right and left. Mikkel saw him twirl through the throng, until the yellow plume on his hat disappeared at the opposite end of the hall. Then he was back again, capering in delight, with the young girl's face constantly raised to his with a quiet, blissful smile.

Mikkel shifted his weight from one foot to the other. There was a great flourish in the music and the cold blasts of November reached in through the windows. Even though his eyes were open,

Mikkel could see nothing now—reverie had overpowered him. Something had begun to gnaw at his being: a feeling of wretchedness over his own rectitude and a burning desire to kick up his heels for once, just like these other frivolous fools. He was over forty now, Mikkel was, but he was no wiser than when he was twenty. Of all his great yearnings not a single one had been abandoned or fulfilled. They had merely been prolonged. But it was not too late for a frolic or two.

The music began a crescendo which ended in a frenzy of madness, pounding out the final measures. The fiddles ran wildly up and down the scales and the dance ended with a compact and sustained burst of pure exultation. Then the dancers scattered on the floor, chatting and laughing.

Axel came over, clapping Mikkel Thøgersen on the shoulder and congratulating him on his new position. Now they were serving together. Later, when Mikkel was relieved, or perhaps tomorrow, they must go out and toast their comradeship! And then Axel disappeared.

During the intermission the king moved through the hall, accompanied by the most distinguished guests. He stopped to talk with several men from the town. The king was clothed in sable, and the Golden Fleece hung around his neck. Now and then he laughed loudly, clearly in the highest spirits. Jens Andersen was busy targeting first one, then another with his wit. Beside the king walked Archbishop Matthias of Strängnäs, aged but nevertheless sprightly, and his sumptuous robe trailed behind him over the floor. He delivered a couple of threadbare jokes, probably the only survivors from his long-lost, joyless university days, and then he beamed about the hall with his toothless mouth.

When they were going out the old prelate turned, his eyes brimming with benevolence, and he nodded to all the young people with his whole wrinkled face enlivened by joy and an inner radiance.

As soon as these high personages were gone, the music burst forth with the blare of Judgment Day, urging everyone to dance again. Mikkel looked for Axel, but he didn't seem to be on the floor.

Soon Mikkel forgot everything going on around him. Once again he was thinking of his misspent life, its hope and its defeat. He felt tired from the many leagues he had journeyed in pursuit of the impossible. For whatever reason, he had banished all happiness from his heart and become a wanderer among those who were happy. As he stood there leaning on his halberd, he composed four Latin hexameters, and their content was as follows:

In Denmark I lost the true springtime of my life—lost in a yearning for happiness under foreign skies. But there I found no happiness, for everywhere I languished for my native land. When at last the whole world failed to beguile me, then Denmark had also perished in my heart. And in this way did I become a wanderer.

# 18. The Galley

No, Axel was not among the dancers on the floor. He was sitting down in the servants' hall of the castle, where they had set out food and drink. He had been dancing with only one young woman, and now he had maneuvered her onto a bench over in the darkest corner. Her name was Sigrid, and she was the daughter of a town councilor.

Axel was lavish with attention to Sigrid's every wish. Unfortunately, she was declining nearly everything—neither strong Prussian beer nor cakes could tempt her. Axel pondered the situation. He was at a complete loss, since it was clear that Sigrid had learned to say no quite automatically. He himself ate without appetite and without pleasure. But finally he got Sigrid to nibble at a cake, and then his heart sprang and he cast himself over the food.

"Drink with me now, Sigrid!" Axel begged. Her answering "No" was a bit irresolute. Would she or wouldn't she? No, she wouldn't. Axel looked suddenly and with great longing at her mouth. It was as delicate and moist as a flower in a glade. He sat there, mug in hand, in complete rapture. At this point Sigrid laughed heartily and Axel, after drinking from his mug, also burst into laughter. In a moment both were laughing hysterically. Then Sigrid sat quietly, her eyes twinkling with merriment. How young and tender she is, thought Axel. May God watch over her hands, so dainty and delicate they are.

Sigrid's face was of the type that reflected the child she once had been and, at the same time, the mature mother she one day would be. Her gentle face seemed in this way a mysterious picture of man's three ages. One could become quite breathless when contemplating her fine blond hair. Axel's eyes moved furtively over her dress, a brown garment with cutouts at the throat and elbows through which silk could be seen.

Finally Axel sighed deeply.

Later Axel and Sigrid hurried back to the hall above. The music was more insistent now and they danced and danced, breathless, the whole enchanted night. Sigrid was tireless. As the night wore on she became quieter and quieter, but each time Axel asked her to dance she accepted, and she never wearied. Her small hands were damp and cool, and her breath came in light, almost imperceptible puffs. At the end of each dance she would smile without knowing why.

Deep in the night, time had turned to eternity for them. From the moment of creation they had been dancing like this. Axel was struck by sadness, like a very old man thinking back on the past. Then he pressed Sigrid's hand. She looked up in his face and awoke from her reverie. Her smile was without reservation, full of trust and surrender. But he did not know how he was to approach her chaste spirit. They danced ever slower, pressed gently from all sides. They danced on, as if borne up in a dream.

Soon after, Sigrid's brother came to take her home. Axel wanted to go with them—to the door . . . just down the steps. He begged like a condemned man, but Sigrid said no. This was her final no, reluctant and gentle.

Then Axel was standing on the steps and watching her go down, wrapped in her heavy cloak. At the bottom she turned and nodded. In the torchlight from above, her lovely face gleamed under her hood. Then she was gone.

There were not many dancers now. Most of the guests were sitting below, drinking.

Axel found Mikkel Thøgersen there, sitting alone over his tankard. He had taken off his armor. Axel was so glad to see the taciturn soldier that he could have embraced him. They had a couple of hearty drinks together.

They sat chatting for a while and Axel was touched by Mikkel's soft voice. There was an overwhelming commotion here in the large servants' hall, with the clink of glasses and outbursts of mirth on all sides. Distorted reverberations billowed down from the vaulted ceiling. The German mercenaries were getting drunk, and here and there fights were about to break out. Most of the townspeople had gone home.

Now Axel was leaning across the table, fixing his eyes on Mikkel Thøgersen's. He was suggesting something with a quiet intensity, as if there could be talk of nothing else. Mikkel tugged at the tip of his nose, a rare expression of humor from him. In his inner eye he saw *The Galley,* and he nodded and stroked his beard.

The reason for all this was that a flotilla from Lübeck lay in the skerries off Stockholm, merchant vessels that King Christian had urged to come and sell provisions to the army while he was besieging the town. Some of them had sailed off now, but a large and celebrated caravel, whose cargo consisted exclusively of lusty ladies, was still anchored there. This ship was commissioned by a great merchant in Lübeck, and it sailed around with its wares to all the places where soldiers were found in significant numbers.

Axel and Mikkel got up immediately, took their weapons, and went out into town. It was dark and there was fog in the air. It must have been about three in the morning. The streets were deserted and without light, so they stumbled and fell several times over rubbish and debris. Finally they reached Southgate and talked their way past the guard. Below the bridge under the

116

wall there were usually a number of yawls that could be rented. Tonight there wasn't a single one, however, so they moved stealthily east along the narrow shore. Some distance from town they found a boat, which they cut loose and rowed out in.

The ships lay quite far out off Slotsholm, and it was some time before the lights from them became visible in the fog. The one they were headed for lay at the far left. After rowing for ten minutes in the unpleasant dampness of the night and the sea, they came to the caravel anchored there. The poop loomed up in the darkness and mist.

But they had *heard* the caravel long before they reached it, for there was great festivity aboard. Three lanterns, one on each mast, spread their light out over the tackle and the decks, and many figures could be seen moving about. In the fog the three red moons of light seemed to have great rings around them.

"There are all the yawls," said Axel quietly, grinning as they slid in under the bowsprit. And indeed, a dozen or so small boats formed a shoal around the anchor chain.

The voice of the ship's harsh German skipper challenged them from the bow, where the figurehead, a bloodthirsty dragon, showed every fang in its gaping jaws.

"Good friends!" shouted Axel in German and jumped from the bobbing yawl up into the ropes. The skipper gave him a hand onto the deck. Mikkel tied up the yawl and climbed aboard.

In the light around the masts lay barrels of beer, and scattered around the deck were hideaways that had been con- structed of sailcloth. There was light in the poop, and here could be heard the resonant ring of pipes and shawms, clinking glasses and cries of joy. The voices were those of women. Oh, how warm they sounded out here on the salty sea! It was homelike and heart-lifting to hear their soft voices on this brine-soaked, Spartan brig. The tarred planking shook under the festivities, above and below, and the whole ship rocked languorously in the sea. Featherbeds were sticking up out of the hatches.

Light footsteps sounded on the deck just beside Axel and Mikkel—nimble feet, but nevertheless the planks gave under the weight of a hale and hearty, full-grown creature. A girl in bright clothing had sprung up from the hold and hurried over to them. She snuggled in between them, welcoming them with a caressing sound but no words, and they suddenly felt the warmth and wonder of her nearness.

Together they walked toward the light, where mugs were being raised to them, accompanied by cheers. When Axel saw the girl's face he leaned forward quickly—her eyebrows joined at the nose—and asked in broken German: "What is your name, you with the white teeth?"

She answered in a quiet, sultry voice, as if she had known him for a long time and knew that he would come.

"Lucie."

# 19. History's Great Trap

Mikkel and Axel were back in town about noon the following day. They went up to Axel's quarters, a garret in a large house overlooking the central square. Here they sat with a tankard of beer, both of them weary and worn. But—with a sly glint in the eye—each was enjoying his headache and his heartache.

Especially Mikkel felt an inner exhileration, and there was an almost provocative merriness about him. Wasn't there a certain softness in his expression? Didn't he look as if he wanted to embrace the whole world and, at the same moment, deal out death and damnation!

Axel couldn't understand him. He examined him with curiosity, for there was one thing Axel was certain of. During the night out on the ship he had heard someone screaming. The sound was coming from down in the hold, long-drawn screams of torment. There was something especially terrifying in the sound of these cries because they did not sound human. And when Axel hurried to help, he was told that it was his friend, the one with the red beard. He was dead drunk, that was all. But Axel went down into the hold, and there he found Mikkel lying unrecognizable, his face contorted like a criminal's on the rack. It was as if Axel could still hear the horrible screams that came from Mikkel as he lay arched up on his head and heels, staring into the air in anguish, choking and grinding his teeth. But now he seemed to be in a good mood—in fact, in high humor.

Axel looked at the round green windowpanes, now refracting the rays of the sun. He threw the window open to the sunshine. The roofs were bathed in a whitish light. Down in the narrow waterway a pram was creeping along with its tiny sail, and far out gleamed the big tower on Södermalm, in sharp contrast with the woods behind it. The pock marks in the wall from the shelling could be seen clearly. The square just below was still covered with mud and puddles from the rain the day before.

"Look, Mikkel," cried Axel, "now there's going to be another celebration at the castle!"

Along the street up to the castle rode a long procession of nobles and dignitaries.

Mikkel jumped to the window. "Then I'll have to go," he muttered uneasily. It was bad to be away so long if something was afoot. He'd probably be in trouble now. Mikkel went out immediately.

Axel stood and watched the entire pride and opulence of Stockholm making their way slowly to the castle. There were knights on long-tailed stallions, with ornamental clasps on their barrets, fur trim on their capes, and golden spurs glittering at their heels. Archbishop Matthias rode bent and decrepit in the saddle, his red velvet cape glistening like a great poppy in the sun and hanging down on both sides of an unremarkable little dapple. Stately burghers walked, bearing with dignity their starched linen and their long staves, while distinguished ladies passed in carriages pulled at a deliberate pace. Many came from the side streets and joined in. Gradually the column moved forward and was absorbed by the round stone arch of the castle portal.

When he tired of watching the procession Axel turned back to the room and stretched, not knowing what he should do with himself now.

Sigrid! Now he stretched really luxuriantly and smiled with deep feeling. The blood pounded in his head and in his breast with longing. Once again he glanced around the room, littered with his weapons and saddlery, and he despaired. Then he threw himself on the bed and slept.

A few hours later he awoke and went out in the town. The sun was sinking and it was strangely quiet in the streets. Only from the inns could sound be heard, the din of soldiers, but even their carousing had taken on a curiously hushed sound. This was the third day of festivities in town.

Axel walked the streets with a nebulous hope: he was looking for Sigrid. And when he couldn't find her he went out to one of the wooded skerries and wandered around aimlessly, as if Sigrid might be found behind a chance tree.

Here he was standing after the sun had gone down, with the town rearing up out of the blood-red waves, black and jagged against the yellow sky. The vesper bells sounded across the water. High, dark cloud masses were gathering in the north, but in the south lay a low fog bank, which might well be the still visible remnants of the day that was gone.

When Axel returned to the town it was dark and quiet everywhere—very quiet. He went up to his room. But as he came in he heard a woman's little squeal of abandon, like the song of a bird, and she threw her arms around his neck in welcome. It was Lucie!

But how had she gotten here? It was forbidden for her to show her face in town. And how had she found her way to his room? Oh, yes, Axel had himself told her where he lived. And as for getting into town—well, she had simply stolen past all the watchmen.

Axel brought out food and wine.

Meanwhile, Mikkel Thøgersen was standing watch in the great hall of the castle, and there he was witness to a cataclysmic event in the history of the North. Although he was only a spectator it marked him to the end of his days.

121

What was about to happen no one had sensed. The great hall hummed as the entire distinguished assemblage held genteel converse with each other, polished and proper in their finery, basking in the royal radiance. Suddenly . . . dead silence, and then a single, brittle voice was heard under the high ceiling, an emotional voice, rising and falling. It was Gustav Trolle who was speaking. The voice itself was ominous, like the hacking of a woodpecker on a dead branch deep in the forest in the threatening stillness before a storm. And the portent of his words caused the knees of the listeners to tremble. More than one of them felt the blood rising to their head. It was fateful matters the archbishop was raking up.

No longer was Gustav Trolle's face the one Mikkel knew, the Gustav Trolle who had dominated his thoughts because he idolized him. Like Jens Andersen, Gustav Trolle was the most learned man in his country and at the same time the mightiest, a man of supreme intellect and a man of decisive action. He was the most saintly and the most profligate. In him the knowledge and accomplishment of his time were conjoined with property and wealth. His command of theological and juridical finesse, as well as of practical application, was unequaled by any other man's. When Mikkel had seen his face before, however, it had been marked and scored by misfortune, harried by hate and also by intimidation. The gravity that he assumed in order to conceal many hidden things–this only gave him an air of dejection. No, a smile was not his characteristic expression, and he sometimes looked like nothing more than a lackluster and ludicrous scribe.

But now the archbishop's face had finally found a different cast. It had become cold. In exactly the same way the befuddled solicitude of a lover is transformed in the course of time. The imploring sweetness in his eyes becomes merciless judgment, and his courting becomes harsh command.

122

This archbishop of theirs the Swedes had treated brutally, as one does a brutal man. As well as demolishing his castle and fortifications and plundering his cathedral, they seized all his properties, threw him in jail like a thief, and tortured him. They were convinced that his enemy, Sten Sture, would remain on the throne. Northmen always treated other Northmen most harshly. Now Christian had become king, with violence and against the weapons and wishes of all the Swedes. Now it was their turn.

Because of his ability Jon Eriksen's life had been nothing but a series of bitter misfortunes, and now it was this man who read the written condemnation aloud to those present. He had languished for three years as a prisoner in this selfsame castle, a formidable fortress, and his ankles had not yet healed.

While Jon Eriksen was reading, those assembled in the hall murmured and shuffled uneasily, and then they began to rage like animals in a pitfall.

On this day the proceedings took their inevitable course, as when two people—alike and yet incompatible—finally part. Thrown together by fate like two children in a family and not able to be without each other, they nevertheless torment each other ceaselessly, wielding weapons with skill and will—until they are finally separated, each with death in his heart.

The evening's horror included an extra flourish that not even the evil spirits could have devised. It was provided by a woman, Sten Sture's widow. Because of her view on matters of state and the present circumstances, she carried papers on her person—official papers, that is. Hardly more than twenty years old, she was the only one to answer the charges, producing a document that proved that all the crimes against Gustav Trolle and the church were the result of a decision by Sweden's entire State Council, attested with the seals of the country's leaders! However, the State Council's action, the substance of the case, was

123

dismissed as being of less importance than the essence—but, of course, the certified names of the perpetrators could now be entered into the record with great ease. Water usually quenches fire, but it can also spread it when the fire reaches its most majestic power. It was Satan himself who laid that document on the table.

Then the doors were thrown open and the guardsmen entered, in armor and with bared swords, and they began to take prisoner those who had been charged.

Jens Andersen assembled the legal experts and the court was declared to be in session. This great man of God and dealer in oxen knew well how to adjust the letter of the law to the technicalities of the case, following in such matters the inclination of his passionate heart. And its counsel was certain. But even the most profound truth, the diabolical truth, failed here. It could not save the North. The Northman distinguishes himself by such a great aversion to happiness that it is precisely the most extreme and radical salvation that kills all hope forever. So mystical was the discord among the Nordic peoples, so obstinate their fate. The realms of the North burst into three parts like a stone exploding in a fire.

The date was November 7, 1520.

But the man who held everything in the palm of his hand, who had brought these hotheads together, who in his struggle for royal power was using the gifts, the malice, and the guile of these vindictive men—this man sat alone now in his chamber, while his henchmen prepared what was to follow.

Mikkel Thøgersen saw King Christian sitting at his table. He sat erect against the back of his chair, etched darkly against the flames in the fireplace behind him. Mikkel took a candle in to him. He saw the King's face, which was tense and relaxed at the same time. He looked like a man still trying to make a decision on a matter which has long since been resolved.

# 20. Lucie

L ucie, the Child of the Twilight . . . how young she was! She was a fallen angel, yes, a human being. Her brow grew together above her eyes, where the twilight had signed her forehead with a bat on the wing.

Lucie was quite unable to laugh. She could only produce a mirthless grimace, like a dumb animal baring its teeth, just as an amiable sign of warning. Only on occasion would she show pleasure, and then her smile was like a September day in Denmark, when carefree birds swoop in great flocks under the brilliant sky, while the withered flowers stand quietly in their greater wisdom. Ah, Lucie—she was not yet twenty, but her breasts were already less than firm, and untender as fallen fruit.

Lucie! She could sing fragments of songs, but without any sign of happiness. She understood nothing—except floating down, like a sinking soul, toward the bottom of the sea. This was of her own free will, and this was why there was a forbidding coldness about her. But, knowing nothing of this, she could only show her simple wonderment, like a dung beetle that has fallen over on its back in a rut and flails away with its legs in the air for the rest of its life . . . until a crushing wheel comes along.

But there were moments that night when Lucie glowed in the sacrosanct splendor of sin. About her dark head was a halo of insatiable desire, of terror, and her soul burst out in a wild, mute stare, like the look in a crusader's eyes when he suddenly sees the blood-red roses springing out around the consecrated cross on his breast.

Axel dozed off.

He slept and dreamed. He had slid into another reality, an ephemeral world where he was sitting at the seashore with Sigrid at his side. It was as if he were weary unto death, yet he got up and staggered into the water in order to make a bed for Sigrid and himself. For a long time he fought with the billows, arranging them and reaching out for a white wave to use as a pillow. But everything that he managed to lay in place then vanished from his embrace. He grasped at the corners of sheets that rose up and then flowed off into nothingness, and he struggled with the swaying pillows. Finally he gave up.

A little later Axel and Sigrid flew up from the earth. For a moment they hung quietly in the air and Sigrid took his hand. Then they flew on to celestial heights, but from the depths of slumber Axel felt that they had to go still farther out into the heavens. He sensed that there was a panorama at the edge of creation that they must see. But when they had flown for a long time Sigrid began to waver. She grew heavy and started to murmur, and then they both came crashing down.

Axel woke, slept again, and dreamed again of wondrous things that he could not remember.

"If you have a birthmark somewhere, show it to me so I can know who you are in hell." The day was breaking, and Axel spoke half in delirium.

Lucie laughed in shame. She was nearly weeping with joy, and she showed him the weals on her back from the public flogging. They were like a bed of yellow rushes and, like rushes, they were topped with brownish blossoms where the knots of the lash had kissed the flesh.

Once again Axel's eyes have closed without his knowing it. Once again he is flying, but this time alone. He is flying through the streets of Stockholm, up among the eves of the houses. In a standing position now and pressing his arms tightly to his sides

126

like a runner, he holds himself in the air with his own inner power, and he glides forward silently and with great force. The streets lie empty in the threatening dusk. Far ahead in deep alleys he sees shadows move and scuttle away with their back turned, but where he is flying there is no living being. The sky is burning, a bright yellow, as if it were proclaiming joyous tidings.

Then the street is blocked by a tall house and Axel is afraid that he will fly against the murky wall. Indistinct faces peer out of the windows. He gathers his strength and manages to raise himself at an angle, and he just clears the top ridge of the house. Then he glides low and his feet touch bushes and trees. But suddenly, with great effort of will, he soars again, the air becomes even deeper and more yellow, and he shoots aloft and sways above all the towers like a speck in the bright, open air.

Axel flies on, and far below him the water swells with soundless waves. At a sharp angle below he sees a ship a short distance away, and he calculates anxiously whether his present course will bring him to it. He is flying under his own power, but it is as if he can manage to bear in on it only with supreme effort. But he reaches the ship's deck in safety.

It is the Ship of Fortune.

At the bow stands a Wildman holding watch, unaware of the world around him, only staring ahead to warn of ocean fog. Like a phantom the ship sails and bobs lightly over the water.

It is Columbus's Ship of Fortune. Columbus himself, the shipwrecked skipper, stands at the helm, bowing his ghostly face over the compass. The course is straight south. On each side of him he has a forest dwarf, naked and red, their hoariness dripping maliciously all about them. The sails swell out from the spars like spider webs, pierced by the stars.

But aft in the abrupt wooden tower, on the deck and under the deck, in every nook and cranny, women from the whole world lie waiting. There is one from each of the thousands of different areas of the earth. Many are white, ranging from those of tender years with slim, boyish legs and budding breasts, to the portly type with knees chafed by their rough garments. There are fair maidens who wash themselves both morning and evening, and there are peasant girls with the smell of milk in their mouths and with robust, hairy limbs that strike like cudgels. There are girls with dusky complexion, with eyes full of bold innocence. There are women with flaming red hair and feet as white as snow. Negro princesses with rose-red lips and tiger teeth encircling their flat, coal-black loins. Arabian maids, lean and supple as leopards. Buxom beauties from the rich farms of Poland, small, flower-bedecked creatures from hidden Asia, and still other women, as yet unseen by Europeans, from far-off islands.

All are different in height, age, and form, as well as in temperament and thought. One smiles casually with a saucy mouth and speaks from the omniscience of her young heart. Another laughs heartily, to be sure, but conceals her sadness. Some flaunt their clearly visible blemishes, others lower their eyes and are embarrassed over their flawless figures. One is not entirely straight, because the Ship of Fortune must also have one of the world's misshapen creatures. One is perhaps less than fair, and another's wondrous expanse makes its presence felt—there are, after all, enough slender beauties on the Ship of Fortune. Each one is perhaps never quite perfect, but no single one can be done without. The common goal that all are striving toward is perfection. Those on the Ship of Fortune are almost identical in one respect: every one is captivating. Like a phantom, the Ship of Fortune sails and bobs lightly over the water. The Ship of Fortune—Axel was dreaming his way aboard. And he was feeling the presence of Sigrid.

Then he woke up suddenly with Lucie.

128

It was broad daylight. Ardent and arrogant flourishes were heard from down on the square.

"Just a trumpet tooting," murmured Lucie groggily, snuggling deeper without opening her eyes.

But Axel got up and threw the window open. There he saw two long, stationary files of soldiers with halberds, stretching from the castle across the square all the way to the town hall. Otherwise the square was deserted. Right in front of the town hall portal . . .

"They've set up the scaffold," said Axel, moving away from the window. He grabbed his clothes and dressed hurriedly. Lucie turned over on her back and looked at him, wide awake now but saying nothing. Axel left the room to go down to the street.

But he came back up quickly. He had discovered that the door was barred and that the town criers had just published a ban on all movement outdoors for each and every resident of Stockholm.

Axel stood by the window and waited. A half hour passed, then a whole. The longer Axel stood there the more eager he became to find out what it all meant. But nothing happened. Two men worked around the scaffold and put things in order. Otherwise there were only those two straight, orderly lines of soldiers across the square and up to the castle. Their hushed murmuring and whispering could be heard. The weather was frigid. From time to time an officer galloped briskly along the ranks and dressed them, but otherwise he remained up by the closed castle portal.

When Axel went to look again an hour later, the lines of soldiers had not moved.

# 21. The Bloodbath

S tillness lay over Stockholm. The only sound in the streets was hoofbeats as cavalrymen rode about, making sure that all doors were still barred.

What was happening? What could the people who were restricted to their houses be imagining? They sat mutely indoors now, but at every window was a staring and bewildered face, at every crack a spying eye. The whole town rose up on its island, compact and wattled as a great ant hill. At each end the drawbridges reared in the air like gaping jaws, and in the thousand rooms of the town, souls were confined—with the result that they broke out in wild speculation, running rampant in fear. An acrid odor comes out of an anthill where the ants have been stirred up and dash about in a blind frenzy. Such an odor lay over Slotsholm, invisibly poisoned by the fantasies of fright.

Only toward midday—Axel was half mad from staring at the everlastingly straight, trim, and rigid military formations down in the square . . . only toward midday did it happen. All the same men who the day before had paraded to the castle in their finest finery and the deepest conviction of their own civic importance—now they were coming out.

It seemed that Sweden's highest officials must have spent the night in a single activity: practicing an even better formation. They had come in no particular order, but now the order was determined by their standing: the high ecclesiastics first, then the nobility, ordered by rank, and finally Stockholm's honorable mayors, councilmen, and rich merchants. No one was riding now—they were walking, tractable and all equally close to the earth, like timorous sheep. The chief executioner had been waiting since early morning and he was eager.

They reached the scaffold still in procession. The arthritic old bishops did not maintain a particularly erect carriage, but among the nobles there were a few who stamped like defiant rams, and an occasional burgher tossed his head like a sheep trying to throw off its tether. Most of them, however, moved along in the flock without protest. There were about seventy or eighty in all.

Because of his high rank Archbishop Matthias of Strängnäs was entitled to be executed first. He still had on his red velvet cape. Axel recognized him when he dropped to his knees, raised his small face, and folded his hands. But there was no time for that. The archbishop rose and began to remove his garments under the open sky and the eyes of the executioners.

At this point a violent tremor went through Axel. He turned to Lucie, who was standing behind him, and he pushed her back into the room. "You mustn't see this!" he cried with such great agitation that Lucie began to tremble. She lay down on the bed.

When Axel got back to the window it was over. Archbishop Matthias's body lay on the ground clad only in trousers and hose. His head rested a short distance away. The red cape . . . no, it was his blood that lay spread out under him.

Even as Axel was looking at that poor, severed head, he heard the executioner's sword sing and set, and he saw another head hop from the block to the ground, followed by a stream of blood. It was Bishop Vincents of Skara. Erik Abrahamsen Leionhufvud was removing his clothing. There was tumult around them now, with many shouting and screaming.

Axel remained at the window, shaken and flushed. He saw a tall, very corpulent nobleman thrashing in the air as he spoke, but his wild voice made it impossible to understand him. Up in the houses across the square many faces could be seen at the windows, and the frenzied man seemed to be hurling his words at them. But they did not answer. Axel saw low gray clouds drifting over the roofs. Now and then they would drop down and fill the square with a thin mist.

Axel saw one after the other being pulled forth, and among them he recognized the highest officials in Sweden. Some tried to disrobe themselves, fumbling in their haste. Others let the executioners rip off their garments without resistance. The flock huddled together, and around them stood the armed soldiers. Axel could see Mikkel Thøgersen and several of his comrades down there.

Now Axel was calm once more. He saw how Jørgen Homuth was supervising and directing the executioners, pointing with his gloved hand. He was in full regalia.

Many heads were lying on the bloody ground now, or rather sitting there, like swimmers treading water. The blood spread out over the square and took on the shape of a gigantic letter of the alphabet. Every time Axel went to the window this rune had been expanded with a new dot or bar, suggesting some new interpretation of its message. The executions were being carried out quite methodically. The weather was dreary and it was becoming more and more overcast, threatening imminent rain. The flock thinned out and the bodies lay in piles.

Axel drew his breath softly. When all the inviolable men of noble birth had been cut down and the headsmen with renewed energy began to hack away on the burghers, he felt an attack of giddiness, for all this lay beyond his comprehension—that the king could have such monstrous and unfathomable power as to ordain this. He visualized him, the king of the North, the short, sturdy figure with the powerful shoulders and beam-like arms. Here was a man who could bear heavy burdens and rip stones out of the earth and lift them right up to his commanding countenance. He remembered the king's eyes, like poised lances, and the king's brow, ever changing. He thought of the king's voice, casual because of the man's pride. He felt touched by a breath of this, the king's autocratic decree. He bowed before the might of such majesty.

Finally Axel moved back from the window and closed it.

He and Lucie decided to eat. Lucie displayed no curiosity about what had happened. Afterwards they lay down and slept. It was raining heavily outside.

It was dusk the same day. Axel was awakened by a sound outside his room, the steps of someone trying to run noiselessly. The footsteps moved across the floor and died away. Axel remembered the empty room in the gable out to the courtyard. He jumped up and ran over to it.

Just as he opened the door he had the feeling that someone was hiding somewhere in the room. He stood in the doorway looking around. The only thing in the room was an empty alcove, and the roof hatch stood ajar. Then someone rose from the bed in the alcove. It was a young man in fine clothing and with a thin, pale face. He stretched his legs down from the bed and smiled at Axel, alarmed but with a show of gaiety. He was very tall, with narrow hips and a dark shadow on his upper lip. Something seemed to be missing in his attire. Suddenly Axel realized that he had no weapons, and at the same moment he noticed the red rope marks around his wrists.

So Axel knew what the situation was. He ran into the room and both of them started talking at the same time. "Come here," said Axel hurriedly, while the other said almost apologetically, "They're after me. My name is . . ."

Just at that moment the steps below creaked violently and a harsh voice broke the silence in the house. The fugitive turned his head, looking for a hiding place, puzzled but not afraid. He

133

shook himself and tried to smile, ready to run but not moving. Heavy boots were heard on the floor outside. Axel gave the stranger a shove, as if he at least wanted to get him into the corner where it was darker, and the young man took a couple of hesitant steps, still half smiling. Then he straightened his back and knotted his brow. A burly mercenary in leather and clanging iron lurched in through the door, like a raging ox with harness and singletree on his hocks. His long sword struck against the door jamb and rattled in its scabbard. Axel was in his tunic, without a weapon, and it was as if he were blown aside. His hand brushed the sloping roof and he broke off a piece of a crumbling lath. He hardly knew what was happening. A quick step, a short, twisting struggle between the other two, like between a buffalo and a colt. The lath broke into pieces as Axel struck the soldier's helmet. He heard his hot snorting, and then suddenly the fight was over. They all drew back. The young stranger stepped backward, hesitated a moment as if catching his breath, then gave a loud, sharp scream.

The whole thing had lasted no more than three or four seconds. The big, half-mad soldier reached the roof hatch in a single bound and twisted through it.

"What the hell, man!" Axel shouted instinctively. He knew it was forty feet to the ground. But he saw the soldier's coarse, sweaty face over the sill, saw him take a deep breath and hold it, then swing over the edge. He was holding on to the sill with only one hand, and then that disappeared. Axel rushed to the hatch, and he saw the man crawling nimbly sideways along a cornice toward a high gallery over the dark courtyard.

When Axel turned back to the stranger he saw that he was staggering. "He's stabbed me," whispered the young Swede with an apologetic look. He pushed his chest sharply forward and pressed both hands to his sides. His eyes fluttered a little, as if in pain or pleading. Suddenly he turned to the empty alcove and stretched himself out on the bed, with his back pressed against the side. A single sound of pain, a wheezing noise, wrenched itself from his throat. When Axel reached him he was dead.

He had gotten it straight through the heart. His face was still quivering slightly and his upper lip twitched a time or two. The young man was no more than eighteen. He was remarkably thin and he seemed to be old beyond his years, perhaps from hunger during the recent besiegement. Axel stretched him out and sat looking at him, and he was crushed by sorrow. His whole being dissolved in misery, and he was completely beside himself with grief.

There were light steps outside, the door creaked, and when Axel looked up it was Lucie. She saw what had happened and she kneeled quietly beside Axel, her hair falling over the face of the dead man.

Axel came to think of something as he was sitting there. It was a winter night by the fire in Tiveden's frozen forests. He had been lying with a blanket wrapped around his head, thinking of Man's fearful impoverishment in death. It was when the report of Sten Sture's death reached the army. The Danes rejoiced at the news, and there was revelry in the frigid camp the whole evening. The snow squeaked merrily under their boots and the stars hung among the desolate treetops in all the colors of the rainbow. They speculated with relish on how this dangerous man had died. But Axel had, with his own eyes, seen him wounded on the ice over Bogesund, and he had rejoiced at that time over the sudden downfall of their enemy—horse and rider crashing into the reflection of rider and horse on the ice! Now Axel began thinking of that lonely man who died in the sledge over Mälaren's frozen waters, with a crushed leg under him. He died. He had to die.

The snow sifted down in the black air—or was it the sky itself that was tilting, threatening to fall? The lake gave under the sledge, sighing as if the whole world now doubted whether it could hold out. Then a human heart burst with kingly cares. The expansive land of the Swedes disappeared from his sight, like the ice and the sighing lake. Sten Sture's royal concerns and his anguish and his pain ended in the narrow sledge like a child's sobbing which stops, like a cradle which is stilled. When they looked back at Sten Sture, he was dead. The snow was no longer melting on his face. As far as the eye could reach there was only ice and snow, Sten Sture, and you sat quietly. Far out from the frozen wasteland came sounds like weak cries for help, and then their slight, tinkling echoes: Oh, Sten Sture!

Later in the evening Mikkel Thøgersen came. He found Axel and Lucie sitting with the body, each holding the stump of a candle. Mikkel said nothing. His face was empty and haggard. When he had looked a while at the dead young man, who was now lying on the floor, he suggested that they lower him to the courtyard so that he could be taken away. Axel and Lucie went in and lay down, and they heard Mikkel talking half-aloud to himself.

When Mikkel came into Axel's room after having seen to the removal of the body, Axel was asleep. Lucie lay awake but she paid no heed to Mikkel. When he went out she was staring into the candlelight, meek and dejected.

Lucie was the first one to awake the next day. The candles on the table had burned down but it was already daylight. She sat up and looked around, moving her eyes back and forth as if she were listening, as if someone were calling her. Then she opened very carefully the horn capsule around Axel's neck, took out the piece of parchment, and hid it in her sack. Axel had told

136

Lucie about his treasure—he had even talked about it in his sleep. Just to be sure, Lucie lay quiet for a few minutes. Axel was fast asleep. Then she edged out of bed, put on her clothes, and slipped quietly away.

# 22. Miserere

Without a proper dawn, the gray November morning took form somberly over Stockholm. The first sign of life and movement was something rising up from the scaffold and flying round and round.

As the day wore on people began to come out to see what had happened. The decapitated bodies were still lying in the square in puddles of blood and rain. Soldiers stood guard, keeping up their spirits in the harsh weather with beer and wine. Shortly after noon the executioner set to work on another group of confirmed heretics and traitors.

It was a hushed day, and it seemed more mean and stunted than other days, moving directly on toward evening without amounting to much of anything.

As it was setting, the sun burst forth in a blaze and all the clouds slid out of the sky—it was like an eye opening slowly. When the sun had gone down the sky remained clear and pale for a long time. Far out at sea lay a dozen vanishing specks, the ships from Lübeck, which had raised anchor that afternoon. The afterglow of the sun deepened in the west and the heavens pondered. The waning dusk was infinite, and the evening chill so tranquil.

In the stillness the bells of St. Nicholas's Church rang out with a mournful sound. Yes, yes! came the immediate answer from the Cloister of St. Klara on Nörremalm and from St. Jakob's Church. And from Södermalm the bells of the Church of Maria Magdalene chimed in. While they were ringing, each with its own tone of accusation, several bells from the small chapels quickly joined the animated lament.

There lies the city now, like a murky mound out on the water: the Isle of Misfortune, where every sound is one of grief, where tongues of steel torment the air, shouting so that the air sighs under a heaven shimmering with pain. The air heaves to and fro, like a living person rocking in agony. The lamentation is born weeping loudly, and then it dies like a ripple in the air. The same sound of grief returns, the air moans, the unseen throats gasp in their merciless affliction, and the air is a maelstrom.

But when the bells of the city had anguished for a long time, they began suddenly to peal in a mad storm of sound. And at once a prolonged screaming was set free in the air from the tumult of the bells. Clear, sharp yells burst out on high, and wild sounds more pure than any earthly sound were born in space itself. It was as if invisible beings were thrashing about up in the air, which was as yellow as fire. Great white forms traced the air with the power of lightning, crying out and singing, wailing and singing . . .

Mikkel Thøgersen passed over the bridge from Södermalm. He heard the bells as he came into the town and walked about there. Never before had he known how lowly man is as he walks the earth. More than ever in his confined life he felt he was at the very bottom. Even the wretched houses rose higher than the man who walked beneath them. He looked up at the gloomy wooden hovels, then bowed his head and went on like a beast under the yoke. At the foot of the houses on one side of the street lay the gutter, full of dirty, stale blood that had flowed down from the square. The wind was blowing and the clear air seemed almost famished. It was bitterly cold.

Mikkel crossed the square where all those who had been executed lay, a pile of utterly motionless bodies. He went on toward St. Nicholas's Church.

On the steps outside, the sick and the crippled raised up and turned to Mikkel, eagerly displaying their afflictions. As they got up, they shook the smell of putrefied sores from their clothing.

A man in white homespun rags put forth both his hands. They had already begun to rot away. He pursed his lips in a plea for alms. A boy made his way hesitantly toward the sound, staring out of two bloody holes that had once been eyes. A young cripple sat with his naked leg on a board. Festering had increased its weight greatly, and it was flushed and fetid. Here on the steps it was warm from the bodies of those sweating in fever.

But far down in the growing dimness at the foot of the church wall sat another creature, only a bundle of rags and a head. It was the head of a woman, misshapen and bloated with dropsy. She had no limbs, and she moved only her eyes, staring up through the gloom. As Mikkel looked down on her with compassion, he was terrified by the evil expression in her eyes, a brutal curse on him and all others.

When he came into the church Mikkel could smell incense. The arches soared majestically, and the heavy, square-hewn stones seemed to be wrapped in a veil of sound. It was the organ, playing softly and reverberating up in the darkness under the vaults. Only a few candles were burning here and there on the splendid altars.

Mikkel did not go far into the church, but held instead to a corner close by the door. He felt that his legs were breaking with fatigue, so he sat down on the floor, deep in the darkness, and closed his eyes.

Quiet tones continued to come from the organ. They comforted him, but they also weighed heavily on his heart. He was the one who was standing on the outside, as always, and for this reason the soothing music sounded stifled and distant. He was outside it all, homeless.

Then, just as Mikkel was thinking this, the music welled up mightily, as if all the great portals were opening, and a hymn

140

was heard from a choir of pure voices. All the organ's small pipes blazed forth, youthful and brilliant, together with the deeper, grief-filled tones and the somber, bleeding sounds. The hymn grew louder.

Mikkel's heart collapsed. "Lord Jesus!" he breathed, and he delivered himself up to the Almighty. He felt the burden of his years of loneliness melting away.

Yes, he had been lonely, and the man who is lonely is condemned—this becomes clear with time. Thought congeals as days and weeks pass disjointedly. All simple truths veer off and disappear. The invincible gifts that you perceived in yourself, with the proud thought that they resided only in you—these are weakened by doubt. Where is the power of your fantasy if it cannot sustain the world? You are like all the others, no stronger. And yet, it is your lot to be alone in the world. Yes . . . lonely.

And how had it gone with you? What happened to the natural gentleness of your heart, to your deep impulse to return goodness to all those who filled your youth with nighttime fears? Life would not deliver you from your consuming passion for happiness, but rather it had driven you to revenge and hate, and you had become a wanderer. Finally you talked foolishly of feeling at home in some exotic place far away in the world, there to lament and dissolve with tears your unfathomable suffering. But no, life would not even deliver you from your soul's boundless burden of lamentation and anguish.

Now the organ swells with deliverance. Pain and passion finally flow together in a poignancy of sorrow. The tones of the hymn bring healing visions to the spirit and the heart stirs suddenly in the breast with its own life, like a child quickening in the womb.

Hear now how the clear voices are singing with such sweet suffering! The organ rages and storms, then whispers. The voices

141

of all creatures join in, and the tongues of dumb beasts add their wild song. The trumpets of Judgment Day and the pure flutes of heaven sound.

Then a light glimmers so that the road from the Kingdom of the Dead into the Great Summer can be seen. All toilworn souls move together down this road, from the battlefields and from the towns. They leave their plows, they land at the coast and leave their ships, they rise up from their graves, and they gather to follow this road.

The shrill winds of withered hope blow about them. They seek compassion, for they found only evil while they were among the living. Their teeth chatter, and in their thousands they weep and wring their hands because life in the Kingdom of the World was only bitterness. While they move along the road they raise a tumultuous dirge, they lift their pale faces and commit their frenzied prayers to the mercy of the stars.

From the inimical earth a rising sound tells of these events, a rushing sound of all that time destroys. It is the wind of the world's eternal desiccation and the disintegration of all created things. It is the coldest wind under the heavens, more ruinous than any winter can be. It holds its own echo, like ice needles crackling as they revolve slowly in the clouds. The echo is that of hoofbeats and laughter and life, life that hurries away—an echo of quietly plaintive harmonies. Hush! Secretly, a rattle of bones! The innermost sound is like a slight settling in the coffin.

Hush! If you think at all, your memory is filled with the whistling wind. The icy breath of oblivion blows over you. In your bleak recollections you hear only the song of drifting snow. A pain explodes in your being, forcing on you an unbearable darkness.

And so the unfortunate who have been placed upon the earth listen, and they are afraid. They flock together, not like those who feel a sense of concord, but rather like cattle on an island in an autumn storm, pressing out on the farthest point and sending their urgent cries toward land.

Here they live in twilight, without warmth. Those who are banished to this place live as outcasts, not knowing human kindness. He who freezes sees to it that it also blows on his neighbor. He who feels loss and harbors rancor drips malice into the heart of his fellow prisoner. The nights are long and without peace for the lonely, for the unprotected.

But now Mikkel sees the Prince of Agony! He hears him in the hymn. He sees the Lord and Savior take the disconsolate to his bosom. One by one they are gathered up from the road, naked but acceptable to God. The Merciful Savior comforts with his warmth. Mikkel sees righteousness bestowed on all the oppressed souls. They rise up and share in the Kingdom of Heaven. Music pours down upon them. He sees all those he has known in his life and who were scattered by the years. Now they are brought together again. Wretched faces Mikkel only glimpsed among those who fell on the battlefield—he sees them again, resurrected. He sees his father, Thøger Nielssøn, step forth before God, dishonored by age, as seen in the somber evidence of his body. Mikkel sees heaven opening, and he feels his heart bursting in the presence of God. On his knees he moves slowly out into the church, and there he collapses.

# 23. The Little Destiny

It was snowing. The main square in Stockholm lay under a soft, shining blanket, and the snow continued to fall steadily. It was not completely dark but lighted candles were seen in the windows.

From all the streets that led to the square came folk in their finest clothing, walking through the new-fallen snow and all heading toward the steps of the town hall. There the glowing windowpanes proclaimed a festive evening. A banquet was being held by the city of Stockholm in honor of King Christian. When dinner was finished in the hall the young people came streaming in. They had been crowding together at the doors for a long time. Now the time had come for dancing.

So the music began, and Axel was the first one on the floor. For an hour he gave himself over to the music with abandon, thinking only of the dance itself, not the girl he was sharing it with. When he came down to slake his thirst and looked out, it was as dark as the inside of a bellows. Snowflakes were darting through the door like moths seeking the light. Axel dashed out and ran a few streets over to look in on Mikkel Thøgersen, who was sick. Mikkel had been in bed for a week, and it seemed that he was weakening.

In the modest inn where Mikkel was quartered a group of mercenaries sat drinking. Axel greeted them as he passed them on his way back to the room where Mikkel lay. It was dark there and the air was very close. From his sickbed Mikkel asked who it was. His voice was weak and feverish. Axel lit a light and pressed Mikkel's sweaty hand, asking how it was going.

Things did not look good. Mikkel was flushed and his brow was dripping. He was alarmingly emaciated. From the depths of exhaustion he opened his bloodshot, glazed eyes, then closed them again.

"Oh, oh," said Axel, shocked. He sat down on the wicker-work chair by the bed and stared at the sick face for several minutes. Mikkel drew his breath in gasps and turned his head restlessly, as if he wanted to shift his position but didn't have the strength. Axel held some water out to him, but he refused it by tightening his lips.

It looked like Mikkel was going to die here in this barren room. This was what he had come to. On the whitewashed wall hung his broadsword with a hilt worn by his hand. But now Mikkel's hands had grown feeble and limp. His jutting mous-tache, which was beginning to turn gray around the nostrils, was matted with mucous. His high forehead protruded, strangely angular, stern and at the same time humble, like the uncom-fortable household furniture made by a carpenter. His cheeks were gaunt.

Axel could not say anything. But what was there to talk about anyway? It was so dreadfully sad. He would have liked to dry the mucous from Mikkel's moustache but he could not bring himself to do it. He sat there for a long time, seeing how Mikkel bore his sickness in his characteristic way, turning in upon himself.

"Ah, yes," mumbled Axel at length and then he stood up. He tried to catch Mikkel's eye as he bent over to blow out the candle. Then he grasped the burning hand, said a faltering fare-well, and left.

Outside it was pitch-dark, and, to make matters even worse, Axel had to squint because of the snow. He ran straight into some-one, and his laugh was answered by a short, girlish laugh.

"Sigrid! Sigrid!" cried Axel in delight, reaching out his arm in order to touch her again. But he could hear from the footsteps that there were others with her, and they were silent. He realized that it had been a mistake to cry out. They were just at the steps to the town hall, and as the door opened he could see from the light that Sigrid was accompanied by her brother and an older woman. He greeted them respectfully.

Axel had not been able to find Sigrid, even though he had thought ceaselessly about her since the evening they first saw each other. Now he was unsure of what approach to use. But Sigrid met his eyes evenly and they were dancing immediately. Sigrid was still cold from being outside. Her dress wafted coldness against Axel, her hair was full of pungent coldness, and her fresh face was radiant.

"How can it be that I haven't been able to find you?" whispered Axel ardently as they danced.

Sigrid danced on thoughtfully, and then she answered demurely, "Yes."

The candles flickered eagerly on the walls, as though the lively flames could not fall to rest while they were sucking and drinking the tallow. The floor resounded under the feet of light-headed couples. The great hall was only poorly illuminated, with the corners lying in darkness. Out on the floor there were more limbless shadows than there were people. The wall hangings rippled in the cold draft. The music blared, the dancers twirled, and ephemeral shadows vaulted over the dark chasms in the corners.

"You are different from the way I remembered you," whispered Axel as he danced, enraptured. "I remembered you in a completely different way. But you are . . ." He was quiet for a long time, breathing heavily. "Sigrid!"

Sigrid danced on in an enigmatic enchantment. "Yes," she said softly.

146

The musicians, men of enormous skill, were certainly not played out yet. The clarinet fluttered lightly from note to note, the horns added their round tones, and the drum marked the insistent rhythm.

The dancing night moved on, unchanging, and Axel and Sigrid danced together outside of time. Then Axel saw how pale Sigrid was.

"You look almost as if there were blood coming from your mouth!" he cried, and then he nearly stopped dancing. Sigrid raised her round dark eyes and turned even paler. He drew her close with his trembling arm and led her very slowly on in the dance.

Then they were sitting on the cushioned bench by the wall. As Axel spoke, Sigrid's response became more and more vivacious. She looked frankly and directly at him, as if to test him, and he answered with an instinctive and self-assured movement of his body. His full blue sleeves were slashed to show the yellow silk within, and he was wearing green hose and square-toed shoes. Sigrid's dress was of blue velvet, open at the top and showing the fine linen at her throat. Her soft hair, like golden barley, billowed about her cheeks. She showed Axel her ring, a glistening diamond on her short, firm finger.

"We have the same kind of hand," said Axel. He lowered his voice. "Would you like a ring from me? I have many of them, Sigrid."

Sigrid interrupted him, but without answering. He asked again. She said lightly "No," and shook her hair back.

"Say yes!" begged Axel, destitute at her rejection. His eloquence failed him and he was silent, but his eyes were insistent in their supplication and he sighed with deep feeling.

Then Sigrid nodded, but she did not look at him. His expression was now disheartened and he was silent. At once Sigrid began to laugh and his face changed. He leaned closer, captivated, and began breathlessly to tell about his treasure. She would have all the valuable neck rings, all the jewels, now sparkling in the bosom of the earth, coming to her fresh from their slumber in the dark loam. She would have solid bracelets and incomparable chains of precious and pure metal. She had only to indicate her desire.

"Shall we dance?" was Sigrid's response, and she laughed. She rose and breathed out heavily, as though she had been thoroughly bored by his talk.

Axel danced, hurt but also deeply happy, and this mood drew Sigrid in, so she smiled lovingly at him with the special warmth of a girl being courted. She danced, youthful and delicate, near and yet far away.

The night wore on. Each time Sigrid gave him hope, Axel was strangely sad. When she teasingly blew all hope away, he suffered—but happily. Then she would take pity on him, feeling drawn to him and abandoning her aloofness. But when he began to rue his victory she would laugh, and he was miserable and enthralled. . . . And so the night wore on.

At three o'clock Sigrid's brother and the older woman came. It was time for her to go home, and this time Axel was permitted to accompany them. The snow had stopped. The night was clean and cold, and the snow sparkled. Finally Axel had learned where Sigrid lived. When he went home to his room he was elated and determined to win her hand.

Several days later Axel and Sigrid plighted their troth. The betrothal was not approved of by everyone in her family, since at first they did not really believe Axel's story about his treasure. But he tapped his chest and showed them the capsule. Would Mendel Speyer—whoever he was—have lied? Why couldn't there be a large inheritance for someone even though they didn't have a family name? If there were some dark question about his ancestry,

148

why then, so much the better. When he received the inheritance (although there really was no hurry) he would surely also discover who he actually was. And that is where the matter rested. After all, who could resist someone who was incapable of doubt? The betrothal was celebrated with great ceremony.

. . . The town of Stockholm lay under the chaste snow, which fell and fell, burying all traces. Every day there was some small celebration, and nearly every evening there was dancing in the house of one or another affluent burgher.

One night Axel put a ladder up to Sigrid's window, but he was pulled down by her brothers in a scene of great hilarity. Then Axel was obliged to treat everyone to wine at the town hall. The wedding date was set for shortly before Christmas.

Yes, there was merrymaking in Stockholm under its shroud of snow. Party-goers in the streets night and day! Late one evening when Axel was walking home, he saw the figure of a woman in front of him. She was walking slowly, close to the houses and with her hood down over her head. She was alone, and she was crying. Axel could only see that she was young. Why was she walking alone on the street and crying? When he spoke to her she didn't answer, but when he took her by the hand she came with him. While they were together she did not utter a single word. She cried and sighed inconsolably the whole night. Each time Axel awoke he heard her speechless sorrow. He did not learn why she despaired. In the morning she put on her black clothing and left, crying as she had come.

The same day that he and Sigrid were betrothed, Axel went to see Mikkel Thøgersen, who still lay without hope of recovery. Mikkel was no longer suffering. All his strength was gone now and he was failing fast.

Axel saw how deathly pale Mikkel had become. And Mikkel himself seemed to be aware that the end was near.

Numb and heavyhearted, Axel sat with the dying man for an hour. When he was about to leave Mikkel opened his eyes and whispered good-bye, but as Axel turned away Mikkel called to him. He wanted to say something, and Axel bent down to him gently.

"The treasure . . . shall I read the paper for you now?" said the dying man, almost inaudibly.

Axel straightened up and tears came to his eyes. But then he looked at Mikkel quickly and steadily.

"No," he answered brusquely. Then he turned his hat in his hands with embarrassment. "Well, ah . . . I think . . . wait and see, Mikkel. You'll get better!"

Mikkel Thøgersen lay silent, but when he saw Axel's back in the doorway he was consumed with rage. He vowed revenge. Once again, he hated.

The next morning Mikkel Thøgersen was on the road to recovery. And recover he did.

## 24. In the Primeval Forest

Mikkel Thøgersen and Axel did not see each other for two years. When Mikkel had regained his health he followed the king down to Denmark. But before this, Axel had vanished from Stockholm. It happened just before Christmas, two days after his wedding. He was seen no more, and of course this occasioned a great deal of comment. It was a wild story. There was talk of family members who fainted dead away. Sigrid had become a widow all too soon.

The one least affected—but at the same time most—was Axel, the unrepentant. In one way it was a simple matter, seen from his standpoint, but in another way exceedingly complicated. Two days after the wedding he was taking a morning ride out in the country south of the town. And being so incredibly happy with the very thought of Sigrid, so robust and with all his senses alive, he began to think of Kirsten in Denmark. The call was actually from the depths of his heart, but in his ears it seemed to come from a great distance. His heart was rejoicing in its fullness of Sigrid, but he heard this as Kirsten's voice. At once he became so ardent with passion that he rode off at top speed. The memory of Kirsten filled him now—he had to see her.

Axel forgot that their last meeting had been nearly a year earlier and that hundreds of miles lay between them. He rode at full speed west on the King's Highway, but after an hour's unbroken gallop the horse slowed to a trot, and then Axel remembered that, to be sure, it was a long way to Denmark. He couldn't be there immediately. But what started as mad impulse had now become sober determination, and Axel rode on at a moderate pace and examined the new situation. At any rate, he intended to travel to Denmark in order to visit Kirsten, last year's love.

By evening Axel had already come a great distance from Stockholm. He stopped at an inn, and there he sat by himself in the common room. Many peasants were there, all talking of Gustav Eriksson Vasa, but Axel was not listening. They asked him politely for news from Stockholm, but Axel had little news to give them. Then too, the others kept their distance when they heard he was Danish. Axel didn't want to talk. He was thinking of Sigrid.

The morning of the same day—far away over forests and towns in the snow, and separated by a remaking of the spirit, with the face of fate now turned in profile . . . that same morning Axel had kissed Sigrid. He had gotten up first and wanted to go out, but she thought it was much too cold. When he kissed her she slipped her white arms from the featherbed and wrapped them around his neck. She was a wonder of delicacy and whiteness. And when Axel came out in the fresh air he had to throw himself on his horse and ride like the wind in order to dull his rapture.

So that is how it happened. In a certain number of days, when he had covered the distance between them, he would see Kirsten. In his eagerness he twisted his hands together so that the bones cracked. Kirsten. Oh, Kirsten!

He could almost *see* the farmhouse there on the bluff, with the crooked apple tree hanging over the roof. The brackish lakes would still be lapping the sand below, just as on that day in March when he had turned in the saddle and seen it.

Axel slept well that night in the inn. But once he awoke suddenly, with Kirsten's face just above his, her lips not an inch from his mouth. "Sigrid!" he whispered, and then he drifted back into sleep.

The next day he rode on in a frost so hard that the world turned brittle. The road was stony and difficult and it heaved tortuously, but he held his horse to a full gallop while the strong wind whistled about his ears. In the midst of the staccato beat of the horse's hooves and the thundering of the air, Axel sang. His voice added one more searing sound to the clamor of the ride. He rode and sang like a tempest, with the snow and stones rushing beneath him. The snowy fields flashed by in the sunlight, a few red log cabins appeared, and great frost-covered boulders reared up from the earth like the skulls of buried giants. He flew through pine forests, he shot into narrow openings in the rocks and out again. And he sang. It was as if he were bending over a greedy grinder and letting his song disappear like a thin stream of grain down into its compact mass of sound.

In eight . . . no, ten days . . . Now suddenly Axel could no longer bear to ride west, seeing that he *had* to go south as well. Why follow the road? It must be shorter to travel at an angle across the country. So he pulled the horse sharply off the road and rode out into the trackless forests.

He rode all day long, but toward evening the land began to rise and become more rocky. Ancient and fantastically shaped fir trees leaned out from the boulders, with bushes filling the space between them. There was snow everywhere and Axel had to dismount and lead his horse. It was disheartening to see how little progress he was making. When it was nearly dark he managed to come down into a narrow and desolate ravine. The bottom was flat enough to ride along, so he followed it until far into the night. But then the ravine ended and he had to pull his horse deeper into the heavy forest, step by step. The terrain was still rising, and the forest was growing ever more dense.

The night was utterly still. The trees were sleeping in the frosty weather and not a sound was heard. Axel did not think of his unhappy plight. Two days had passed, and now his fate was to pull his horse behind him in a hopeless forest, in the night and the biting cold. That's just the way his life was.

At midnight Axel found a hut in the forest and there he was given shelter. In this hut he remained—because the woodcutter's daughter was lovely.

The man's name was Kese and his young daughter was called Magdalene. When Axel came down from the loft the next morning, Kese had gone into the woods and Magdalene was standing by the open hearth making food. Axel looked at her, and they moved quickly toward each other, testing each other—and they were on intimate terms immediately. He reached out for her and laughed, refreshed by sleep, and she laughed too, ready for battle with lifted ladle. Then Axel took her resolutely about the waist and probed the depths of her eyes. Magdalene avoided his eyes, but he kissed her firmly. And in an instant they were clinging to each other.

When Kese came home he walked around silently for a long time in the little room, and then he nodded several times to himself. The young people took this nodding as a favorable omen. And so it happened that Axel became the son-in-law in the hut.

"She's yours," said Kese several days later, suddenly lowering his ax when they were felling trees. He looked up at Axel as if he had used the last few days just to think this thing through.

"She's yours." Kese leaned on his ax and pondered the matter. It was little more than by chance that *he* had gotten her, he declared. It happened in quite a casual way when he had a woman working there. Later she ran off, leaving him with the child that had been bestowed by chance upon them. Magdalene, he called her, just because it was a name. But that wasn't really her name—she might just as well . . . In short, she simply existed, seeing that she was walking around there, just as strong and pretty as any other person.

154

"So take her!" said Kese. "Easy come, easy go!"

Kese spit in his hands and swung his ax against the tree. After that he made no more speeches.

The winter grew more severe and it became frightfully cold. All winds stilled and the air perished. The sun glistened in the sky at midday, white and cold like a chunk of polished ice far away, and in the late afternoon it sank into a dark sea of blood behind the forests. The stillness of the long nights was broken only when a listless bird flew close enough to brush snow from the trees, or when wild animals in the distance gave voice to their hunger and their heavy heart.

In the hut in the forest they were able to keep the cold out. It was padded from top to bottom with moss, and there were sheepskins to sleep in. The fire burned day and night. In the corner by the hearth lay pieces of wood from the forest, freshly cut and damp. The moss on the bark came alive in the heat, and then the fine, knotless wood began to exude resin as the frost thawed out of it. The wood was eager for the fire, and it expanded just as soon as the flames had a grip on it. The smoke permeated the room and settled on their face so that the taste of the forest was on their lips. The wood gave off a wonderful fragrance in the fire, its vitality filling the air with the pungency of spice.

But they didn't have much of a Christmas. They had nothing to eat but bread and tough old salt-cured meat. Soon they also ran out of fodder for Axel's horse. But why have a horse anyway? asked Kese. The day this was discussed his bearded face livened up and he became both energetic and thoughtful. So they agreed to slaughter the horse, and Kese assumed this duty. He put it off until the following day, however, and in the meantime he kept his own counsel.

Early the next morning Kese woke the two young people and led them outside ceremoniously. The horse lay dead by the door, still warm. Kese began to cut it up, somewhat hesitantly at first, but then with gusto.

When Axel realized that Kese was a heathen he felt a bit uneasy. But he thought no more of it, and when he had taken the leap and whetted his appetite, he was seized by a zest for the forbidden and gave himself over to the carnage. And Magdalene helped too, all three pitching in with exuberance.

In utter silence Kese cast several bowls of blood out toward the east and the south. He seemed almost shyly embarrassed at his skill in butchering the horse. He pointed with the tip of his knife at the delicacies as they reached them. "Oh, yes . . . yes, that's right," he said, nodding.

"It was eight years old," he whispered, squinting confidentially at Axel. And when Axel confirmed this, Kese opened his hand and showed the blood-covered little bone he had used to judge the horse's age. Kese was lying with his nose to the incision in the belly, and he was working at full speed, with both arms in up to the elbow. He was satisfied. The slaughter could not have been more elegant. It had been a healthy and spirited horse. It was difficult work because of the warmth of life still there. You could almost burn your arms inside the horse.

Late in the forenoon Magdalene called them in for the first meal: the finest parts of the beast, boiled and steaming. Kese's mouth watered when he saw the warm meat. He was ready to have at it!

But Magdalene looked devotedly at Axel and set the horse's heart before him. She had roasted it over the open fire, and steam was coming out of its veins. At first Axel ate as if he were not interested in it, but after a few bites he set to in earnest.

156

There was clear, quiet weather all day, with heavy frost. Most of the day they went in and out, eating and butchering. It was as if the fragrance of the boiled and roasted meat refreshed the memory of the newly opened, odoriferous carcass, and of the intestines when they were still functioning. The reek of the butchered horse filled the hut, and the vapors billowed out of the low door and rolled up over the roof. The snow in the eaves over the door melted, then froze again to reddish-brown icicles.

Toward evening Magdalene began from the beginning, baking blood pancakes. The two young people had fallen silent, but the old man could control himself no longer. He began to wallow in the food. He sang and feinted at the sun and the moon in ecstasies. He had been eating almost since morning and he was covered with juice and grease to his eyebrows. He lay far out over the table now, with his leather-sleeved arms embracing the abundance. He chewed and stuffed suet back into his mouth at the corners. He purred and sang. Magdalene went back and forth, also taking a tidbit in her small teeth from time to time.

. . . During the whole of the quiet night Kese lay dreaming up in his moss bed in the loft. In his sleep he laughed and talked of demonic things. The young people woke up and heard him. And once in the black, inert night they heard a trembling out in the forest as a breath of wind passed over the trees. When the frost and the hardened snow fell down from the roof there was a soft, rustling sound as the forest wept over its impotence.

Axel looked out through the windowpane, made of green glass. He saw the horse lying in the snow with all its ribs sticking up in the air. It looked like a shipwreck. The shanks were frozen stiff, casting shadows on the snow in the green light of the moon.

157

The next day they ate again as long as they could. For Kese this meant until his eyes closed with fatigue. But before this happened he had frightened Axel and Magdalene with outbursts of sheer lunacy. He gorged and glutted, he glared at them. Then his sensibilities left him and he sang a little ditty about dead horses whinnying in hell. Hair and beard bristled from his head, stiff with grease. Gleefully he pronounced mortal threats against the young people, and in the same breath he extended his gracious mercy again, gasping with compassion. He contemplated his own inner being with much shaking of the head, and he weltered in reminiscences. In Kese's monologue, Axel heard him mention several traditional women's names, and he could only imagine that Kese was moved by maudlin memories of long-lost sweethearts, one blonde and buxom, another slender and dark-haired, one with happy eyes, another wild-eyed and sleek as a fox cub. ... Kese pawed the air with blood-covered hands and rolled his eyes as he sang and mauled the food.

When he collapsed they carried him to bed.

They also feasted on the third day. Then Kese sobered up and things were back to normal.

And the Swedish spring came, although it took a tremendously long time. One day the sun shone with tongues of fire high in the soft blue of the heavens. There was not a cloud in the sky, but even so, the earth lay covered with melting water. The snow slid off the trees, cleansing itself. The light was refracted in water and in drops of water everywhere.

When the first cool, snow-free day came, with shadows dashing and the water rippling, Axel went out in the forest. A solitary bird chirped from a treetop where the white clouds drifted, lofty tokens of spring in full blossom. The smell there was that of a forgotten summer, with the withered grass and the wet tree bark giving off compelling scents. . . . Where was his horse now? Where was that horse!

The quarters were very cramped now in Kese's hut. It was like a ship's cabin after months at sea. The main room was encrusted with the filth of confinement and daily routine. Magdalene sat there—how mature she had grown, how beautiful! Even as she was sitting there a blush spread over her face and throat.

There was more and more warmth in the sun. One day Axel raised his face, and warm air wafted over it while the sharp sun pricked his eyelids. He took payment in advance and promised himself summer immediately. He became uneasy when he realized that summer had already come to Denmark. One time he had ridden over the heath in lovely, gentle Denmark and met a girl herding sheep. She squinted at the sun and came toward him with grass and flowers between her toes, while the burial mounds behind her stretched for miles.

That same day Axel left Kese's hut.

# 25. The Capsule

As for Axel, the young man who had no birthright, it can be reported that he traveled far and wide, with many changes of fortune. The decision to go to Denmark and to Kirsten—and then back to Sigrid, of course—did not remain the trunk of his Tree of Fate, but became only a withered offshoot between other robust branches nourished by the tree's vitality. Axel was impelled by a shifting infatuation with the young women of the world. It should be mentioned that his sublime experiences with the loveliest of these girls led gradually to a surfeit. Not so much so that he avoided them—no, not at all. It was only that he was just as thankful as he was insatiable. When it came his way he was happy with a drop of joy—but also with a flood, of course.

Axel, the one who bore no grudges—he got on well with all people. One of his natural traits was that he saw all developments as being equally good. Even when everything went against him, he thrived. He could only *receive*—there was no time for losing. He knew only credit, never debit. His heart he moved with him wherever he went.

Eventually Axel came to Denmark, for the great summer was waiting there for him. A year or so after he took the little jaunt following his wedding in Stockholm, he arrived in Denmark again, following chance byways and accepting whatever befell him of fate and fortune.

Much had happened in the meantime. Denmark had lost Sweden and there were rumblings of war and rebellion everywhere, from all points of the compass. Christian, the great king, was setting the whole of his kingdom in jeopardy.

And this is what happened: Mikkel Thøgersen was traveling in Jutland on a mission for the king. He was coming from Thy and had just been at Spøttrup Castle in Salling when he got the idea of making a side trip to his home area, since he was so near. Who knew when he would be in these parts again? Maybe never. The king had promised Mikkel leave, and he intended to make a pilgrimage to the Holy Land the following year.

In an inn in Salling, not far from Hvalpsund, Mikkel heard some strange news. The innkeeper told in disjointed detail of a great celebration a mile up the coast in the village of Kvorne. It had begun the day before and it would likely continue for a day or two more, even though it was only a betrothal. A strange story it was—the young man who was betrothed was supposed to have money to burn. His name was Axel, and he appeared to be of high social standing. Then too, he was an officer, but where he actually came from no one knew. They said about this fellow Axel that he had an enormous treasure. At any rate, he came to the festivities dressed like a duke. But the bride was hardly naked herself. It was Inger, daughter of the rich farmer Steffen in Kvorne. Yes, now they were betrothed. They were holding the celebration on the farm and it could be heard all over the area.

This was the story that the innkeeper told, and Mikkel paid close attention, an appreciative listener. He asked questions and discovered that Steffen's wife was named Ane Mette. And Ane Mette—yes, there was a story to tell about her too. Inger was not Steffen's daughter But Ane Mette had been Steffen's wife now for over twenty years and they had children from their marriage, so the whole affair was almost forgotten. There was actually no one who knew the real story. Some said that Ane Mette had been carried off and violated by a university student in her youth.

That student was Mikkel Thøgersen, but no one would be able to see that now. No matter—he was of no account. A stranger, standing here and gossiping for the sake of business in his inn— this stranger had unwittingly informed Mikkel that he had had a daughter for twenty years without even suspecting it. When the innkeeper had provided this appropriate verbal accompaniment for Mikkel's beer, he left him there, sitting alone at the table. Yes, Mikkel was sitting by himself, *alienus*, an outsider—that was his refrain.

*Alienus.*

What was said about Axel was true. He was to have Inger, the daughter of Steffen in Kvorne. After seeing a good deal of the world, Axel had ridden some months earlier to this nondescript place. Inger's fame had reached him already far south in Jutland. He came, he saw, and now their betrothal was being celebrated with great ostentation. Steffen in Kvorne was the area's richest farmer. As well as his share of the common land of the village he owned a grove of oak trees, and he also engaged in extensive fishing and production of salt.

Mikkel Thøgersen left his horse at the inn and walked up along the shore of the fjord. It was getting on toward evening. He came to Kvorne much sooner than he would have wished. When he heard the violin from the farm buildings where the celebration was being held, he stopped, leaned up against a garden fence, and came no farther. The evening was so cool and endless—the bright nights of summer had already begun. The frogs croaked sonorously in the village pond, and from out on the beach the chirping of a vagrant tern could be heard now and then. There was an elder tree in the vegetable garden Mikkel had stopped beside. He knew the fragrance of its leaves, and the old memory that it revived left him so desolate that he was filled with fear of himself. He turned and walked back to the inn in the warm evening air.

The next morning Mikkel was standing at the same place, and again he left. He came back in the afternoon, and this time he moved closer to the farm buildings. Finally he was standing on the road right in front of the port, but he could not go in. The courtyard was full of fine carriages, and from the house came the sound of festivity and commotion.

A child came out into the port, then ran back and said that there was a big soldier outside. When several came out to look, Mikkel went away, but he did not get far before someone came running after him, shouting his name.

It was Axel himself. He was enormously glad to see Mikkel again, and he could not get over his astonishment. However, he was upset when Mikkel could not be persuaded to join the celebration, even though he had come. Axel could not understand this. They stood in the middle of the road and talked awkwardly. Axel, dressed in fine clothing and bareheaded, did not know how to express his warm feelings. Mikkel lowered his head, endlessly rubbing the graying stubble on his chin and having little to say.

Mikkel could see that Axel had changed—he had become more calm. But it seemed that all his former unrest was now concentrated in his eyes, which gleamed with a zest for life.

Wouldn't Mikkel do him the favor of joining him for the celebration? begged Axel for the twentieth time. He knew Mikkel's peculiarities but he would not give up hope. Just to see Inger? He had to! They would like so much to say hello to him. There was food and drink on the table.

"Inger's mother grew faint when I talked about you," said Axel, laughing lightly in jest. "Come on, you must make her well again!"

Mikkel's turned his shining eyes away. He didn't say no, but he didn't want to go in. Axel tugged at him, but Mikkel resisted and rubbed his chin, deep in thought.

"Ah, yes." Axel sighed in disappointment and gave up. But then he would visit Mikkel down at the inn. Surely there was no great hurry for him to move on. Mikkel had to promise to remain at the inn until the next day.

"All right, but come alone!" said Mikkel harshly. Then they parted.

When Axel came down to the inn the next day Mikkel was pacing about outside, ready to travel. His horse he had already sent over with the ferry. He was impatient to leave. Axel looked gently at his old comrade-in-arms. When he saw that he was anxious to be away, Axel suggested this himself in order to avoid embarrassment for Mikkel. But then Axel would like to go with him across the sound.

At first they sailed in silence. Mikkel was still filled with misgiving. But out in the middle of the sound—with the sun shining down deep in the green water and the coasts lying bright in their summer splendor in front and behind—there Axel looked up at the sky and smiled. He could not contain his joy any longer. He began to talk about Inger, about how it would be for them. He would buy a manor. Soon he would dig up the treasure, at long last. . . . Inger . . .

As Axel spoke, his voice became infinitely warm and tender. His eyes were lost and he was moved in his innermost being. From time to time he chuckled with deep feeling over what he had said. He became restless, he shook his head, and his face was full of emotion as he looked at Mikkel. He had forgotten everything else. . . . And Mikkel felt that the young man's divine goodness was unfair, something measured out mercilessly.

Axel hardly noticed when they left the boat over on the Himmerland side. He continued to tell of his dreams while they walked up the road together.

Mikkel was no longer listening to what he was saying. He bent far forward as they walked. They came up onto the heath and were soon enveloped by the stillness there. The midday warmth coaxed forth fragrant scents from the dry herbs in the ground cover. A bee buzzed above the road and the music of grasshoppers sounded like gasping breaths in the clumps of heather. There was no sign that the countryside was inhabited except for the broad roadway. There scores of ruts wove in and out, crossing each other as the road wound farther and farther on toward the horizon. In the distance lay the Graabølle hills. The bright sky stretched in a great arch across the land.

Here—in their complete solitude on the heath—Mikkel took his revenge.

It was impossible for Mikkel to forgive Axel. He had never seen Inger, and Ane Mette was far from his thoughts now, except in his most profound torment. He was thinking only of Axel's insult when they were in Stockholm. Yes, his hatred for him was beyond restraint. But his heart was in his throat, and he felt his weakness growing just as fast as his resolve to take action. He was nearly paralyzed, like a man who cannot say that he loves and wants desperately to say it. In fact, this was really a simple matter. But Mikkel hesitated in order to increase his pleasure, in order to enjoy the pain of it all. He was prostrate with humiliation, he was robbed of his senses, his heart burned with pain. He felt that all of creation was conspiring against him—against him alone. Finally he succumbed to the darkness, but he could still not perform the deed of darkness—until the moment came when it was as if another being than himself took action.

It happened like this: Suddenly Mikkel staggered and then stood still, staring at Axel. Axel broke off his reverie. Then Mikkel drew his long two-handed sword and moved in on Axel, who was unarmed. Mikkel slashed out with the blade in a strangely awkward way, like a child in a rage. But when Axel finally took a blow, it was a solid one. He did not say a word. He kept his eye on the sword, trying to protect himself with his arms and seize the blade with his hand. Then he took a cut to the knee that rang through every bone in his body, and his skull danced at the end of his spine. He sank to the ground, unconscious.

Slowly Mikkel put his sword back in its scabbard. He passed his hand over his beard and thought for a moment. Then he bent over and put his hand in under Axel's collar, groping on the warm chest until he found the bone capsule. He drew it out and took a few steps away before he opened it.

The capsule was empty. When Mikkel discovered this, he threw it out into the heather and set off at full speed down the road.

# 26. No Quarter

Several hours later Axel came to his senses. His leg could not bear his weight and he was in great pain. He dragged himself a dozen steps down the road, then he sat down in a rut and waited—breathed deliberately and waited. His head was so full of pain that he could hardly see. His knee throbbed, and for a long time he did not have the courage to look at it. Finally he loosened his clothing resolutely and examined the injury. There was only a small blue gash on the outside of the knee. It was not even bleeding, but the joint was swollen and unbearably painful.

It was nearly evening. The birds were singing to the setting sun and a gentle breeze wafted over the heath. Just beside Axel there was a crowberry bush, but the berries were hard and green.

Far away he heard the creaking of a wagon coming from the ferry landing, drawn by oxen and slow—maddeningly slow. Finally it came close enough for Axel to hail the driver. He did not want to be taken back to the ferry. He asked where the nearest inn to the east was. Graabølle Inn was the closest, so he was driven there. It was nightfall when he got there and, although he had been lying on a large bunch of soft heather, he was in miserable condition.

He was laid in bed in the inn's only guest room, and there he dozed off.

When Axel awoke in the morning and saw the pale dawn at the windowpanes, there was to be no deliverance from his agonized dreams. The first thing he felt was a slashing pain from his leg, and he was frightened when he realized he was not dreaming. And when he looked at his leg icy needles of dread shot through him. The knee was double its normal size, red and

167

throbbing. Then Axel lay back and burst into tears, quivering like a straw in the wind. He clasped his hands and bemoaned his fate, with salty tears flowing down into his mouth.

During the morning someone came in to Axel, a small man with a brownish complexion who gave his name as Zacharias. He was an itinerant barber-surgeon, just now in this area by chance. When Axel saw him his spirits rose immediately. "Good morning," shouted Zacharias cheerily in a voice like wood. "Well, let's have a look!"

He threw back the featherbed and seized the injured knee with both hands. Axel gave a single, penetrating scream.

"Oh," growled Zacharias. He continued his examination with claw-like fingers, but Axel lay back and was silent. "Oh." Zacharias bent forward, beginning to savor the situation. Yes, just as he thought. He straightened up and told Axel that he would have to lance the knee, but that it was not a serious matter. So he made his preparations, bringing a basin of water and unpacking his bag.

Axel followed him carefully with his eyes and he got an indelible impression of the man. His skin was grayish brown and wizened. His flat lips were spotted and his gums and half rotten teeth looked as if he had been drinking corrosive acid. There was a reddish glint in his eyes, and under them were shadows as blue as gunpowder. His hair was like hay spoiled by dampness, and even his little moustache seemed stained, like fermented hay. Zacharias's tongue was as quick as a lizard's, and his dark hands looked like they had been in all kinds of muck. And there was a smell about him, a dry, rancid odor, like toads and other reptiles.

While he was arranging his knives and small brass forceps on the wicker chair, Zacharias told a story, completely meaningless and nonsensical, with no point at all. Then suddenly he laughed, with great guffaws rolling up out of his throat.

168

"So." He was finally ready, and now he became very serious. Slowly he stretched his hands out to the knee and felt for a place to begin. While he cut, he said nothing.

At first Axel was almost paralyzed by the unbelievable brutality of the pain of the knife in the wound. But he braced himself, held his breath in with all his strength, forced his ringing head down onto the pillow, and drifted slowly into unconsciousness.

When he came to he saw Zacharias's face above him and heard him ordering: "Breathe out! Breathe in!" It seemed dark in the room. The door was open and a pair of faces looked around the door frame.

Axel leaned out over the edge of the bed and threw up. Then he fell back, exhausted. And the pain was there, heavy and horrible. It throbbed gently but with a frightful power. "Oh, no! No!" But it went on and on, and Axel writhed on the bed like one who has fallen on the ice. He nodded weakly and his teeth chattered as he sucked breath into his heaving chest. With his tongue he wet his lips, and they felt burned or mutilated.

"There, there," said Zacharias soothingly. He stood mixing a black potion in a clay pot. "It'll be over in a few minutes. See, here's a good ointment. It's got seventy-seven different ingredients and the whole of nature's potency in it. Just as soon as we put it on . . . Hmm . . . ."

Zacharias smeared the salve in the wound and Axel fell unconscious again. When his senses cleared, his leg had been straightened out and bound up. The burning of the wound seemed to have lessened a bit, as if the pain's first hunger had been satisfied. But not for long.

Zacharias had gone.

The rest of the day Axel lay in pain, pain which thundered over his head—or else in deep exhaustion. Food was brought to him and he ate it, feverishly and with chattering teeth, making haste to get it over with, and then hurriedly closing his eyes and taking up the battle again.

When he opened his eyes hours later he thought it would be night. But it was not dark yet—the time of the bright nights had come. And when he saw that it was a bright night he understood in a visionary flash the nature of his anguish. He was suffering intensely. There was a rhythm in the pain of the knee, as if it were a beast that had reduced its attack to a system. He was alone. Mighty sobs swept over him, and he lay awake the whole of the bright night, growing sicker and sicker.

But when the sun rose there was a pulsing in his heart, a hymn of power and might. He felt like God. Every heartbeat renewed the consciousness of pain in his head. A thunderous roar seemed to envelop him, though he lay in perfect silence. Oh, God, how comforting it was to hear this clamor in the air! He grew immensely in strength, sensing his monstrous doom.

Axel slept, then suddenly reared up in bed with corruption flowing from a place on his thigh, as if Death had clamped its mouth there and was sucking. Sweat poured off him. But he was trembling with fatigue, and he collapsed again.

Faces appeared before him. Just as his fright subsided a hare ran toward him, its eyes bulging. Horseflies buzzed with metallic wings on the featherbed in ever increasing clangor. The song of a giant grinder! And Axel accepted his fear and succumbed to it totally. But then he awoke again and rediscovered his torment.

Zacharias came and took off the dressing. He pursed his lips in disapproval—there was a great deal of inflammation in the wound. He cut a bit more and laid on a new and powerful salve. Then he sat by the bed and fired off a few more stories. It was going better with Axel now, the siege of pain was less intense, and he was able to rest.

And what did Zacharias tell Axel? A merry little tale about a strange town down in Germany he had once passed through. Everyone was a cripple there, and if you wanted to get through town alive you had to bind up one of your legs and hobble through on crutches. Now that was reasonable enough, wasn't it?

Axel saw Zacharias's face as if in a fog. That carefree grin—he thought that the barber-surgeon looked like a big beetle.

Axel heard bits and pieces of another story. It was also of one of those small, fortified towns down in Germany. Zacharias had traveled through it and had seen people disperse in the street as if by magic. Doors and gates seemed to suck them in, or they just blew away. Why? Well, because a single mad dog with froth at the mouth was marching down the middle of the street.

Axel dozed off.

Zaharias recounted a legend. It was about a monk who was taking a shortcut to Jerusalem. First he came by two sparkling lakes, then over a little hill, and then around a hollow. After a long journey up hill and down dale, he came to two great white mountains, and there he rested. Then he traveled for miles over a domed plateau, up one side and down the other. From the top he had glimpsed the Garden of Gethsemane. Then he came to Jerusalem.

. . . Suddenly Axel was wide awake at something Zacharias was telling. He saw the merriness in the discolored face.

It was a most repulsive story about a young girl in Holland. She had come to Zacharias, saying that the master of the house wanted some rat poison. She was a big buxom girl in her twenties, the early-maturing, full-blooded kind. And there was—notice this now—a sort of languor about her. Yes, she was the type of girl that had taken her fill of forbidden fruit for perhaps half a year, no mistaking it. So two days later Zacharias was summoned to inspect a body. It was the same girl, and she was with child. Ha, ha. She had swallowed four ounces of rat poison, just the amount she had gotten from Zacharias by deceit. There she was, lying on the table. In death she looked as if God Almighty, when He breathed the spirit of life into her, had really puffed in an almighty way, so that a big bulge had formed on her. . . .

At this point Zacharias cackled with laughter. It sounded like a pile of firewood that suddenly came tumbling down.

But Axel looked at him in horror. From the story he had nothing but a sharp image of the dead body, right there on the table. Then he thought of Inger, who had picked a flower on the meadow and held it in her hand like a candle, walking at his side. His entire being rose up and denied the possibility that all this was happening. Away with it! He closed his burning eyes, turned his face to the wall, held his breath, and cried.

# 27. Danish Death

Axel, the carefree young man, died in the evening under the open sky. In the last hours of life he was fully conscious. The third day after he had been wounded came his final struggle. He had been racked by physical torment for two days, an eternity that had consumed him. When he felt the final flush of fever he asked to be carried outside, and he cried like an animal while he was in their arms. Outside he sat in a chair the whole day.

When he opened his eyes in the sunshine—the ducks were scratching near the well—he saw Mikkel Thøgersen. He had been standing there for a time.

"Can't you get better?" asked the old man miserably. Axel shook his head listlessly and closed his eyes. After a long time he looked up, and Mikkel was still there.

It was stifling warm and still. A potsherd lay on the ground, glistening in the sun.

"The bees, they're swarming," said an honest peasant voice from the door of the inn. In the snow-white air above the vegetable garden there hung a swarm of bees, a round, undulating cloud just beside the sun, flaring out, then contracting around its teeming core, and sometimes disappearing in the brightness of the sun. From it a sultry, seething sound drifted down.

Axel heard Mikkel say that the capsule had been empty. "There was nothing in it, Axel!" But Axel didn't care. In the midst of life doubt had never darkened his mind. After all, he had the paper. Now he was going to die, and it made no difference that it was lost.

"Will you forgive me?" begged Mikkel in profound wretchedness. This was only a further affliction for the dying Axel, and he did not move. Soon he saw that Mikkel was gone.

Only Inger was in Axel's thoughts now. Had they forgotten him? They hadn't come. He had not sent word to them, but he felt in his heart that they would find him anyway. A little before he would not have wanted to see her, but now . . . Why hadn't they found him? Mikkel had! Then why none of them? His heart wept. He sat completely still. There was no relief. He couldn't even swallow to help ease his burning breast. His throat was parched.

Late in the afternoon Axel awoke, and he sensed that all his pain was gone!

Yes. He felt so thankful that his color rose. The pain stayed at a distance! He was constantly aware of his deliverance, and inner delight overwhelmed him. In enormous exhaustion he lay motionless, transported to a realm wondrously free of pain. His heart stirred silently in his breast from time to time, like a tired child, laughing and sobbing in joy as it is put to bed.

His mind had become so lucid that he remembered things long forgotten. The past and the present flowed together in a unity of time without pain. The torment of memory had left him. There was no sting in death. When you can die before the moment of death, then dying is less hard.

Axel remembered incidents from his childhood, when he had been so proud that harsh treatment or a thrashing suited him better than kindness. That boulder was surely still there, the one he had clung to for more than an hour. It weighed at least a ton, but in a blind fury Axel wanted to throw it at another boy. When he couldn't wrench it from the ground he fastened himself to it with hands and feet, like an enraged ant. They had to pull him off. It seemed like it happened only yesterday.

Axel thought of the times he had sneezed several times in a row. He remembered a toad he had seen in the rain and evening murk, crawling through the nettles on its stomach like a spy. He remembered a frayed spot on the sleeve of a coat he had once had. He died with such fragmented recollections before him, forgotten trifles that sear like molten iron, but the anguish of memory had now become one with the blissful awareness that it was ceasing. And thus Axel died, living. Like snow melting. He went living into death.

Inger! Oh! She was far away, but present in memory now at his death. Dear Inger, farewell! But it was not hard to die.

It was the eve of a holy day, and the peasants in Graabølle were preparing for the festivities. When dusk—summer's gentle twilight—was falling, the sky burst forth in gold, and dew gathered on the grass. Great heads of heavy green grain hung over the fertile fields, giving off a pungent odor from all the thousands of young heads of grain. Down in the pastures by the stream the cows were bellowing for their milkmaid. Far away on the hills of Graabølle Heath there was a prick etched against the boundless sky. It was a shepherd boy, on his way out now at evening.

Under the sky there lay a nocturnal stillness and a fragrant coolness. The twilight itself seemed green, as if the air were a life-giving sea. All sounds were hushed when they reached the ear. Every shout in the distance sounded like tidings of happiness there where it came from, transformed into a peal of joy on its way to the ear under the beneficent sky. True night would not be seen—it was the season of bright nights.

When the cattle had been given their feed and the evening meal eaten in peace, the people of Graabølle gathered together on the road by the inn. Music from a single violin was heard, sounding like a human voice.

One or another person stood for a few minutes looking at the stranger who sat by the inn. There was general agreement that his condition didn't look too promising.

Soon all the folk in the village, young and old, moved up to the church, where the celebration was to take place. The fiddler led the procession. Only an old woman stayed at the inn to watch over the sick man. She sat in the doorway with her spinning wheel and spun, hour after hour, making not the slightest sound.

Time passed. Now and then a faint swell of voices could be heard from the church. Then a gust of wind brought louder sounds—laughter and shouts from those who were dancing.

Axel opened his eyes and, even though he was half unconscious, he saw that the night was bright.

Song was heard from up at the church and the sound of the bung being knocked out of a beer barrel. And then—perhaps as accompaniment for a ring dance—loud and boisterous singing broke out. The celebration became so lusty that it could be heard far out in the countryside.

Axel opened his eyes once more and saw the bright night.

The heavens were like white roses.

Far, far away, a joyful bonfire blazed on a hill.

A silent bird flew swiftly by and on into the cool dusk. The willow tree by the well bowed quietly, with all its gentle leaves white in the bright night. A delicate, ash-white moth fluttered in the night air. The sky was misty with the light of stars. Axel closed his eyes.

And he flew upright in the bright night and descended gently on board the Ship of Fortune. They were sailing on the sea under the light of the moon and the stars. And when they had sailed for a long time, they came to the Land of Fortune, the low land of glorious summer. With closed eyes you breathe in the sweet odor of the turf, and the earth is soft and green as a newly made bed in the sea—a bed for birth, a bed for death. A benevolent sky arches over it, clouds hang motionless above it, and waves reach in and stroke the dazzling beach. Two blue seas fondle the coasts, where the sand is fine and the grassy sea bottom is strewn with round, multicolored stones. Inland there is a fjord which can never be forgotten because the pillars of the sun are found there. The coasts and islands of the Land of Fortune rise up enchantingly from the sea, the fjords sing, and the sounds are like gateways to the Land of Plenty. Here all colors are vivid. The earth is deep green and the sky meets the sea in a fusion of blues. This is the great Land of Summer, the Land of Death.

# 28. The King Falls

**B**efore Mikkel Thøgersen received leave from the king's service and journeyed to Jerusalem, the king's time of tribulation had begun. Mikkel took part in some of this—he was with him the night the king sailed on Lillebælt.

King Christian was now reaping the harvest of what he had sown in his manhood. The stones he had flung at the heavens began to fall down on his head. The king's deeds of might were now seeking revenge.

History tells briefly of the king's most fateful night. It was the tenth of February 1523, the night of doubt and desolation, and it was a direct consequence of the seventh of November 1520, when the king's power plunged. Yes, the king's power came to an end even as he used it.

King Christian had received in Ry the Danish nobles' letter of annulment, an abjuration of their pledge of loyalty to him. His situation was now precarious. But if his cause was so hopeless, it was because his own gigantic design was collapsing around him. He had conquered Sweden by evil means and bound it to him by brutality. Now it was wrenching itself from his grasp. His reign in Denmark had been unbending and ruthless, so now the Danes were implacable and defiant. He who will rake must learn to take.

Now at the end the king had sought an accommodation with his uncle, who aspired to the kingdom. He had undertaken difficult trips to and from and about Jutland, written letters, negotiated—all to no avail. He was exhausted, and his scheme seemed to have floundered hopelessly. Then he was stricken by doubt.

During the evening of the tenth of February he abandoned his cause. He went aboard the ferry to sail over to Fyn. Sjælland and Fyn and the other islands were steadfast in their loyalty, and the whole of Norway still supported him. But as things stood he knew that he was giving up his cause—Denmark's cause—when he left the negotiations and sailed from Jutland. Lillebælt was the water that Charon's ferry plied.

It was bitterly cold that evening, and neither dark nor light. It was not raining but the air was heavy with moisture. The king boarded the ferry at Høneborg Castle, together with ten of his men. When the horses were put on board there was some commotion, but otherwise everything was done quietly. The others in the king's party remained in Jutland and were to follow the next day. They stood on the shore with torches while the ferry moved out on the dark water.

The king sat aft in the ferry and all could see his face in the torchlight from the bow. Everyone sensed the state of affairs and no one said a word. But when they had been on the water for a time the king himself broke the silence with a casual question about the current and the driftage. His manner was so composed and his voice so even in tone there in the open boat that those who were with him felt strangely moved. They were frightened, and they remained silent.

A little later the king inquired about one of the horses, one that had shown signs of lameness that day. Mikkel Thøgersen gave as much information as he could. Then there was silence again. The water heaved about the ferry. In the bow there was a man with a torch, and it seemed that the waves were trying to reach it. Everyone turned their eyes to the torch from time to time to see if it was still burning well. All the men were sitting at the railing with their back to the water. The stillness plagued them, oppressed them.

"We do not wish you to be silent!" said the king softly and suddenly, with a touch of the characteristic menace in his voice. "It shows insubordination, he added, wronged and angered.

Then most of the men cleared their throat, pulled themselves together, and started asking each other about the price of armor, how often they had been in Hamburg—whatever they could think of saying. But they talked like sick men, chattering about the draft from the window . . . and meaning death. When their tongues were loosened, however, the king relaxed. Their voices held his spirits up—as with a girl who find herself walking alone through the woods with an unknown man. She talks and talks, listening to her own faltering voice among the trees.

The ferrymen rowed steadily, sitting in their damp sheepskins and bending over the oars. Their caps were pulled down over their brows. They were mesmerized by the king, and their devoted eyes did not leave his face. The horses in the middle of the boat held their balance as best they could, but they snorted and showed the whites of their eyes, apprehensive at the nearness of the water. The light of the torch flickered against the rough, tarred boat. Conversation on board was flowing smoothly now.

The king was able to turn his eyes inward. As long as Jutland's coast could be seen he felt a measure of calm—he was leaving! He had abandoned his cause. All the thousands of details and complexities in his shattered imperial strategy ran once more through his head. He surveyed his entire position, calculated the factors of time and distance, considered the various possibilities and alternates—and when at the conclusion of this painful effort he *saw* the net result, he had to bow his head and let the matter lie.

But when the torches on land had burned out and sunk from view, when the ferry lay out on the open water where its forward progress could not be felt, the king was not so sure. And when he could see the lights in Middelfart, he thought of the territory he had given up. It was, after all, his kingdom. In a vision he saw Denmark, a reality in the sea, a variegated whole of separate land areas—a *country*.

It is an eternal truth that Denmark lies between two blue seas, green in the summer, bronze in the fall, and white under the winter sky. The Danish strands are wonderfully inviting and the Danish fields undulate in gentle harmony, clothing themselves with grain and then yielding it up. The sun's rays stream down from behind the clouds and spread over the hills by the Limfjord, whose waters are the playground of the western wind. The day's rhythm in Denmark is always different and always the same. The smaller fjords and inlets create and recreate Denmark a hundred times, and Øresund is like a gateway leading to the country itself. Here the streams run out to the sea and the forests grow near the coast. You see a gull, catch a glimpse of a hare bounding over the heath, feel the sunshine and contentment. This is Denmark.

But now that the king *had* abandoned his country—inasmuch as he had been absolutely certain that he was abandoning it—the thought of Denmark became so powerful in his heart that he could not abandon it.

"Put about!" commanded the king suddenly, standing up in the ferry. The sounds of the many voices on the ferry stopped as if they were coming from a single mouth. The ferrymen hung motionless over the oars and stared. King Christian gave them the order again in an impatient but quiet voice. They obeyed and got the heavy ferry turned in the water. Soon they were on a steady course back out into the strait and the lights of Middelfart disappeared. No one dared to ask the king about the reason, but they were all greatly relieved, and this led them to remain silent—until they remembered the king's earlier command and saw to it that the conversation was kept lively.

The king's courage grew quickly as soon as he was moving in the opposite direction, for now he was turning back to his royal goals and his life's plans. As they rose up in his consciousness he was strengthened. In the very decision to sail back to Jutland lay an assurance that the difficulties could be overcome. Now he was thinking only of his plans. He looked forward to the ever-enduring North, and he envisioned the peace and general acclamation he would enjoy at the midpoint of the kingdoms. He reaffirmed for himself the measures he would implement. He regarded the laws and the reforms he had instituted, and he found them beneficial. He remembered his scheme to stem the stream of trade from Lübeck and divert it over his own territories. Once again he considered how excessive and harmful the privileges of the nobles were, and he was gladdened by the thought of the market towns that would be developed, of the peasants who would be free to plow the riches up from the earth. In his mind's eye he saw the estates in his kingdom as enormous plateaus and terraces, miles across, and he saw how one vast level would rise while another would sink until they were equal, all in response to a steady pressure on the scales in his reigning hand. And then . . .

King Henry sat on the throne in England. By what right? England had been Danish earlier. Danish fleets had once had England as their goal, and a unified North could surely turn its claws to the west once more. A certain amount of money—when law and unity and trade and agriculture had concentrated wealth in the North—a certain number of ships and mercenaries . . . and, no matter what storm and weather had to say, a broadside of Danish cannonballs would ram the cliffs of Dover.

Emperor Karl in Germany was the king's brother-in-law. He knew him, and he had little regard for him. Neither was King François in France any extraordinary figure. No matter—if they should remain on their thrones, then he, King Christian, would fight with them over the domains of the New World, which Columbus had prostrated under Europe's heel. Ships, ships! The North didn't have its share of the New World yet, but they would get it. From it there would flow money and new power and new ships. Ships! The Northerner would reach much, as long as there were worlds to conquer.

Yes. But the king's confidence died when he saw Jutland again. There were no lights on the shore, The ferry went in close, and the coast and Høneborg Castle loomed suddenly in the gray night. The ground lay covered with patchy slush, and crows and jackdaws rose screaming from the naked trees. The castle was like a tomb and the night lay dark and dank everywhere.

The sight of the coastline struck the king like a blow. He sensed how true it was that the land was in revolt. The situation was deadly serious, and since its hopelessness had already been manifest for him one time, the path was short to the same bitter acknowledgment again. There were impressions and recollections enough to dispirit the king, experiences from all the years he had been at the helm. Endless adversity and disappointment, daily recalculation and strain for ten whole years. Sweden he had conquered twice with the sword. This had cost him dear in many ways and had led to irreparable losses. And what gain did he have from it all? On Denmark he had spent his utmost effort, night and day. Their thanks was to cast him off as an unfaithful steward. Was there anything to be done with this obstinate folk? On every farm in his widespread realm was pigheadedness, in every man shortsightedness which he had to fight or circumvent. Everything for a goal that no one could see. It was an unequal struggle. There were many heads filled with obduracy, and only his own with royal visions. It was a fight against tortoises. And now the lowly and the oppressed, those he wished to lift up—they could see no further than to the needs of the moment. They had poured out of their huts from Skagen to Vejle Fjord with their axes and flails—all because he wanted to lay a tax on them to save the kingdom. No, there was nothing to be done. Small heads and hard necks everywhere in Denmark. Closed hearts and pockets, obstinacy, churlishness, stupidity.

The boatmen had tied up and were just going to put out the gangplank when the king ordered them to cast off and sail back to Fyn. His voice showed lack of resolve, but when they did not respond quickly he jumped up in a fury. The king's men were deathly silent. And while they sailed over to Fyn for the second time not a word was uttered.

When the king came to Middelfart he left the ferry immediately and went up to the nearest house. It was the middle of the night, and when the people there were roused they were greatly confused. The king ordered that he be given lodging, and while preparations were being made he had a candle brought in and he sat down to write. He wanted now to make a final effort, and he was writing to several of the fomenters of the rebellion. When he had seen Jutland's coast again he had been seized by a loathing for Denmark and the whole situation, but this had disappeared the instant he made his decision and turned back toward Fyn. When he had finished writing these letters in Middelfart he was calmed and filled with secret hope.

The king ate a little supper with Ambrosius the Bookbinder, who was with him that night. Then they had a heated conversation for an hour. The king became vehement and Ambrosius was also carried away. He was against all negotiation and would have the king assemble the army on the islands and get underway with an extermination of the wretched curs in the land. Ambrosius quivered at the thought of the Danish rabble.

"Yes, yes, yes," said the king, agreeing that he was right, but his gaze wandered and he was not listening. The candle smoked on the table in the unfamiliar surroundings of the modest room. It was past midnight. The king went to the window and threw it open to see what the weather was like. The night had not changed—it was still damp and cloudy.

"Yes," said the king, turning back from the window. He paced in a small circle, then he stopped, raised his head, and nodded. The decision had been made. Ambrosius the Bookbinder was stunned.

"We will return to Jutland. That is our decision," said the king in a deep voice. Half an hour later they sailed.

The king's resolve was unshakable. His thoughts were far ahead, in Jutland. In his mind he was already on the way to Viborg by horse. For he had now decided on the most serious and most difficult course of all: he would strike a bargain. Yes, he would relinquish his right for the sake of the ultimate goal. He could bide his time if just for a while he might regain control. . . . He would summon the estates in Viborg at the Assembly and promise them the compliance they demanded.

While the ferry labored its way over, the king was absorbed more and more in this thought. And now he understood the error of his action that time in Stockholm when he had struck. No sin, no wrongdoing—no, it had to be done . . . but it was wrong in that the consequences were so great and so ruinous. He had forgotten to consider his subjects' opinions, which are a reality even if they are absurd. In the future he should certainly take into account the common man's spite, stupidity, and ignorance, just as it is necessary to aim above the mark in order to compensate for the arrow's fall. He would come to terms, make concessions! When he had regained power there would be opportunities to shorten by a head the good folk who would now help themselves to his concessions. He estimated there would be about one hundred Danish leaders—and he specified them to himself—that he would yield to.

But the king did not come across the strait. Halfway over he became uncertain. His heart pounded and he felt great emotion and weariness. When they had almost reached the coast of Jutland he gave the order to put about. He wanted to go back to Middlefart and at least spend the rest of the night there in peace.

So he did sail toward Fyn. Yes, it was the king that was sailing away from everything again. So overwhelmed that he was trembling, so despondent and shaken . . . and now it was this fatal irresolution itself that struck him with terror. He saw how impossible it was for him—sailing to and fro—to make a decision for one course or the other. It was doubt that assailed his heart. He perceived it, and it grew more powerful. No longer was it the cause he doubted—no, it was himself. The fate of his kingdoms, the movement of the armies, attack and counterattack—everything shrank and became mere strategies in the head of the king, and he was conscious of this. And in this way doubt destroyed his sovereignty, leaving nothing more of him than a feverish and indecisive man.

And yet King Christian turned when he saw the lights of Middelfart, for when he had realized that his malaise was doubt, he felt so destitute and defeated, so utterly drained of hope, that he reached a sort of peace in *despair*. He became secure in his doubt, and this with such certainty that, in a peculiar and converse way, he gained hope again.

His strength failed, however, and when he neared Jutland he realized that now he would never come to rule Denmark again, since Denmark had turned him into a doubter. He had to leave the country, like one leaves a woman who has seen his defeat. He sailed back to Fyn, sick with sorrow and suffering.

But the ferry had not passed the middle of the strait before the king felt drawn to Jutland, Denmark, as one feels drawn to a woman who has seen his weakness. For where a man has suffered defeat, there must he seek redress. A man can conquer the whole world, but until he is victorious there where he has failed he will know no triumph. The king ordered the ferry to turn and sail to Jutland. But he was tired and frightened, and as miserable as a mortal can be.

This was King Christian's night of despair.

It broke him. He sailed back and forth until dawn came. When the sun rose he was on the Fyn side, and there he stayed, simply because he happened to be there.

But no . . . it was not by chance, and it was not the sunrise that put an end to the king's agonizing indecision. No, it is written that he who doubts will always, always end in default, letting die that cause which is the wellspring of his doubt.

# 29. The Treasure

In the year 1523 four German mercenaries came to a Jewish merchant in Amsterdam and presented him with a document written in Hebrew. It was a claim for payment of thirty thousand gulden. The claim was authentic enough, and the merchant had the money in safekeeping, but he contended that—according to the paper—the money should be paid to a certain Axel, or Absalon, the grandson of the man who had deposited the money with him, Mendel Speyer.

The soldiers explained, however, that they had received the document from a girl named Lucie, and she had gotten it from the inheritor. Now they had had it deciphered, and they maintained that the money was due the person who held the document.

When the merchant refused to turn the money over to them, the four soldiers brought the case before the courts, which sustained their claim. The large amount of money was paid out to them with the same thirty thousand pieces of embossed gold that Mendel Speyer had deposited many years earlier with the merchant.

Wealthy men now, the four soldiers divided the money and scattered in as many different directions.

Just as soon as he had received his portion, the first one bought an ox cart to carry it in. He drove off leisurely and was murdered the same night in a village outside Amsterdam.

The second hurried back to his homeland on the Rhine, and there he buried all the money somewhere. He died alone and in great wretchedness, without having touched a penny.

The third gambled himself into beggary in Turin eight years later.

And for the fourth it also ended badly. He died of riches, revelry, and rapacity, in his ninety-seventh year.

Axel rested in peace in the churchyard at Graabølle.

# 30. Inger

But Inger was full of sorrow. She wrung her hands and wept for her betrothed ceaselessly. Every night she gazed out over the fjord toward Himmerland from the window of her room, and she wept. It was the time of the bright nights, and the heavens were open day and night.

And Inger was full of sorrow. In his grave in Graabølle churchyard Axel heard her weeping. Then he raised his weary head in the moist earth and rose up. The churchyard lay so open to the wind. Between the graves jogged the three-legged Hel-horse with its tidings of death. It whinnied patiently after him, but Axel went out through the gate with his coffin on his back.

He went out over the heath toward the fjord, through the bright night in Denmark, and his gait was toilsome and weary. The sky was white and yellow, while the earth lay shrouded in dusk. The fjord gleamed, and the bluffs rose peacefully over in Salling.

Out on the heath a dead man walked in a circle. He stopped, and his careworn eyes followed Axel until he disappeared with his coffin in the sunken road. Then he began his lonely circling once more.

The sun hid itself beneath the land to the north where the sky was yellow. The wind blew, filled with dewdrops and the heavy fragrance of flowers. All growing things slept, dreaming luxuriant dreams.

Axel came to Hvalpsund, and he saw how the waves on the sound faithfully followed each other. He went over without stopping and came to Kvorne.

He stood in his burial clothes before Inger's door and knocked. He was so weary.

"Get up, Inger. Let me in."

Inger heard his voice, but she lay quiet for a moment, listening. The wind whistled very softly in the keyhole. Was it perhaps only the vagrant wind that was pleading out there? Then a foot moved on the doorstep and there was a very gentle knocking.

"Get up, Inger. Let me in."

She got up and her warm tears began to flow unchecked. But then she was afraid and she hesitated. She wondered if it could be Axel.

"Can you say the name of Jesus?" she asked, crying again. "Then I will open the door."

"Yes, I can," came Axel's answer. His voice was hoarse. "Yes, I can say the name of Jesus just as well now as before. In the name of Jesus, Inger, let me in."

Trembling, she opened the door and saw him standing outside, bowed under the black coffin in his long, moldering clothing. She could see that it really was Axel.

But when they were seated together, Axel had nothing to say that would comfort and soothe her. Inger's sobs welled up from the depths of her being. Her lips parted and great feeling racked her heart. For a long time she wept. Her overwhelming joy, even in sorrow, brought such strength she was almost crushed.

The night was still. Only the sound of the wind could be heard. Inger had cried and cried—she was so full of joy. And now she combed Axel's hair. She continued to cry, but her tears were mingled with laughter. Axel's hair was cold, and his head was as cold as a stone on the field.

"You have earth and sand in your hair," said Inger happily and tearfully. "There are pebbles on the backs of your hands."

Axel turned his lifeless hands thoughtfully. Yes, and he also had earth in his mouth.

"You are so cold!" cried Inger, and her voice was choked with the chill that shook her from head to foot. She sat quietly, she cried and laughed, she sighed. She combed and combed, and Axel bowed his head toward his beloved.

The night was still, and the yellow glow from the north lay on the windowpanes. The wind sang gently outside.

"Tell me, what is it like down in your grave, under the black earth?" asked Inger lovingly, full of concern and compassion. They were sitting so happily together in the transfigured night in the bright room. "And why do you have your coffin with you?"

"I have my coffin because otherwise I might be homeless. It is my home," was Axel's honest answer. "I am happy in my grave. I am happy when you find consolation, Inger. When you sing and are happy, then all care leaves me. Yes, my coffin is full of roses. I slumber on roses in the dusk of heaven. It is wonderful to rest in the earth when you are singing in your room and are happy."

"Then let me come with you!" cried Inger in a storm of tears. "Take me with you down into the earth!"

"When you mourn and lament, Inger, when you weep, then my coffin flows in thickening blood! Then it is frightful in the grave. Dear Inger, why do you long for me and grieve for me? Why do you love me? I am dead, and the dead must remain in the earth."

Axel said this patiently, but with the power of a proverb. He had grown immeasurably in wisdom, and his voice was husky with what he had endured, now a part of him for all eternity.

"Won't you kiss me?" Her whisper was hardly audible as she drew near with trembling. He did not move. She wanted to warm him, and with great tenderness she pressed her heart to his, to warm him, but he was not alive. Timorously she called him by name, believing that he had swooned. But he lay awake. Yes, he was awake.

192

And the night passed.

"Now the cock is crowing to welcome the day," said Axel. Inger did not want to let him go.

"Now the sky is brightening, and all corpses return to their graves," said Axel, and he stirred restlessly. But Inger laid her head against his dead breast.

"Now the panes are growing red and the sun will soon rise," said Axel falteringly, his voice faint. "Now I must return to the earth."

But when Axel had gone Inger was so heartbroken that she forgot his words. She ran after him, wringing her hands, and she overtook him down in the dark woods. Weeping with every step, she followed him until they came out of the woods at the shore. Then she saw that Axel was languishing, and that blood and water ran from his mouth.

"Take me with you!" she begged, beside herself with grief and horror. And he took her with him over the sound with its glistening waves. As they were crossing the heath it flamed in the east.

When they stood in the churchyard the sun burst forth. In the sharp glare of daybreak Inger saw that Axel's eyes were vanishing and his cheeks melting from the bone. His naked feet under him were crumbling from the roughness of the ground.

"Now you will never weep for me again." As he spoke to his beloved, Axel's voice was weary and trembling from the cold.

"Weep no more for me!" he begged and insisted. But she could not let him go.

Axel laughed very quietly.

He stood there for a moment, moldering, and yet majestic.

"Look up at the sky," he said, laughing with infinite tenderness, even with longing. He was consumed with weariness and yearning for his grave. "See! How blissful the night!"

Inger looked up at the faint stars in the sky. And the dead man passed into the earth. She saw him no more.

193

# WINTER

# 31. The Final Homecoming

An old man with a pilgrim's cowl over his head and a mussel shell hanging from a cord around his neck reached the top of the hills south of Graabølle. He folded his arms around his staff and stood for a time looking out over the valley, the arm of the fjord, and the low hills. It was Mikkel Thøgersen.

He had come home again. The area had not changed, but he thought it seemed more level. It was in September and there was a cool edge to the sunshine. Sparrows and starlings were flocking around the stacks of grain in the village over on the other side of the valley. Down where the stream ran into the fjord lay Mikkel's birthplace. He saw that a large new house had been built beside the old one. And there were fields where it had not been cultivated before, all the way up to the bluffs. I wonder if Niels is alive, thought Mikkel.

Yes, Niels was still alive, but he was marked by the years. It happened that Niels was alone in the house when Mikkel came. He was sitting at the end of the table, sleepy and with straw and chaff in his gray hair. He had just gotten up from his afternoon nap. The edge of his beer mug was black with flies, and they lifted buzzing in the air when Mikkel came in.

When Niels saw his brother in pilgrim's clothing he crossed himself without a word. First surprise and then pleasure showed themselves slowly in his face. Mikkel sat down quietly and they kept their voices low, so they would not disturb the stillness in the house.

"The boys are sleeping," said Niels. "Welcome, brother! Are you tired? Yes, you must be. Aren't you thirsty? These cursed flies! Just a minute . . ."

197

Niels drew fresh beer and sat down again to talk. He glowed with inner happiness, and a curious mixture of questions and exclamations came from his mouth in the strange, awkward way that had always been characteristic of him. But the look in his eyes was livelier and his manner much more straightforward— hardly the Niels that Mikkel remembered from the past. But, of course, he had been working here on his own for many years now.

"Well, the old man is gone now, your father and mine," said Niels in a quiet voice when his thoughts turned to this. "Not many weeks after you were home to see him we laid him to rest. It must be twelve years ago now. Yes, he was old."

Mikkel said nothing. The flies buzzed and crawled about on the scoured table top.

"I hardly thought you would step inside our door again," laughed Niels, avoiding Mikkel's eyes. But suddenly he looked at his brother, moved. "Yes, we're getting old too, both of us."

Mikkel raised his face thoughtfully and nodded.

Niels talked about other things, growing more lively now. He stood up.

"Well, look, you're here!" he said. "This is a day to remember. I'll rouse the others."

Niels stood outside the door in the courtyard, calling his sons in high spirits. There were three names: Thøger, Anders, and Jens. Mikkel sat in the room, looking around and moving his weary legs. "Yes, all right!" came the voices of Niels's sons from out in the barn, awakened so abruptly. One of them cried out for a time, only half awake, as if he had been terribly frightened, and Mikkel heard Niels chuckling outside the door. Just then the door to the kitchen area opened and Niels's wife came in. His sons turned up one at a time, each one staring in surprise at the pilgrim on the bench. They were strapping lads, all three of them.

"This is your uncle!" said Niels, deeply pleased. Mikkel gazed intently at the young faces, and he recognized the family features in them all.

Food was set on the table, and the whole family sat around Mikkel while he ate. Niels looked eagerly at his brother who had come home, and he was happy that he had brought his appetite with him. His wife and sons sat quietly and discreetly, but they watched Mikkel constantly with enormous and friendly curiosity. As Mikkel ate he gave answer to everything that Niels asked.

"That big mussel shell—what does it signify?"

"It's from Jerusalem," said Mikkel. "From it we ate whatever people would give us along the way."

"Well, just think!" Niels fell silent, just thinking. Suddenly he looked shyly and fondly at his brother. He wanted to ask a question but he gave up, yielding to something he did not understand. He sat with his thoughts for a few minutes.

"Well . . . yes, you'll stay with us a bit, won't you? You must tell us a lot—you've seen so many things."

Then Niels stared fixedly straight ahead. Suddenly he stiffened his back against the wall. "Something's afoot here in this part of the country," he said in a low voice. "But surely you've heard about how things are?"

Mikkel glanced up from his food and shook his head. But Niels's look told him that this was something they should talk about later. The others knew what Niels was referring to. His wife lowered her eyes quickly with an expression of fear, while the face of Thøger, the oldest son, became hard and alert, like a man ready to spring.

That afternoon Niels and Mikkel were out looking around the farm. Niels didn't spend much time in the smithy any more. He had bought land and worked it, and now he had a good-sized farm. Elkærgaard, as it was called, was one of the largest along the stream. Suddenly, while they were standing in a field, Niels became strangely restless, but he relaxed immediately. He took a straw up from the stubble on the ground and spoke with a degree of composure that frightened Mikkel.

"War is breaking out—no way around it," he said. He paused and let air out through his nostrils a couple of times. Then he continued in quite an ordinary voice.

"No, you don't know much about how things are, since you have been out of the country so long. Yes, there'll be war, for us in this area too. Listen now . . ."

And then Niels gave an account of the situation. There had been turmoil in the country for too long. The nobles were holding the king imprisoned in Sønderborg Castle, King Christian, but now the peasants in the whole country wanted him freed. They were going to take things into their own hands. The peasants in Vendsyssel had been set on this course of action for a long time, and those in Salling had also begun to band together.

"The rest of us, here in Himmerland—we don't want to be the last to join in," exclaimed Niels, controlling his emotion only with difficulty. "We've begun to sharpen our axes."

Niels passed his hand over his eyes, which were glowing now, and he cleared his throat noisily.

"Here, come along. I've got something to show you!"

Niels led the way home. There he took Mikkel into the little smithy, where everything was unchanged, exactly the same as in Thøger's time.

"We've had plenty to see to lately," whispered Niels. "But both Thøger and Anders are good with a hammer. We've put a lot of scythes in order for folks, and we've also had time to take care of our own needs. Look here!"

Out of the corner Niels brought a big, newly forged ax. The head still shone with the colors of the rainbow from the firing.

"We've made a lot like this," said Niels in a hushed voice. He reached back for another one.

"Look, this one is mine. Do you remember it? Yes, I've set new steel to it."

Mikkel knew the ax. It had been his father's as far back as he could remember.

"The old man would never part with it," said Niels, "because it was taken out of the hand of our grandfather when he lay dead on Aagaard Meadow, up in the district of Han. That was ninety-three years ago. It was the time the peasants fought and were beaten to smithereens. We mustn't forget that now."

"Thøger, Anders, Jens!" called Niels with unusual authority in his voice. The three tall youths were there almost immediately. Then Niels lifted his unexceptional head, laying his hand on the ax of their forbears. His sons stood around him, looking tensely into his face. He said nothing, but they understood him.

Mikkel lowered his eyes. He did not want to look at this brother of his with the warlike heart. It seemed dishonorable somehow. Mikkel felt bitter shame, but he remembered their father, who had been a more worthy man.

In the days that followed many come to Niels Elkær with all kinds of implements to be made into weapons. There was a lot of talk, sometimes quite heated but usually quiet and restrained, about what was coming. Mikkel got the impression that Niels's words had weight among the people of the region. It was another man, however, one up in Graabølle called Søren Brok, who was the acknowledged leader. Final authority could only have rested on Old Thøger if this had happened in his time.

The unrest grew quickly. Almost every day an unknown rider was seen flying down the road, and peasants never before seen in the area were often met. Time passed, and soon it was the end of September.

"We could easily get you some other clothes," said Niels one day to Mikkel, coming out with what had been on his mind for a long time. Mikkel smiled.

"If you want to cast your lot with us, that is." Niels handed him a complete set of clothing.

But Mikkel shook his head, and as he thought about this he felt that he *had* grown old.

"No, Niels," he said gravely. "No, I've had enough fighting in my day, even though it was in places where I was not involved in the cause. But I'm tired now. There are grown men now who were babies when I began to serve as a soldier. No, if I'm to serve the king it will be in another way. But you might let me stay here and see how it goes."

Niels nodded, disappointed but understanding.

A few very quiet days followed. Everything was ready and everyone was only waiting, feeling that the war must begin from outside. No one knew just how it would start. Every day Niels combed his thin, iron-gray hair with water, as if for some solemn occasion. Only the most necessary work was being done on the farm. The boys were away most of the time—they were with the other young men up in Graabølle. Niels's wife knitted stockings, sitting all day long very erect on a bench and hardly breathing.

During these few days Niels and Mikkel talked a lot about their father. Niels busied himself with small tasks on the farm and reminisced about Old Thøger. Mikkel walked beside him in his white pilgrim's cloak, listening to him tell of small incidents from the old days. When he got started Niels was a lively storyteller, with his own special warmth and humor, and every little story fed Mikkel's fantasy. For his part, Mikkel said almost nothing.

Then the last day Niels talked of something he had apparently been putting off for as long as possible because it had to do

202

with Mikkel personally. A little over two years earlier a strange pair had come over from Salling, and they had asked for Mikkel. One of them was a fiddler called Jakob, getting on in years and with a liking for the bottle. The other was the little girl he had with him, a deaf-mute. She was a strange and sickly little thing. Jakob said that he had taken her because no one else wanted her. She was the daughter of a girl named Inger and a man who was probably of a certain standing. His name was Axel and he had been killed. It was said that he lay buried in the churchyard in Graabølle. Now Jakob wanted to help the little girl find her family so they could take care of her. The reason they were searching for Mikkel was . . .

Here Niels broke off the story and looked at his brother, as if to prepare him for what was coming.

"Yes, Ane Mette is dead," he said gently

Mikkel did not move, It was a blow for him, but it was like something he had been waiting to hear for a hundred years. It did not hurt. He had *known* it—or maybe this part of his consciousness was dead.

"Yes," continued Niels after several moments of silence, "it happened a long time ago. She has been dead for many years. But now I think I should tell you what that fiddler was here for. He said that the little girl's mother, whose name was Inger, was supposed to be the daughter of you and Ane Mette. So you are the grandfather of the little girl Jakob brought with him. He called her Ide. They were here a few days and then they went away. I don't know where."

Niels was silent, letting Mikkel take it all in. When Mikkel didn't say anything, he went on: "You see, Steffen in Kvorne probably never really liked Inger, his stepdaughter, although he took good care of her, as a father would have done. But things went very badly for her. The man Inger got—people hardly knew who he was—he died. Yes, he did."

Niels stopped, drawing several deep breaths. It was a moment before he could continue.

"Almost before they had been properly united. And then she died herself, in childbirth. That was when Ide was born. But when Anne Mette also died Steffen didn't want to continue providing for this stepfamily of his. And so that's how Ide came into Jakob's care."

Niels fell silent.

"We'll see Steffen with all his sons when things get started," added Niels in a moment as his line of thought changed. "As well as some girls, he had six boys with Ane Mette, brawny fellows, all of them. Same age as my boys."

They were out on the fields when Niels told all this. Darkness fell, and now there were long periods of silence in the conversation. Mikkel walked with his head hidden in his cowl. Niels went across the field to move a couple of sheep. When he came back he stood quietly beside Mikkel, wanting to say something but unable to come out with it.

"What do you want to say, Niels?" asked Mikkel sharply.

"I've heard tell . . ." stammered Niels with great difficulty. "If it is true—of course, it doesn't make any difference to me . . . But I want to talk about it because it may be that we won't see each other again. People in Graabølle have said that it was you that killed that fellow Axel—your own son-in-law, sort of—to . . . to take his money. In any case, you were in this area at that time, but I didn't see you because you didn't come to visit us. Is this true, Mikkel?"

"Yes," answered Mikkel with the same composure and defiance that Niels remembered from their childhood, and which also now he yielded to immediately.

"Then you had your reasons," said Niels, subdued and relieved. "I won't pry into them. But you shouldn't have passed my door. There are lots of things that people like me can't understand. . . . Let's go home and see what the wife has for supper."

When they were standing outside the dark house Niels whispered quickly, "If you should live longer than I do, Mikkel, will you keep an eye on what we have here?"

"Yes," answered Mikkel, and his voice was desolate.

They went in.

# 32. The Red Rooster

That same night the people in Graabølle saw the manors burning over in Salling.

But they still didn't know what action they themselves should take. At midnight they saw torches moving out on the fjord, and an hour later three large prams landed at Hvalpsund with armed peasants from Salling. They sprang ashore with loud shouts, they laughed and sang, and many of them were not entirely sober. When the Himmerland peasants heard ordinary people like themselves snorting and bawling like livestock on the loose, the blood also began to pound in their heads.

The body of men on the shore seethed and heaved in the darkness. Steffen of Kvorne, the leader of the Salling group, took counsel with Søren Brok. Without anyone really knowing how it happened, the whole troop began to move as one, and both groups, united now, swept away into the countryside.

Mikkel remained at home on the farm. Except for him there was only Niels's wife, but she went to bed crying. Mikkel stationed himself up on the hill, and from this vantage point he could see four big fires over in Salling blazing up and dying down. But at one of the places the conflagration was at its height, and the flashes from it came pulsing all the way across the fjord. Up in Graabølle the white gables on the west side of the houses glittered and glowed, reflecting the flames. Otherwise the night was still. But nature was now showing its brutal side, with this alarming red glow reflected in the water and the clouds. Tonight many hidden accounts would be settled, openly and with blood.

All sound from the throng of men had died out, but still Mikkel could sense how far they had come. When about an hour had passed he knew they were nearing Moholm. His ears strained in the direction of the manor but he heard no sound. Ten minutes later he could make out a bloody red gleam at the place in the darkness where the manor lay. The fire grew rapidly, and a high, curving tongue of flame leaped into the air. Soon he saw naked flames springing out of the windows. The manor could now be seen in the blaze it was feeding, the smoke erupted, thick and greenish-yellow in the night—and still not a sound was heard.

Then Mikkel sat down, and time seemed to stop. A little later he felt sleepy and he went down to the house and lay on the bench. It was daybreak when he awoke. Niels's wife was still crying under the featherbed. Mikkel went up on the hill and saw that Moholm was as good as destroyed by fire. A great deal of smoke was rising from the ground, and there seemed to be a copper-red halo hovering over the whole ruin. Here and there blackened and splintered fragments of walls could be seen through the fumes. It was the quiet time, just before sunrise. The smoke lay everywhere over the bed of the stream and the valley, drifting slowly to the west. When Mikkel could smell the fire he sensed how searing the heat had been, and his heart began to pound.

But as he turned he saw a new and violent blaze a little farther north. That would be the manor at Stenerslev. The flames leaped up in the dawn, white and almost invisible—stark, naked flames—and the smoke pulsed like a wheel turning high up in the air above.

Now the sun was rising. Mikkel could hear the fish snapping at flies down in the stream.

Half an hour later Jens, Niels's youngest son, came home. Mikkel saw him come running far away across the fields, and his speed did not slacken. When he reached the farmhouse he dashed over to the spring and drank right from the trough. His lips were so dry that he couldn't close them over his teeth, and his chest was working like a bellows. When he raised his head Mikkel could see in his eyes that he had seen blood, and that it had a-roused a frenzy in him.

"Where is your father?" asked Mikkel harshly.

"He's all right," answered Jens. "I'm supposed to give the news to my mother."

The lad was incoherent and Mikkel could not get any reliable information out of him. Jens buried his face in the trough again.

"Take care of your mother," said Mikkel reprovingly, and then he hurried off along the stream toward Moholm.

When he got there the peasants had left the manor. Only a handful were poking about, busying themselves with the household effects that had been pulled out of the burning buildings. Mikkel knew one of them who was from the area, and he asked him what had happened.

The man answered him with great nonchalance. Yes . . . well, ah . . . they'd torched the manor, as he could plainly see. It was a pretty short show. And now all the others were up giving Stenerslev the same treatment. When they came back they'd gobble and guzzle here. . . . The man pointed to a pile of meat and barrels that had been dragged out. The heat near the smoldering ruin was unbearable.

"But wasn't there any attempt to defend the manor?" asked Mikkel.

Well, ah . . . yes. His High and Holy Lordship had known quite a while what was up, so he'd gathered a flock of his folk on the property. But the fracas was over before it got started—there were a lot more peasants. The manor wasn't fortified, so they could march right in. Otte Iversen and one of his boys got it right off and then a slew of their farmhands. The rest of the family was lucky—they managed to get away. A dozen or so peasants bit the dust and a lot of others were chopped up pretty bad. Steffen of Kvorne was shot just as they set boot in the courtyard.

Mikkel looked around. One of the men was picking up some lead that had melted off the roof and hardened in the grass. It was still hot, and he cursed and blew on his fingers. The others were also busy gathering up and watching over bits and pieces of the manor they had just burned.

"Where have you put the bodies?" asked Mikkel.

"They're lying in the vegetable garden," said one of the men casually. "We'll throw them out of there when Søren Brok comes back."

Mikkel went along the hot, smoking wall and into the garden, and there he saw a score of corpses lying in a row in the grass under the apple trees. They had been laid in order carefully—the peasants in one group and Otte Iversen and his men in another. Mikkel did not know any of the peasants except Steffen of Kvorne. He was a very stout man, with silver buttons on his coat, and he was lying at the far end of the row. A few steps away lay Otte Iversen, with his young son placed close beside him. Both their heads were crushed. When Mikkel saw the enemy of his youth, his heart ached in his breast. He felt how everything had collapsed, even time itself. Now there was nothing left. He sat down in the grass between Steffen and Otte Iversen. Yes, they were dead, lying there with livid wounds.The portly farmer lay with his chin pressed down into his neck, and his abdomen had fallen in on one side of his body. Someone had closed his eyes. But Otte Iversen's eyes were wide open and his eyeballs were shrunken. Otte Iversen was bald and his beard was white. His features had been scored by life, and now in death their expression was one of bitter discontent. At his side, under his dead arm, lay one of his sons with a crushed, bloody mass that had once been hair and brow. He had a small moustache, just like Otte Iversen in his younger days.

Here we are, Anne Mette, all three of us, thought Mikkel. His mouth opened without a sound, like a fish dying in the grass. Now we are together—the one you loved, and the one who loved you, and the one you married. Ane Mette, here are your men!

# 33. The Defeat

Late that evening Niels came home with Thøger and Anders. They were covered with dust and grime, and Niels, who was no longer a young man, could hardly drag himself through the door. As well as Moholm and Stenerslev, they had taken part in the burning of another manor farther east. But the whole affair had left Niels dejected. He threw himself on the bench and told Mikkel what had happened.

"I don't like it," he said with a heavy heart. "We could have spared Moholm if it hadn't been for that Salling bunch. They say it was folk from here in Himmerland that got things started over in Salling, so now they were going to return the favor. Well, Otte Iversen probably had it coming to him, but anyway it seemed to me he hadn't provoked them when they struck him down. Steffen breathed his last there too . . . Oh, we went to work cruelly, we did! I hardly knew who it was I was using my ax on. The nobleman at Stenerslev screamed like a pig when they killed him. But now we've begun—no denying that—so now we'll have to see it through. Tomorrow we're going north to join up with those from Vendsyssel. Yes. . . . But I thought war was something different. You bet I did. . . ."

The next day they set out, and Mikkel went with them. Jens stayed at home to watch out for his mother and the farm. It would surely be quiet there, thought Niels, now that the noblemen around them had been killed—so maybe it was a good thing after all that they had done it.

So it was that the peasants all over Jutland rose up. For fourteen days total anarchy reigned. The peasant bands roamed the countryside, burning and carousing and hardly knowing what they were doing. It's a bad business when peasants are uprooted and cast out into the world's wantonness. As long as they know each other there is a sort of solidarity, but when men are from different regions they are automatically half-enemies. When two bands are united under one leader, at least one of the bands doesn't trust him. Then the many leaders begin to disagree among themselves. What they need is one leader right from the beginning.

When the peasants from all of North Jutland had gathered, Skipper Klement assumed command over them. There were six thousand men—with almost as many different kinds of weapons—when they massed outside the town of Svenstrup. Here they engaged the noblemen, only six hundred strong, but mounted and in armor. Victory went to the peasants.

Mikkel Thøgersen stood on a hill that October morning and saw how disastrously it went for the nobles. The two forces moved toward each other at sunrise. They didn't really take up much room in the landscape. It was rather like two dark patches, unequal in size, approaching each other in the broad countryside under the vast sky. Nature was indifferent—the morning was gray and the ground cold after a rain. Mikkel looked out over the low-slung hills and thought how it is—that only the land is eternal, while generations pass over it like shadows of clouds.

Then the two groups joined battle. But there were too few noblemen. Even from a great distance Mikkel could see how the peasants flocked around every single horseman and literally flailed him out of the saddle. The visibility was good, and Mikkel saw the puffs of dust rise from the riders' clothing under their armor as the peasants thrashed away on them. From time to time the wind bore the din up on the hill where Mikkel was, and he could hear the clang of the peasants' axes on the horsemen's armor.

But the mounted nobles also cut down a large number of peasants before they gave up. The skirmishing thinned out more and more, and the scattered harquebus fire had stopped entirely. When a nobleman was overpowered and beaten to the ground it was just as thick with peasants around him and on him as with flies at a lump of sugar. Many of the nobles began to wheel their horses about and seek shelter.

Below the hill where Mikkel stood, a farmhand was plowing. While the battle raged he didn't even stop his draft horses. He could easily plow and watch at the same time.

At length the nobles had to give up the battle, as could be expected, and they fled at full speed south in the land. This time they had relied too much on their dignity, and they had forgotten that all are equal before the ax. Many of them lost their life in this battle.

But it was the last time the Danish peasants struck with a right to fight, because it was the last time they were victorious. Two months later they lost this right and were judged rebels because they lost. And on this occasion the Danes ceased to be a Nordic people.

It was a sad day. Mikkel was watching when the peasants defended Aalborg and suffered defeat. Winter had set in and the weather was miserable. Johan Ranzau led the noblemen, who were now more numerous, but he also had his German mercenaries and soldiers armed with guns.

They set to work with vigor. The peasants were wide-eyed when they faced the modern firearms that Johan Ranzau used against them. Every shot that came whistling through the air was an enemy they could not see and not get hold of. They were unnerved, for the only kind of war they knew was fighting hand-to-hand. And neither was strategic calculation a thing they had learned at their father's knee. It finally came to close combat and they were able to satisfy their lust to use their bare hands, but then it was too late, for the battle was long since lost.

The situation was hopeless, but the peasants scuttled out like badgers between the dogs. When they realized what had happened they fought desperately, each man with the strength of three, nearly slashing the nobles to pieces with their scythes and chaff slicers when they could get them within arm's reach. But soon their ranks were split and they were surrounded. They were doomed and they knew it.

At the end there were two thousand peasants from Vend-syssel who couldn't get over the Limfjord and home. They were slaughtered. The veteran mercenaries fenced them in and the nobles trampled them. There they were, all packed together. They cut and thrust to all sides while the victors were killing them. They cried in the bitter winter weather. They toppled sobbing into the snow with their heads split open.

The last little cluster of peasants defended themselves frantically, screaming madly. They cried through clenched teeth, but the sword was upon them. Iron and lead ripped through their lambskin coats and into their trembling bodies, while maces crushed their hands, cut through their fur hoods, and smashed their heads. No mercy was shown, and they were wiped out to the last man.

If King Christian had killed all the noblemen in Stockholm instead of only a few score, then there wouldn't have been so many to give vent to their irascibility later. The story of the blood-bath has been passed down through the centuries, but Johan Ranzau pulverized two thousand men at Aalborg and few have bemoaned that event. There the peasants were crushed so thoroughly that not even the story of the misdeed could be handed down. After that conflict an oppressive stillness fell over Jutland.

Not many came home to Graabølle. Niels Thøgersen fell at Aalborg. His oldest son had already died at Svenstrup. Mikkel sought out his brother's body outside Aalborg and covered his face with earth. Niels had fallen as an honorable man, his back crushed by a cannon ball.

Anders, the second-oldest son, brought the news when he came home from Aalborg, aged and haggard. Later he began to work the farm as a serf under the new nobleman at Moholm.

# 34. Time

Time passed. And Time prevailed. The days conquered all, and the years spread like a contagious evil that lies beyond all power of human control. What folk resolved to do, they only half started. What they imagined would be completed one fine day, Time slung back at their feet as a fiasco. And now all of that had taken place long ago. Old people spoke of it as memories. Their first clumsy attempts were forsaken by Time, and they became reality only when the sun spun its fire and ash into the following century. Men sank forgotten into the earth, but their tentative efforts at action remained as dim monuments along the road for all eternity. Their chronicle looked like a landscape after a flood, where the desolate earth is covered by heaps of rubble and black trees with their roots bared, and with salt and slime as far as the eye can reach.

Gustav Trolle—he was mortally wounded in the battle of Øksnebjærg on Fyn and sank to the ground. He lay there, stretched out in his armor, clad in iron from top to toe, feeling both pain and an inner gladness. Knowing that death was near, he thought back on his life and his deeds. He felt burning anger over having been cut down, but the turmoil of his spirit was so great that, in weariness and misery, he welcomed his final rest. Indeed, there was significance in his death, in that it brought a whole series of absurdities to a meaningful conclusion. He felt no regret except for the regret over things undone. Here he lay, having reached only the beginning, although he was now an old man. He had accepted loneliness for the sake of a cause, and now he was dying in loneliness. His life's course had now come full circle, without encompassing anything more than impermanence and loss. It could be said of him that he had isolated himself and given himself over to misanthropy—all of this, moreover, for the sake of unknown goals. When Gustav Trolle realized that he was in the grip of fate, he felt at long last the serenity of submission. He lay there, warm and compliant, and when he felt the ardent breath of death, he surrendered for the first time in his life.

They carried the bishop off unconscious and he never fully regained his senses. He was laid in a house and guarded like a thief, and those who came and went heard him laughing wildly. The saw him lying there with cheeks flushed and lips twisted with fiendish malevolence. He was delirious, and his burning eyes were penetrating and threatening as they looked out from another world. When his death struggle set in they heard him raling or whining from the depths of his dementia, like a stubborn child. He lay for an entire day, with ever greater intervals between his sobs, as life and defiance ebbed. His death agony lasted for two days. An attack of dread brought to his lips froth and curses on the specters he seemed to see. When the throes of death seized him, his limbs tensed and twitched like bows of steel, or he lay rigid under the onslaughts, his whole body knotted and hard as stone. The final night brought relief from pain, and he cried out from the depths of spiritual anguish. And then, as a wild convulsion seized his entire body, he died screaming.

After the battle of Øksnebjærg, the resistance on Fyn was broken. Now it was only on Sjælland where the Danes laid their life and property in King Christian's hand. When they too were crushed Johan Ranzau had conquered the whole country. He had had to wrench each part of it loose, like the legs of a stubborn horse being pulled up one at a time. The same Danes who ten years earlier had abandoned the king were now prepared to die, if necessary, in their effort to restore him to the throne. Yes, the Danes were now just as pigheaded as they had once been fickle. Copenhagen submitted to siege for a year. During the final months they sank as low as humans can. First it was a matter of the disgrace of the idolatrous—eating the meat of horses, cats, and dogs from the knacker. Then they had to make do with the same food as the most abased savages: mice and beetles. Finally they indulged like beasts in carrion and other offal. As always during hard famine, children died at their mother's breast, and people could also be seen toppling over and dying right on the street. And after suffering such unspeakable misery in order to hold the town for the king, after accepting untold privation and leaving no agony unproved—then they surrendered the town, so that the futility of it all could reach its highest perfection.

Ambrosius the Bookbinder, the childhood friend of King Christian, whose zeal for the king's cause had known no moderation—he took poison. His life and energy had moved in a great arc, ending with a whistle back into his own body like a boomerang.

A year later Jens Andersen Beldenak died, a refugee in Lübeck. His final years were quiet, for age had settled on him now. But he was also a cripple. Jens Andersen, who himself had never spared anyone, suffered mistreatment in the fullest measure at the hands of his enemies when they had managed to lay hands on him. He was an old man when they vented their long-time thirst for revenge on him with prolonged and cruel torture. In his prime he had delivered the barbs of his stinging wit to left and right. Now in his declining years they came back—into his body. They stripped this fallen man of God, anointed him with honey, and placed him in the sun as a target for flies and mosquitos. See him, this spiritual giant, despoiled by age, naked and at the mercy of a swarm of insects! See the great bishop and soldier, the tireless dealer in oxen, jurist and *bon vivant*. The sorcerer, the wizard, casting his spells with the Bible balanced on the saddle horn. Time had fallen away from him and abandoned him. This ruin of a man had once been an indomitable intellect and

218

a daring intriguer. What now was only a low cloud of sickening smoke had once been a blaze of enterprise.

Jens Andersen, a bastard munificently endowed by nature. His head was the repository for the most felicitous union of theology and jurisprudence that has ever been seen in Denmark. Considering the conditions of his time he was an eminent aesthete—and yet he could sum up his life and thought in two very small Latin poems. One of them was a tight epitaph, the other a pyre of spare couplets, an inventory of his torments.

But there was truth in Jens Andersen's lean poetry! His verses rattled like a skeleton of human history, as can be seen in these two:

> *Os, dentes, nares, genitalia, brachia dantur*
> *Torturis, quibus adjunge manusque pedes.*

The King had been a captive in Sønderborg for many years now. Since the battle of Aalborg Mikkel Thøgersen had shared the king's captivity, and for this service he received six Lübeck marks a year.

Now that Mikkel had gained this position as fellow prisoner with the king, he was constrained to live austerely. Throughout his life Mikkel had felt that his fate was wedded to the king's. It was as if their paths were ever converging. The closer Mikkel had come to the king, the farther the king had fallen!

Forty years had passed since Mikkel first saw the king as a sixteen-year-old prince reveling in the shops of rich merchants in Copenhagen. The king's hair was red as claret then, and his hands were still smooth and unmarked by life. Now his wintry gray hair bristled around his head like an abandoned bird's nest, and his bony hands were tapestries of wrinkles and swollen veins.

# 35. Jacob and Ide

But now, while the king and Mikkel Thøgersen reposed in the total security of Sønderborg Castle's fortifications, there were two others who wandered about the country homeless, Jakob the Fiddler and Little Ide.

Jakob was a man of uncertain age, and he grew no older in the many years that he and Ide wandered. But Ide, who was a child when they left Kvorne, grew into womanhood on the road under the open sky.

They left Salling the same day Ane Mette, her grandmother, was buried. While Ane Mette lay in her bed, without the power of speech and with the sanctity of death about her gaunt and venerable head, the object of her final gaze was her grandchild, Ide. All her grown children stood around her, but her eyes searched for Ide. When she had been laid to rest, Jakob took the little orphan girl by the hand and left the churchyard with her.

That was the day the green plover returned. Jakob heard its refreshing, shrill cry as they were walking over the marsh. The sky stood open above them, they were free, and they headed east toward the pale sun hanging over the thawing ground. During her entire childhood Little Ide had seen a hill at a great distance, out there where the sun rested on cloud pillars. They went by this now —yes, they went all the way past, and then an exotic and unknown land opened mysteriously before Ide's eyes, like a gateway to the world.

Jakob and Ide came to Graabølle, and there Jakob tried without success to get information about Mikkel Thøgersen. He was in the Holy Land, if he wasn't dead, said Niels, and with this information they moved on, fiddling through the countryside.

Jakob and Ide spent two days at Moholm and entertained the manor's folk with their music. The nobleman's family they did not see. Little Ide played the triangle to Jakob's violin. She was a good performer, watching his hands in order to pick up the rhythm, since she heard nothing. But the second evening the lackluster nobleman showed his parsimonious face and sent them packing—he didn't want to listen to their sawing and clanging any longer. So Jakob put his violin back into its fox-skin and they left the manor hand in hand, Ide's triangle tinkling at her belt like tiny bells as she walked along.

They went over the heath, farther north in the country. Spring finally came, but only after much persuasion, like a weeping bride. Each morning dawned over a cold earth and the sun could start again from scratch. Spring moved the day to smiles, until it shrouded itself again in grayness. The clouds rose before the moist winds. It was rain in the morning, moisture in the evening. It was the tiresome weather's eternal fickleness— wedded, however, to eternal hope.

The rain washed Ide's pallid hair down over her face and the sun dried it, so that her head was crowned with shining disarray. The rain was more persistent, however, so Ide walked the roads looking ahead through pale eyes under her damp hair, which was as colorless as linen.

"Ide with the Rain-Hair!" said Jakob to himself, looking at her reassuringly.

All of Denmark's birds came home now. The starling sang passionately every morning while the sun came up glistening and wiped the frost from the meadows. The larks warbled as they hung on their wings far above the barren fields. The wind sang in the withered grass on the hillsides and rippled the ice-cold, blue water lying on the plowed fields. The first yellow flowers came up from the earth, and soundless swallows rode the eastern gale. Finally it was calm. Warm nights and growth. From the sikes came the fervid croaking of toads—a veiled and yet cheerful sound. The fields greened, and the frogs sang their endless evening paean to the fertility and fruits of the earth.

The roadsides grew verdant, and there Ide liked to walk because there was so much to see. She picked the white catkins from the pussy willows, raising them to her lips, stroking her cheek with them. She braided cords from rushes, which she loved to pull up by the roots. Ide saw the newborn lambs on the field, still unable to stand, lying under the protective heads of the sheep.

The days turned warm, with brilliant sunshine. On May Day Jakob and Ide played for the dancing in Aalborg and earned good money. Jakob bought new wooden shoes for both of them, and when they moved on they were in fine fettle. People liked to hear music, and these two were never without food and lodging. Finally they came to Skagen, where Ide saw the open sea. Here the sand was the whitest and finest she had ever felt. And when they had come all the way out to the end of the spit, Jakob sang the song he had made about himself and Ide. Their audience was only the sea gulls, swooping down close to them.

Jakob laughed and reached out his hand to them while he sang. Ide saw the white birds open their beak but she heard nothing, not even the purring and rumbling of the sea under the fair sky.

And this was the song that Jakob sang:

> How about a bed for the night,
> And maybe something to eat?
> We're on our way to Lucky Land
> With blisters on our feet.
> How about a bed?

We come from a place called Back-of-Beyond,
Where the street's a rutted lane;
The walls are built of wind alone,
And the roofs are thatched with rain.
How about a bed?

The village goose is a full-blooded bird
With legs both round and bare,
Just like my jug on the inside now—
Have you got some beer to spare?
How about a bed?

And if you doubt this story is true,
Just ask my daughter dear;
She's never known her ma and pa,
And can neither talk nor hear.
How about a bed?

Since Jakob and Ide had now been as far north in Denmark
as they could go, they made friends with a skipper and sailed
with him in the two bright months of summer. They came to the
islands of Læsø and Anholt, they saw the green hills around
Randers Fjord, and they anchored in the Limfjord, where the
peasants were on the beaches fishing and often seemed raised
high up in the air by the reflection of the sun on the water. Those
were endless days.

But when the summer was drawing to a close and all the
fields farther inland turned yellow, Jakob and Ide went on a long
journey with the skipper to the island of Sjælland. They went
ashore in Helsingør, and here they played for many days with
good results. Jakob often got drunk and sang and did the town.
While he was sleeping it off Ide would hide in the nearby fields

223

of rye. There she braided ripe straw in her hair and bathed her hands in the warm dust.

One day there was an unusual amount of commotion in town. Everyone hurried down to the harbor, shading their eyes with their hand, talking with great animation and pointing south in the sound. In the strong wind three large, dark ships could be seen, and the middle one was flying the red flag at the top of its mast. Soon everyone in Helsingør who could creep or walk was down at the shore. A feeling of great gloom spread through the crowd, although only a very few of them knew why. In the wan sunlight of that August day the three warships glided forward noiselessly over the shallow waters of the sound. It took them two hours to reach Helsingør.

Jakob asked someone who was aboard, and he was told it was no less than King Christian himself. Some were able to report that he was coming from Copenhagen, where he had been in negotiation with the State Council after his many years of exile in Holland and Norway, but no one knew for sure where he was headed now. Everyone sensed, however, that they were losing him.

When the three heavy caravels were directly opposite the town, holding course with their sails bellying in the wind, scattered shouts went out to them from the crowd on the shore. It seemed as if the ships only lowered their heads and plowed their blunt bows into the waves. No salute was seen, no cannons were fired, there was no signal.

But all the townspeople in Helsingør followed along the shore for a way. More had joined in—peasants from the coastal area and farther inland who had seen the ships. There were several hundred people, young and old, and they ran along the shore, waving and calling, until they reached the last point. Here they stopped, pressing together, thronging as close to the water as they could get.

"Farewell, King Christian!" called an old man. Those who were standing beside him and heard his feeble voice burst into tears, and then they took up the cry.

"Farewell!" came the chorus of voices, like a gust of wind in a storm. They fell silent for a moment, anxiously following the ships with their eyes. Sobbing and sighing could be heard. They reached over each others' shoulders, waving and waving to the ships. Then they took up their plaintive calls again, but by now the ships were already far out and the cries grew weaker and more dispirited.

"Farewell, King Christian!"

At the back of the crowd was an old woman who had had great trouble keeping up with the others. Now she stood leaning on her cane, wavering from her efforts. Her bronzed and wizened face was framed by a wimple, and she was crying. At the height of the shouting she rasped: "Farewell, King Christian!"

She stood there with her weak back bent almost double with age, hardly more than a yard high. She trembled and whimpered over the shared sorrow, which as an old person she could hardly understand.

This old granny was Mendel Speyer's daughter, Susanna.

And now the lament was raised for a final time: "Farewell, King Christian!"

Jakob the Fiddler tore his violin from its fox-skin and scraped out a sorry tune. Tears ran down into his mouth, which was twisted into a heartbroken smile. Little Ide stood at his side, playing the triangle. She saw how everyone opened their mouth while their body strained, as if something were coming out with great pain. She rolled her tongue in her mouth, trying to understand it all.

# 36. Homeless

Jakob the Fiddler had learned that Axel, Ide's dead father, had had been born in Helsingør. He was the illegitimate son of a Jewish woman named Susanna Nathansohn. Jakob and Ide also managed to talk with her. She lived in a stately house in the middle of town. Susanna spoke of her husband and her grown children, but she also admitted freely to the mistake she had made forty years earlier. She acknowledged that Axel was her son. He had been placed with strangers immediately after he was born, however, and since then she had heard nothing of him. It was quite possible, of course, that Ide was his daughter. The old woman looked at Ide but she did not recognize the features. Ide looked more like her maternal grandfather, Mikkel Thøgersen. But when Jakob and Ide continued to stand there, not knowing what to do, the old woman gave them a little money and something to eat. She really had very little time just then, since it was Saturday.

Jacob and Ide left Helsingør and traveled the length and breadth of Sjælland. This took two years. When war broke out and the roads became unsafe, Jakob sailed with Ide over to the smaller island of Samsø, and here they wandered for more than a year. Ide was growing up. The two of them became well known to the people of the island, and later many tales were told about the poor fiddler without a care in the world. When the war was over Jakob and Ide resumed their wandering, this time back in Jutland. They had begun to yearn for the region they came from. Before they reached home, however, they learned that everyone they knew had been killed in the war. So they did not stay in Kvorne. They went straight through the village without being stopped by a soul. Their home was no longer in Kvorne—in fact, it was as if they had never lived there.

A year later Jakob and Ide reached Skagen again. They went out on the spit, turned their back to the two seas shouldering roughly up against each other there, and looked back over the land spreading out so far to the south that they felt dizzy. Jakob laughed and took his mute comrade by the hand. Then they walked down along the northern shore.

They were buffeted by the fall winds, and they often had to dash up on the dunes when a big wave rolled in and covered the beach where they were walking. It was cool and visibility was good. Gulls wheeled silently against the wind, and bitter foam flew from the waves high up on the shore, then hung on the sand and trembled in the wind like shivering birds. The clouds were low, moving in steadily from the northwest.

In the evening Jakob and Ide came to a fisherman's hut, the only one that could be seen on the desolate beach. Jakob stood outside the door and ran his bow briskly over the violin strings from the lowest to the highest. The door opened immediately and a face appeared, the deeply moved face of an old man. Three or four small children came tumbling out, one on top of the other.

What a marvelous sound! Jakob played again, and it was like gold and diamonds and brightly colored cloth. The violin was like a big star, sending out flames of red and blue and yellow and white. From its impetuous heart it conjured up a vision of flowers.

"Please come in," invited the old fisherman solemnly when Jakob had finished playing. Then they were seated and food was brought to them. The family's joy over having music in the house was unbounded.

Too old to be useful now, the fisherman lived on with his son, receiving from him measured sustenance and meager regard. When Jakob had played a little more the old man suddenly began to pound the table.

"My son's on the water today," he exclaimed with a meaningful look in his eye. "Today I'm the one who decides here. Sørine!"

But his daughter-in-law was so gentle, and the old man's anger softened. He stood up at the end of the table, perky, clad in white homespun and house cap, his hair and beard like yellow straw. Now he was again the man he once had been.

"Sørine, bring the bottle!"

Zing! Jakob's fingers galloped up and down the violin, but then he went over to a soft, caressing melody while the bottle was carried to the table.

It was schnapps, and that evening the hut was not lying there in the shifting sand as a mean shelter from the fall storm and the darkness. The light from the burning peat shone like the sun, and the warmth of southern realms wafted down from the roof. Soon the whole room lifted into the air like a fiery coach. The driver was Jakob, who assumed a devil-may-care countenance and flailed away on his violin, while the old fisherman swayed on his seat, transformed by renewed youth, and the angelic faces of Ide and the children bobbed above this sky-borne conch shell. The waves boiled out on the beach and the storm drove the drifting sand against the pig bladder pane, but it was the stars that dusted them as they rode in state through all the seven sparkling heavens.

Early the next morning Jakob awoke in a sorry state. He woke Little Ide and they slipped away from the family, who lay sleeping with expressionless faces. They continued down the coast.

228

The fall caught up with them and they came into the time of short, destitute days, the time when awareness dawns that all migratory birds have left the land and cold is creeping into the air.

And then one day, when they were wandering away from the coast and into the countryside with the church at Vestervig constantly before their eyes, the first snow of the year fell.

# 37. At Sønderborg Castle

But spring and summer came again. Jacob and Ide traveled over the whole of Denmark. It was as if every part of the country was longing for them. They moved about more and more restlessly, even though they had almost forgotten why. For seven years they tramped the highways and byways. Everyone knew them and opened their door to them when they came, but they were especially familiar to those who lived around the Limfjord, where they spent a good part of the year. Later many anecdotes were told and retold about Jakob the Fiddler, and his songs were also sung faithfully for many years. He was quite a fellow, Jakob was. He was great at singing and playing, and there were tricks and stunts in him when he was on the bottle, which he often was. There was a story about how he played for a dance one night in the grove near Bjørnsholm. He was in his cups, and when they found him the next morning he had lost his bow. This didn't stop him though—he just took his walking stick, put resin on it, and played with it so that everyone marveled. Yes, he certainly had grit!

But then one year Jakob the Fiddler and Little Ide did not come to the Limfjord. People also missed them everywhere else in the country, and they never turned up again.

What happened was that Jacob had finally found out where Mikkel Thøgersen was, Ide's grandfather, and they immediately set out for the island of Als. Ide was nineteen years old now, so it was high time to get her properly placed.

One day early in October they sailed over Als Sound. The woods were billowing on the shore, fading at the edges now, and the red castle lay free out to the water. When they had nearly reached shore a big flock of snow-white doves flew up from the tower and cast themselves out over the sound, disappearing and then reappearing against the pale blue sky. Jakob watched them and nodded to Ide. It was a good omen. They were sitting in the ferry, cheerful and hugging their bundles. Jakob looked at his wooden shoes and saw that one of the straps had broken. Yes, it was high time . . .

But luck was not with them right away. The first day they were denied entrance to the castle, so they had to seek lodging in town. The next day Jakob managed to speak with the commandant, Bertram Ahlefeld, and he agreed to think it over. Indeed, there are many levels of authority to clear on the way in to the king. Finally the third day they made it over the drawbridge and got permission to play in the outer courtyard for the guard and those serving at the castle. But when at noon they were finally received by the commandant again, a new problem had come up. Mikkel Thøgersen, the one they'd come to see, was about to set out on a journey.

They did manage to see him though, but only from a distance. The commandant permitted them to go into the castle courtyard, and just as they got there Mikkel was about to mount his horse. The old man was at the bottom of the steps, and two steps up stood the king, talking to him. Jakob and Ide remained standing under the arch of the portal, not wanting to go in as long as the king was there.

It took some time to get Mikkel underway, what with all the preparations. The horse kicked and scraped on the cobblestones and the king's voice resounded in the high courtyard. There seemed to be little progress. Mikkel Thøgersen was dressed in fine new clothing—green hose and a brown doublet. He kept walking around the horse, sticking his finger in under the saddle cinch and checking the bridle. It was a young and spirited horse, and Mikkel, with weak knees now, did not seem too eager to come up on it.

"You must be about ready, Mikkel," shouted the king, laughing peevishly. "Up with you!"

Mikkel inclined his head courteously and completed his investigations. Now it was time to do it. The young man who stood holding the horse by the bit stretched back as far as he could to give Mikkel a hand. At the same time he looked furtively up to an open window in the kitchen where the faces of a pair of girls were peeking out, twisted with laughter. Mikkel got a foot in the stirrup and pulled himself up, slowly and sedately.

"Careful you don't fall off the other side!" shouted the king with a nervous laugh. No, Mikkel landed safely in the saddle. And when he was sitting properly he straightened his hat and turned his white-bearded face with injured dignity to the king.

"Farewell, Mikkel," said the king, moved now. "Take care that you come back safely."

"Thank you, Your Majesty," answered Mikkel. Breathing heavily, he took the reins and screwed his white moustache resolutely up under his nose. Then the man let go of the horse and it broke into a trot. Mikkel swayed feebly in the saddle.

"No, he'll never make it," shouted the king, pounding the balustrade. "No, no, no!" But Mikkel did make it. He stiffened his body and took control of the horse. The watchman held the gate open for him and he rode through straight as a ramrod, right past Jakob and Ide. The gate was closed immediately behind him, and they heard him ride across the outer courtyard and thunder out onto the drawbridge.

When it was quiet again in the courtyard the king turned on the steps to go in. He stood for a moment, talking to himself, and then he caught sight of Jakob and Ide.

"Who are you two?" he demanded, coming down from the steps and looking over at them sharply. He placed himself in front of them and looked from one to the other with the greatest interest.

Jakob could not answer because he had completely lost his composure. Ide stood there with her fine, empty face, gazing directly at the king. He snorted with vigor and looked at them searchingly.

"Who are you anyway?"

"We're traveling entertainers," stammered Jakob, He drew a breath and found his courage again. "We're the kind that are on the road a good deal. This little girl here is actually the grand-daughter of the man who just rode away."

"Hmm. Well. A relative of Mikkel's, eh? Perhaps you've come to visit him? It's a pity that he had to leave just now. Why didn't you speak to him?"

"Oh goodness, no." Jakob smiled with enormous politeness, lowered his eyes, and made a circle in the sand with his stick.

"All right then," said the king gently. They remained silent while he looked at them.

"Yes, all right," he said again, more strongly now. "Nothing's lost yet. Mikkel will come back. You can . . . you can stay here until he does. We'll just arrange it with Bertram. Come this way. So you play, do you?"

"Yes!" Jakob tapped his violin bag with shy happiness while they were moving off. The old king led the way, clearing his throat and in the best of spirits. Yes! Everything would soon be in order. Yes, yes!

They went to parley with the commandant. Jakob and Ide stood at a respectful distance while the king spoke on their be-half. Bertram Ahlefeld listened obligingly and with equanimity. He was much taller than the king but he did not incline his head.

The king looked up at him, speaking with great spirit and moving around to the other side. His request was honored and he thanked him warmly, but Bertram Ahlefeld maintained the cool distance of a subordinate.

The king himself walked in his worn-out shoes over to the outer courtyard and saw to it that Jakob and Ide were quartered in one of the buildings there. In the evening they played for the king in the tower room, where he spent most of his time. They were treated to wine, and Jakob played his dance tunes with all the finesse at his command. The music sounded so strange here between these walls. The king's spirit was eased, and then he became melancholy, sitting with his jaw in his hand. The wax candles burned on the table where the clasped Bible lay open.

The wine was beginning to liven Jakob up. A slight spasm passed over his face as he obliged with a wild polka. Thin and pretty, Ide stood beside his chair with her triangle.

In between numbers Jakob asked when Mikkel might be coming back again. He tossed the question off carelessly so the king could ignore it if it were improper. But the king answered evenly that it was a matter of ten or twelve days.

Then the king fell silent, and Jakob thought it best to say nothing more. He played everything he could remember. Once while he was sitting with the violin under his chin and trying to think of a new tune, he stole a glance at the king's relaxed and venerable features. At just this moment the king looked up, and he noticed that Jakob was a wreck of a man.

"Shouldn't we have some more?" asked the king warmly, lost in his thoughts.

Jakob played on, stamping out the beat of the Wooden Shoe Waltz with his heel.

The king had them stay with him the whole evening. He felt so alone—this was the first time in nine years that Mikkel had been away from the castle. The watchman had sounded midnight from the tower before Jakob and Ide were allowed to go, and by this time both the king and Jakob were dead drunk. Before they left, the king laid his hand on Ide's shoulder and judged her figure with the restrained boldness of an old connoisseur, now on his best behavior.

Jakob and Ide were passed out through locked doors by the castle keeper, an extremely sullen fellow. The watchman down at the gate was a more jovial type. He shined his light on Ide and discovered how fine and fair she was. Then he raised the lantern slyly so that they were standing in the dark, and he put his big hand roughly on Ide's hip. She cast herself to the side and let out a bellow, deep and primitive, as if it were coming from a nameless animal. It echoed under the arch of the portal and was heard over the entire castle.

Merciful heavens! The watchman staggered and backed away into the portal. Shutters and windows all over the great castle, above and below, were thrown open, and frightened voices called out sleepily, asking what had happened. The commotion died down only slowly, long after Jakob and Ide were safely in their rooms.

Also the king heard Ide's roar. He had been standing at the window, looking out to see what the weather was like, and he sprang far back into the tower room. The hair crawled on his scalp and he stole over to the door, put out his hand, and checked to be sure it was locked. Yes, it was properly locked and bolted. He drew his breath deeply, walked trembling over to a chair and sank into it, mortally exhausted. Then he opened the Bible and began to read with the candles close to him. From time to time he raised his head from the book without a sound and stared out over the sputtering flames of the candles, his eyes fixed and frightened.

235

His calm returned gradually and he ventured away from the table, lighting more candles. Then he gave himself over gratefully to the Book of Ruth. He sat there with his great white head among the candles, eagerly reading the story from beginning to end. When he was finished, a recurring thought began to trouble him—as always when he had been immersed in Scripture and was then drawn back to the things of this world. It was the realization that his friends were dead and gone. All of them had long since perished.

He sat for a while, running his hand through his hair. Then he put out all the candles except for three. He kneeled solemnly in the center of the tower room and said the Lord's Prayer, slowly and half whispering, until his account was settled. Then he got into bed, with the candles still burning, and lay there with his hands folded over the fur blanket and his eyes quiet and wakeful.

In this room he had now lived for eleven years. Here it was that he had stalked from wall to wall like a beast of prey when the first months of confinement had thrown him into a frenzy. Here he had sweated, eaten, and drunk like a madman, fallen asleep in the evening intoxicated and raving, only to wake in the morning with scathing curses in his mouth. Here he had paced up and down, kicking the dilapidated chairs, and here he had fired pewter mugs against the wall so that they fell flattened to the floor. Here he had walked about with the sound of the breath in his own hairy nostrils filling his ears.

The expression on the king's face changed constantly as he lay there in the alcove, looking into the candlelight without being able to fall asleep. Shadows passed over his brow, but then he lay quiet again.

Suddenly he laughed, and it was the deep, happy laughter from the old days. He remembered the young woman that Ditlev Brokdorp smuggled in to him eleven years earlier, when he had lain down on his bed and refused to get up. He had certainly been happy with that girl, and she was truly beautiful. But it was a sin, a grave transgression. God protect her, wherever she was now!

The king sighed deeply and looke˜d into the candlelight with tear-filled eyes. He hoped to fall asleep soon, with thanks to Our Lord, who frees us gently from all distress and turns to dust the impatience of our heart.

# 38. Carolus

Mikkel Thøgersen rode over the drawbridge. But when he
came out in the open air he felt faint and nearly fell off
the horse. The wide vistas in all directions made him giddy and
he felt that he was being torn asunder. He rode the short distance
down to the ferry, hailed the boat, and was taken across. But he
came no farther that day. Sick and confused, he was forced to go
into the ferry inn and directly to bed. The next morning he had
regained his courage, and he managed to lighten his money bag a
bit at the inn. Now he began to look more cheerfully on the whole
trip, which he had feared from the moment it was decided that he
should take it. He and the innkeeper drank a little together that
morning, but then suddenly Mikkel was eager to be off and he
ordered that his horse be readied.

"I'm on my way to Lübeck," he said with an air of importance. "It's a long journey, and I'm being sent on this mission by
the King."

Saying no more, he assumed the silence befitting a states-
man privy to matters of great moment.

"Bring forth my steed!"

The innkeeper learned no more, but his interest was surely
limited anyway. Mikkel was slightly tipsy, and his eyes rolled as
he mounted the horse and tossed a large coin in the dust for the
stable boy. And—wonder of wonders—the hardy old man actually
cut quite a smart figure as he galloped off down the highway, a
veritable hotspur.

Mikkel took his traveling seriously. He stopped at every inn
on the road, and at each stop he let it be known that he was on an
important and urgent mission for the king. People wondered about

238

the decrepit old man and considered whether he might be a demented and defrocked cardinal or a colonel who had been mustered out, or perhaps a senile carnival quack. With his high forehead he looked like a man of rank, but he downed his schnapps like a soldier of fortune. He commanded respect, but nevertheless everyone laughed behind his back. What "mission" was it he was talking about? It must be an urgent matter indeed, one requiring extensive experience, seeing they had sent such a ramshackle specimen out to perform it—and that at full gallop too. But they had to admit that he could keep his lips sealed. No one got the slightest inkling of what he was about.

When Mikkel had been on the road a couple of days, rain and wind set in, with the leaves whistling through the yellow forests. This weather was too much for him, and he stopped at an inn and went to bed sick. Here they thought he was about to go to his reward, but no, he was on his feet again early the next morning. He climbed shakily into the saddle, sped through Schleswig, and finally arrived in Lübeck more dead than alive.

Mikkel took lodgings at "The Golden Boot." The rest of the day he relaxed and ate well. The next day he slept until noon and then repaired to the town hall cellar. But this was the end of private pleasure as far as this trip was concerned. Now the important thing was to see to the mission. He asked the innkeeper where he could find Veilchenstraße.

Veilchenstraße! The innkeeper looked at him with arched eyebrows. Hmm! Well, yes, he could indeed give him directions. He did, and Mikkel set out. By that time it was late in the afternoon and he almost didn't find it. It turned out to be a narrow passage which was quickly sinking into darkness. Up in the windows sat plump young women, and more than one of them called out to Mikkel in raptures, as if she recognized a long-lost, dear friend. Mikkel paid no attention to them, however. At length he found the house he was looking for. It was only a single bay wide and there were no windows in it, just two shutters high up. Over the door hung a brass basin covered with verdigris. The door was locked. Mikkel lifted the knocker and let it fall.

Several minutes passed, but Mikkel was patient. Finally he heard steps inside and then a key was stuck in the latch. Instantly Mikkel remembered for some strange reason the time many years earlier when he had whispered through the keyhole in St. Nicholas's Church in Copenhagen. The door was opened a crack and Mikkel saw a face with large black spectacles.

"Is it Master Zacharias?" asked Mikkel.

"Yes, sir," was the softly whispered answer.

Both were silent for a moment. Then Mikkel began in a quiet voice to explain the reason for his visit. Zacharias had hardly heard mention of the king before he opened the door wide with a formal bow.

"Come in, come in!" he shouted, his voice coarse and harsh. "Ah, so! My dear friend!"

Mikkel stepped across the threshold and Zacharias locked the door again. They were standing in the darkness and Zacharias struck fire, lit a piece of wood, and led the way to the steps.

"Follow me. There's more light up above."

They came up into a large room. Light was coming from a window out to the courtyard, but nevertheless the room was gloomy and sinister. Mikkel saw the skeleton of a crocodile and several bird skins hanging from the ceiling. The floor was covered with books and old clothes, and a globe stood on the table between piles of dusty papers. Shelves on all sides held bottles of many different sizes. There was an unpleasant, stale smell of medicine in the room, rather like rust or fungus.

"Just imagine!" shouted Zacharias heartily, with his earlier astonishment unabated. "Please be seated! So King Christian wishes to communicate with me, his humble, learned servant. But surely it isn't my surgical skill the king has need of?"

"No," affirmed Mikkel, cowed.

Zacharias rocked his yellowish skull back and forth, and his voice became a growl.

"We're getting old, *Mikkel Thøgersen,*" he said, taking Mikkel by surprise. He had stretched his head forward now and fixed his eyes on Mikkel.

Mikkel started and looked up, open-mouthed. "How do you know . . .?"

Zacharias began to rock his head again, enjoying his triumph.

"Yes!" he said. "Yes!" But this was the end of the joke. Now he turned serious. "So!"

There was silence for several minutes. Mikkel shook his head as he looked down at the floor. Here was a man it would pay to keep on the good side of. He tipped his head slightly and looked up at Zacharias innocently.

"Old? Oh! You don't look so old. I'm over seventy. You're not that old."

At this Zacharias sprang out onto the floor, exploded in a violent cackling, and walked about with long strides. Suddenly he laughed even more horribly and snapped his fingers in front of Mikkel's face.

"No, I'm actually young!"

And, taking even longer strides, he howled with merriment and cited for Mikkel:

*Mugit et in teneris . . .*

He hooted in laughter:

*Formosus . . .*

He stalked around screeching:

*Obambulat herbis.*

241

It was a long time before Zacharias's hilarity over this searing surge of Ovid subsided.

Mikkel sat in embarrassment and wrung his old hands innocently. He thought of his reason for coming, and out of the corner of his eye he looked at the globe on the table.

His glance did not escape Zacharias's voracious scrutiny, and he ended his harangue.

"The king wishes information on heavenly constellations?" he asked hurriedly.

"Yes," Mikkel admitted, with an old man's humility and composure. So this man knew everything. . . .

"Tell me!" shouted Zacharias.

Then Mikkel explained briefly why he had come. Half a year earlier he and the king had had a falling out over a question concerning astronomy. In Jerusalem Mikkel had met a German monk who told him he was convinced that the sun did not revolve around the earth, but that it was the other way around. Later Mikkel heard the same thing in Italy. One day when he was telling the king about his journeys he happened to mention this. The king had immediately become frightfully agitated. Since then they had quarreled about it almost every day, for Mikkel had been able to see that what the monk said was quite possible. He had to agree with him when they were riding on camelback through Asia Minor, following the course of the stars at night. Furthermore, Mikkel had experienced something similar, but in a different way. Life had taught him the same thing, really. At first he had believed that he was the center of all that existed, with everything revolving around him. However, gradually he was able to observe that things only appeared that way. But the king could not accept the fact that Mikkel actually believed this, and he was outraged.

Then Mikkel fell silent and caught his breath, struck by the thought of the injustice he had suffered because of this. More than once, when the king had not been able to hold his own in the day's argument, he had gotten up stealthily at night and thrashed Mikkel in his bed in the dark.

So they had finally agreed to appeal the matter to Zacharias, who was famous for his erudition.

Zacharias narrowed his eyes. Mikkel's strangely subdued way of telling the story had rather impressed him. Such a horrendous heresy—turning the firmament upside down—Zacharias would have delighted in proposing, but in quite a different way. He stood up and bustled about the room, putting on his spectacles and leafing for a long time through various papers. Finally he came back to Mikkel. He had assumed a calculating and resolute manner, and he exclaimed in Latin:

"Excellent. We will initiate an investigation. Come again tomorrow."

Mikkel got up with difficulty and thanked Zacharias. He was about to leave, but he remained standing there and directed his eyes slowly and searchingly at all the strange bottles around the room.

"I will show you out."

Mikkel was looking at the bottles and moving his mouth. It seemed as if Zacharias could no longer read his thoughts. He sighed and chuckled.

"I'm so thirsty, Master. Now you don't think it would be possible . . .?"

Zacharias was most apologetic—he had only medicine in the house. Actually he was put out at Mikkel's baseness, and he began tonelessly to illuminate him with regard to learned folks' frugality and thrift. But he did take out a tankard anyway, as well as a pewter beaker that he poured half full. Mikkel drank from it. It was a strong Spanish wine. He drank eagerly, and then he was so fortunate as to remember a verse from Horace. Zacharias nodded in delight, and when he had taken a drink himself and let it run down, he smacked his lips.

They emptied the tankard. Then soon Mikkel recovered the Latin of his youth, making do without the subjunctives. But citations streamed from Zacharias. He told smutty stories from his student days in Leipzig, he imposed small, nasty anecdotes on Mikkel, he screamed with laughter, and soon he became quite wild. At times they were carousing in the grand old classical style. Mikkel tried to ape Zacharias and—to the very best of his ability—create the impression of a debauching alumnus. But he had forgotten many things, and he had and become stiff in his jests as well as his joints. He sat there like a broken-down old organ with holes in its bellows, and when Zacharias trod on him he perhaps produced sound at the right place, but just as often wind. Darkness fell, and the bird skins under the ceiling began to grow and flutter.

Now Zacharias was in a drunken frenzy. He stood up on a chair and recited the entire lovely metamorphosis *Europe and Jupiter.* Suddenly Mikkel looked at him with the pious simplicity of an old man, and he became almost sober. Would he be able to follow Zacharias on this path too? What was it he was sullying now?

"Do you know who I am?" hooted Zacharias.

No, Mikkel did not.

"I'm the one who flew too close to the sun. I've been near the fire. Can't you see that I am singed?"

Yes, Mikkel could. There wasn't a hair on Zacharias's hands or his reddish-yellow head, not even on his eyelids. His skin was shrunken and polished, as if it were nothing but scar tissue.

"It was in Magdeburg twelve years ago," laughed Zacharias, suddenly speaking with a subdued and grating voice. "It was there I came too near the fire. But we got the cart turned around."

His laugh was like the crack of a whip. Then he composed himself and paused significantly, his eyes burning malevolently. Mikkel sat there in complete perplexity.

"Well, shall we go up and have a look at my oracle?" asked Zacharias. "What do you say, my good fellow? You can keep a tight lip, can't you? Come!"

They lurched up the steps and went into a little room on the top floor of the building. It was dark, and Mikkel was almost pained by the smell there—a heavy, unpleasant smell, like small children or spoiled meat.

"Yes, I myself know nothing about stars or philosophy," shouted Zacharias boisterously. "I've always been a surgeon and I haven't concerned myself with the relationship between the organs or with the soul. But since I'm also in general practice as a sage, as it were, I've provided myself with an *alter ego*. There is no metaphysical question brought to me that cannot be answered. May I introduce two honored colleagues to each other?"

With this Zacharias threw open the shutter, light came in, and Mikkel saw that they were three in the room. Over at the wall on a low bench lay a creature, staring at them with deep-set, sickly eyes. But its head, of unnatural size and shape, seemed to have sunken flat on the bench. It was white as tallow and lay in large clumps.

"Yes, just look at him!" shouted Zacharias. "He's tame enough. That's my omniscient partner. His name is Carolus. At the moment he's almost without the power of speech. It takes two hours to warm him up, and it requires a monumental problem. Get up, Carolus, and say hello."

Carolus brought two wraithlike arms out of the fur blanket he was lying under, braced them against the bench, and raised himself with difficulty to a sitting position. At first it was as if the large, soft head would not follow his body, but he finally got it up from the bench. When he was sitting, his head hung like dough over his eyes and down to his shoulders.

"He's very weak today," explained Zacharias, "for he had some mighty matters to ponder yesterday. That's why he must lie in the dark. Lie down again and relax, Carolus.

Carolus sank slowly back and arranged himself and his head on the bench so that his eyes were free. His little face, unbelievably old, took on a paralyzed expression. Only his mouth, turned up like a flounder's, moved with a strange twitching, as if he were in pain.

"When he's lying like this he can be used for simpler tasks, such as calculations or memory exercises. Give him a number to raise to the second power."

"3719," said Mikkel.

Carolus closed his eyes and opened them again almost instantly.

"13830961," he answered in a weak, husky voice, rather like the croaking of a frog.

"Good!—Well, we've come with a problem for you, Carolus, and you can begin with it immediately. The King of Denmark wants to know for certain if the sun revolves around the earth, or whether it is the earth . . . *et cetera*. There you are."

Zacharias turned, still speaking to Mikkel in a loud voice. He directed his attention to a very large bell of grass-green glass, standing in a corner of the room

"Carolus was nurtured in that. Oh, it cost me a lot of money, that glass bell. It was nine years ago that I got Carolus. I bought him from a vagrant, the wife of a knacker. He was two years old then, so he's not so young any longer. I've been lucky with him. Seventeen years ago I started a child in Magdeburg in a smaller bell, but he died of an infection when he was only half as far along as Carolus. But his pedigree was not so impressive. He was the fruit of the primal relationship between quite an ordinary monk and a woman who was herself freeborn and of high rank. Carolus, on the other hand, was born a prince! *Do you know who he is?"*

Zacharias was in a frenzy of joy. He was staring at Mikkel, contempt for death flashing from his eyes. He lifted a leg and passed wind.

"If I tell you who Carolus is, then you must keep it to yourself. He is the son of the King of Denmark! Yes! He was born in Sønderborg Castle! The king had him in his prison! His mother was a girl of the people. The child was taken from her by the honorable Knud Pedersen Gyldenstiærne and given to the Gypsy woman I bought him from. I have written attestation. Yes, Carolus is the most noble branch that has ever been grafted onto the Tree of Knowledge. Carolus, son of the King, Prince of Denmark! His head has proved to be singularly expandable. I remove the skull, you see, and let the membrane over the brain develop into skin, and then I provide rich nutrition and a high temperature around the head. That's why the bell is necessary. In fact, Carolus still enjoys crawling into his bell, where he has sat for so many years, although it is now getting too small for him. He has the best head in Europe. Not only is he thorough—he's fast! There's not another apparatus like him because his body and limbs are fairy robust and not deformed. He also enjoys good health—there's good blood in him for the head to use. His sense of touch is much keener than others'. I need only *show* him a piece of iron and he begins immediately to drool. He can distinguish between metals by touch alone. Lead and all base alloys make his fingertips sweat at once, while gold or silver have a relaxing effect on him. And I must say that he's not overspecialized. He knows the number system, and I've also taught him Latin. But everything else I have kept from him, precisely so that he might be what Plato would call a Norm.

Everything is in him, he is Verity—he has the universe imprinted internally on his membranes. . . . Look at him!"

They stepped over to the bench, and there Mikkel saw that Carolus's head had become darker, with all the soft growths rose-colored now and distended. He was lying with closed eyes. Zacharias threw the fur blanket aside and showed Mikkel the pitiful, thin body, which was drawn up in the embryonic position. The limbs were growing cold and lifeless.

"He's begun now," whispered Zacharias. "See how his face registers suffering. Here, feel his pulse!"

Reluctantly, Mikkel laid his hand on the soft head, which was throbbing and already very warm.

"Yes, we can go now," said Zacharias. "He's deep in the problem. But it'll be an hour before the head is filled and extended. He looks really fine when he's completely blown up and sitting like a stem attached to his own ripe head. . . . Would you like to wait, honored colleague, and hear the result in two hours, or would you prefer to come again tomorrow?"

"Why is he lying there with such misery in his face?" asked Mikkel, with compassion and fear in his voice. He was beside himself with wine, horror, and pity.

"That's only natural," answered Zacharias. "It's simply part of the intellectual process."

"I thought wisdom brought joy," stammered Mikkel, feeling weak.

"Shall we go?" suggested Zacharias. "Ah, yes, my dear Mikkel! Wisdom doubles the number of enigmas. Carolus has told me this, the distillation of all his thought. His head weighs just over eight and one-fifth kilograms before it is warmed up, and each time he solves a problem the weight increases by five grams. Carolus has also told me that after a certain period of time all abstract thought returns to its point of departure. That is, at the same moment that the solution to a problem is approaching, the problem as such ceases to exist. But the process—which, by the way, manifests itself as suffering, and the scope of which is immaterial—the process itself is of interest and value. I don't know whether my esteemed colleague understands this? Shall we go down? I think I have another tankard below."

But Mikkel did not want to stay. He felt sick and stupefied, and he wanted to go home. Zacharias followed him down. He was not completely sober. He chattered on, mercilessly vivacious, but Mikkel was hearing nothing now. Down in the doorway they agreed that Mikkel would come back the next day for the results.

# 39. The Fire

It was evening when Mikkel staggered out onto the street. The lusty life was in full swing there. Women were singing and waving from the windows with large mugs in their hand, and soldiers and sailors moved noisily through the narrow passage. Mikkel tottered along as fast as he could. The soldiers greeted him with salvos of laughter, but he got past them and came back to "The Golden Boot," half senseless. Here he ordered wine and, quaking and choking back sobs, he managed to drink himself quickly into oblivion.

The innkeeper had the old man carried to the bed in the guest room. A few minutes later they heard him crying feebly there, and when they went in to him he was lying in the bed on his back and with his elbows at his sides, staring up at the ceiling like one damned. There was nothing to do except let him sigh and snivel until he stopped. Some hours later when they looked in on him, he was very feverish. Later in the night he fell into delirium, so they had to sit with him. His tongue loosened now, he told what he had seen, and in the morning the innkeeper went to the police and reported everything. An hour later Zacharias was in chains and his *homunculus* in the custody of the court. Now the citizens of Lübeck certainly had good reason to cross themselves.

For two days Mikkel lay seriously ill. Then he began to recover and was able to be up and about, but he was very weak and he walked with two sticks. The same day that he left town in the afternoon, Zacharias and Carolus were burned in the morning. Mikkel was at the square to see it. All of Lübeck was out, crowding into the square from early in the morning, but Mikkel got a good place up front because he was infirm. The pyre had been laid and it looked promising. There were over five cords of the very best wood in it. The executioner had piled it skillfully so that there were air ducts to create a draft, for Zacharias was supposed to be burned alive by the flames, not suffocated by smoke. The fire itself should reach him. People were expecting something special from this execution for, after all, Zacharias had some experience with this very sort of thing. He had been at the stake before and had bathed his feet in the flames. That was in Magdeburg, and for the same evil deed as now. This had been discovered during the investigative proceedings. However, on that occasion Zacharias had been pardoned at the last possible moment because he had once saved the life of the electoral prince.

At eleven o'clock the procession arrived, and the soldiers of the guard cleared a path through the crowd with their halberds. Zacharias walked behind the executioner, flanked by two of the executioner's assistants. He was barefooted and had only a shroud of course linen on his body. It was smeared with brick-red paint, which was supposed to represent flames. On his head he had a high, pointed paper cap, painted with snakes and toads and scorpions. Zacharias was hunched over against the cold and he clasped his hands to his chest. He was bitterly cold in the sharp October air, and he did not seem to have any other feelings.

Folk screamed and raged against him, stretching their clenched fists over and under the picket of lances that the soldiers had formed to restrain the crowd. Zacharias looked neither right nor left. Behind him came another of the executioner's assistants bearing Carolus, who had been placed in a sack. No one could see him. Then came the Town Council and the judges and the clergy in procession.

251

While the sentence was being read aloud Zacharias seemed indifferent—there was not even a defiant look on his face. From time to time his whole body would shiver and he seemed about to collapse, but this was because of the cold. His face was frozen stiff, and indeed the day was beastly cold. Those standing nearest noticed that the malefactor's arms and legs were a reddish color, covered with dried blood and water. He had been put to torture and washed afterward. Both his thumbs were blue and they dangled broken from his hands.

The judge finished reading the sentence, and the executioner led Zacharias forth to the ladder. He went up without protest. Then the assistant bore Carolus up on the heap of wood and took him out of the sack. Tumult broke out—the crowd screamed and brandished their fists when they saw the horrible monstrosity. Some of them swore oaths, while others sang hymns. Carolus was laid beside the stake, rising up in the middle of the pyre. A chain was fastened around Zacharias's waist.

Then the executioner went down and lit the fire. There was dead silence now over the whole square.

At first there was a great deal of smoke, and the fear spread among the spectators that the victims would suffocate. But the wood was completely dry, and as soon as the fire had bitten fast and begun to rumble in the air ducts the smoke disappeared. The wood crackled and split open with loud explosive sounds as the first bright flames leaped up voraciously between the pieces of wood, lashing out at the sinners.

Then Zacharias came forward from the stake, as far as the chain allowed, and called out calmly:

"Is Mikkel Thøgersen here?"

Mikkel was struck by a terrible fear. He averted his eyes and managed to stand there like one completely uninvolved. He hunched his shoulders and turned the crown of his hat toward the fire so that Zacharias would not be able to see him. Fortunately not a single person suspected that he was the one whose name had been called out. He let out his breath in relief.

The flames grew in intensity very quickly. As they roared up, the concussion and the heat could be felt at a considerable distance. Zacharias was moving forward and backward to avoid the fire. When no one answered his question he stood still and seemed to be preparing to say something.

At just this moment a long, ravenous tongue of flame shot up, burning his shroud and paper hat off in a single lick. He stood there naked and the crowd guffawed. He bent double and crept in to the shelter of the stake. But now the flames were leaping up on all sides and Zacharias could not remain sitting at the stake. He stood up and began to jump about in the fire in a most lively fashion and dance across the burning planks. Suddenly animal-like howls burst from his mouth:

*Mugit et in teneris formosus obambulat herbis.*

Mikkel remembered the verse, and he roared with irrepressible laughter and mortal pain.

Zacharias, silent now, collapsed and crumpled in the flames. One of his hands hung out over the edge of the pyre, and Mikkel saw how one finger after the other swelled in the fire until it burst dripping, and then turned black.

"Look! Look!" came the mighty cry from a hundred mouths among the spectators. And when Mikkel looked he saw that Carolus's head had raised up from the pyre. He was lying in the middle of the flames, apparently still alive, but his head was not sagging. It bulged out from the brow in two clearly separate halves, each of which was further divided into plump whorls.

"Look!" screamed the crowd in horror. And it was a loathsome sight. The blood throbbed in the grotesquely distended head,

253

and the veins, thick and contorting, pressed out against the skin. The entire head convulsed as if it were about to leap, as if a great struggle were taking place inside it.

"Look there!" came the hysterical scream. "Look there! Look! Look!" The veins had burst open and their black blood crept out like worms, writhing in the fire. The head split open in several places and began to char as small flames broke out all over it. But above it the fire quickly paled in color to a venomous green, then turned red again and formed crimson swirls.

The conflagration had now reached its greatest fury, a single storm of flame. There was only a little black clump left of Zacharias. Then the whole pyre collapsed and turned into a white-hot heap. The heat from it was so great that it blistered the faces of those standing nearest, and tumult and panic broke out. But then it was over.

Later many would claim that they had seen Satan dancing in the flames, blue as molten iron, and then leaping up with the smoke when the pyre collapsed.

# 40. The Voice of Winter

The king had ordered the tower watchman to sound welcome when he saw Mikkel returning. And a little more than two weeks after Mikkel's departure, the watchman did begin one forenoon—only to stop in the middle, as if he were unsure. After a moment's hesitation he began again, blowing with all his might. Mikkel returned riding, but not on his horse. He was in a cart with his horse walking behind, its saddle empty. It was raining.

Gate after gate opened before the cart and closed after it, and finally it reached the castle courtyard.

Up on the steps stood King Christian with his faded scarlet cape and a barret on his head. He had positioned Jakob the Fiddler on one side of the steps and Little Ide on the other, and now they stood formally and proudly under the dripping eaves. Jakob was supposed to play a tune in welcome. He had his violin ready, protecting it from moisture under the lapel of his coat.

The king waved to Mikkel and was all smiles. "Ho! Welcome home!"

But Mikkel remained prone in the back of the cart without returning the king's greeting.

"Good God!" The words burst from the king, and he went down to the cart, greatly agitated. "Are you in a bad way, Mikkel?"

Yes, indeed he was. He lay there colorless and with half-closed eyes, looking as if he were dead. The king laid the back of his fingers quickly on Mikkel's face and could feel that he was still warm.

"Carry him up," ordered the king, pale-lipped now. "Jakob, get the watchman from the gate. Where is everyone? Call Berent! So—grab hold of him now!"

Mikkel livened up a little as they carried him up, but he was extremely weak. They got him into his bed up in the tower room and the king sat down beside him. After an hour Mikkel began to look better. A little color returned to his cheeks now that he was lying there safe and snug.

"How is it going, Mikkel?" asked the king anxiously.

Well, not so bad. . . . But suddenly he turned weak and pale again—he was so afraid that the king would begin to talk about the mission he had sent him on.

"Where are you sick?" asked the king

"My left side is paralyzed." Mikkel's voice was not clear. Something seemed to be wrong with his tongue.

"Hmm!" The king sighed with great uneasiness. They were quiet for a time. Then Mikkel suddenly grew agitated, fumbling about with his right hand and opening his mouth, looking at the king and then away. It lay so heavy on him, the matter of the mission. Now he wanted to get it over with. Finally the king understood him and dismissed the matter—they could talk about it later. But on the way home Mikkel had prepared a story about the results of the trip, and this he wanted to get told. The king should not know the truth.

When the king saw that Mikkel was determined to tell what had happened, he tried to help him.

"So you made it down there, eh?"

"Yes," stammered Mikkel, breathing hard and looking aside to conceal his distress. "Yes. But I got no information. No, I got no information. I took sick and had to leave." Mikkel's face was covered with warm tears and he turned it to the wall.

"There now," said the king comfortingly. "It makes no difference at all, Mikkel. You should not have been sent on the trip. We have regretted it every day since you left. Now you'll just have to get well again."

The king had many words of solace for his old comrade-in-confinement, and Mikkel lay perfectly quiet in his own good bed, thankful and contrite. Later the king could see that he was falling asleep. The careworn face was beginning to relax. Half-asleep, Mikkel started twice with his eyes closed, while heartache and pain suffused his face. Then it softened slowly, and finally he was sleeping, his features expressionless. The king moved quietly away from his bed and sat down to read.

The next day Mikkel was better and on the way to at least partial recovery. But he never regained his health—he was bedridden all winter and spring until his death in March.

It was a quiet winter. The king aged a great deal in the time he was with Mikkel, watching his decline.

And time dragged on for Mikkel. He seemed unable to die. Now that he wanted to leave it, life would not leave him. Now it was avenging itself. He had never done justice to life because throughout his life he had never wanted to die. He lay quietly and admitted this to himself during the long nights when the king was sleeping and he was alone with his bleak thoughts. The wind sighed deeply and intimately outside the tower, listening to Mikkel's meditations on desolation from the depths of its great experience. The man who does not die every day will never live. But Mikkel had never wanted to die.

One day the king had Little Ide come up, and he brought her in to Mikkel. He thought he would be overjoyed when he saw his grandchild. But Mikkel turned his face to the wall. He knew nothing about any grandchild of his. He had never had any children—he had not been married. He was alone. He was more alone than the man who dies childless—he was doubly alone. Although Ane Mette *was* the one he had cared for, he had never yearned for her. His fate was to lose the very woman he got!

The king let Little Ide leave.

So there they were now, the two stormers of heaven! King Christian, who sprang onto the stage of history as burning impatience incarnate, with grandiose schemes—and became the creator of Denmark's lack of history. And Mikkel Thøgersen, who with his invincible pride and all-embracing longing became the progenitor of a fancied, far-reaching lineage. There they were, imprisoned together, each the founder of a dynasty of the imagination.

The night Mikkel died, the deep and powerful feelings of his youth returned. The moment his heart stopped beating he felt again the warmth of his true nature and the beautiful springtime of his heart.

But Mikkel had to pass through an eternity before he reached his goal. He was disappointed time and again. At midwinter it even looked as if he might survive. He was showing real spirit as he lay there in bed, and his nose had turned red again.

Once more the king had begun to rattle the mug lids with regularity, just as before Mikkel left on his trip, and they resumed their regimen in the tower room, but with one difference: Mikkel lay in bed. No longer, however, was he spared the king's unreasonableness. As before, the king demanded entertainment from him, and Mikkel sat in bed and repeated his stories from the battlefields. He had told them over and over, although his repertory was large. Mikkel had been in all the big and famous battles of Europe in his generation. He had served almost all of Europe's sovereigns and he could tell of their personal traits and appearance. What especially interested the king was battle strategy, artillery, and all the things that Mikkel had been aware of, of course, but without really noting the finer points. The king could ask endless questions, and Mikkel delved into his memory in order to satisfy him.

Mikkel had a spare and direct way of telling his stories. Incidents that he had related earlier he always repeated with exactly the same details, even if they had originated for the most part in his imagination. The king often asked for one or another story that he had heard many times, one that he found entertaining to hear again.

When the king awoke at night Mikkel also awoke immediately, as he had done for years. They could lie for several hours talking quietly, each in his alcove with the fur blankets pulled up to the chin, breathing the cold air that came into the tower room from the fireplace when the fire was out. The moonlight shone in the deep window niches through the frozen green panes. The king would turn the hourglass at the head of his bed. Time passed slowly and Mikkel had to think of some exciting new story, which he would then tell to the accompaniment of the king's "Hmm" and "Well," his approval or his head-shaking.

In the morning the king was always intense and intimidating, so Mikkel remained silent and lay quiet as a mouse while the king dressed and overturned chairs. The door was unlocked for Berent early in the morning when he came to light the fire, and when the cold was gone the king got up. He always got down immediately on his bare knees on the stone floor and said his morning prayers, which, to be sure, often sounded more like furious maledictions. When this had been attended to he would get underway with the heavy stone ball that he lifted above his head a hundred times every morning, fifty times with each arm. Mikkel could hear him counting, and his snorting became less and less bellicose as he became more and more exhausted. While he was washing he talked to himself in hot whispers. Sometimes the water would splash on the floor when he was groping among the pitchers. He would huff and puff threateningly, and if Mikkel should steal a glance at him he would be drying himself with the towel, red from the cold water, his brow and jaw rigid and his eyes darting wildly left and right.

When the king had washed himself he usually read in the Bible, with a threatening concentration, until the bolts were taken from the door and Berent came in with the morning refreshment: warm beer flavored with cloves and ginger. Mikkel received his portion and they drank without talking to each other. If the beer was too warm the king would throw the mug and its contents on the floor.

Then the king went down and walked for an hour or two in the courtyard, followed by his four servants, whose duty it was to accompany him when he moved outside the tower. The king amused himself by tramping on and shattering the white ice blisters in the gutter, or he had a crossbow brought to him so he could shoot at crows in the frosty trees outside the parapet. But if the king had received a letter he always went out in the orchard, sending the servants away and walking up and down alone a-mong the trees. It was his custom to seek this haven when mem-ories were being revived.

When the king came up to the tower room again he would be in a mellow mood and call out brightly to Mikkel. Then began the daily round of meals and devotions. Now that Mikkel was bedridden there was no longer any question of a game of ninepins. Nevertheless, the king had enough to take care of throughout the day. In fact, he was even so busy seeing to a thousand insignificant things that he had to hurry—hurry and worry, all day long! When he laid himself to rest in the evening he was exhausted and submissive to the will of God.

In the Christmas season there were lively celebrations at the castle. The king took special care that food and drink be brought up to Mikkel, who had to lie alone most of the time. There were days when the king was not in the tower at all—he was sitting in the big guardroom down in the outer courtyard, drinking with Jakob the Fiddler and the soldiers. Jakob livened things up a good deal.

When it was getting on toward closing time in the evening, the king would come tacking home, sailing close-hauled across the outer courtyard, holding course on the portal. When he had passed through it, rolling a bit, he would cruise over the inner courtyard, humming and hiccuping. Then he would salute the frosty moon and put about, his shadow following him on the white snow.

Neither was Jakob the Fiddler sober a single day in the Christmas season. And Christmas lasted all the way to Easter.

At New Year's there was such a heavy frost that everything jingled and tinkled. The sound froze over, and at night the mile-wide sheets of ice sighed and rumbled. There was a mad power in the booming of the ice. It was as if the frost were sending out bolts of lightning from coast to coast, reminders of frightful, pent-up powers.

Mikkel heard this from his bed. One night he woke the king, thinking he was dying.

"There's such a fierce ringing in my left ear," he said in an icy tone. The king got up and lit a candle. He was unsteady and his hair was disheveled—he hadn't slept it off yet. When he saw that the expression on Mikkel's face was one of fear, he decided that he probably wasn't dying. "It's only the ice, Mikkel," he said in order to comfort him Then he put out the candle and crawled back into bed.

Up in a room in the castle's left wing was one who heard the deep, eerie reports, a young soldier from the castle garrison, and his body contracted in reflex against his mute and beloved Little Ide. She could hear nothing, but she smiled in rapture when her lover in his mysterious fright sought shelter deeper in her embrace. She saw him—so big and strong—suddenly become timid, as if struck by inner terror, lying there with trembling lips and a look of forlorn confusion in his eyes. Ide loved him. She kissed him, and peace and joy came into his eyes again as he held her in his arms. They were lying in the glow of the candle, which filled the room with gold, and he kissed the fine white down on her virginal breast.

# 41. Grotte

Every night a ringing, rending sound came closer to Mikkel's left ear.

It was like the sound of a millstone, close by his head. Often he lay thinking that now he was dead. Centuries passed while he lay paralyzed, stretching out in this steel-edged song of darkness.

And yet he would wake from time to time, able to move a hand or make out the form of the room around him. But each time when the monstrous sound began again in his ear, it had come closer, boring through him shrilly and more brutally than before.

It was the same sound he had known in his youth, but then it was low and distant, a thousand miles away Later, it began to grow every time it crept in upon him. Now the clamor was so mighty that there was nothing else, and Mikkel was lost in it. It was the sound of a giant grinder.

It was the sound of Grotte, just beside him, which Fenja and Menja turn in the North Pole night.

Their mill-song will beset you. It will come from the center of your brain, like the sound of a crushing millstone. The clouds of dust from the earth that Grotte swirls up, and the shattering mill-song of Fenja and Menja—these will converge in your head.

"We're grinding," sings Fenja, "we're turning the stone, heavy as the earth. We grind sunrise for you, and cattle, and fertile fields. We grind shining skies and growing weather for you, clover, and yellow and white flowers."

"And we grind sickness and drought for you," sings Menja at the same time, "parched meadows and brooks run dry. We

263

grind hail as big as your knuckle, we spin up thunderheads in the west, darkness, lightning, and smoldering ruins!"

"We grind spring and blue waves for you," gasps Fenja. "We make summer ready in time, we grind green woods, full of songbirds. We grind love and oblivion and bright nights."

"And we grind impenetrable darkness for you," sings Menja with a grating voice, "ash-fall, blight, and winter that chills the heart of summer. We sing of fall storms, we hurl hoarfrost and freezing weather out over everything that grows, we grind all warmth out of the human spirit."

"But we also grind a new spring and new crops," sings Fenja in a fury. "We grind the solstice for you and dead calm on the sea. We grind colts for you and quivering puppies and the southern wind. We grind trees leafing out, and trust."

"Yes, and we turn the millstone so that it creaks and groans," screeches Menja. "We grind at birth and in the coffin. We grind snow and despair. My song is the last."

And now they hunch their shoulders, these angry female giants, and they plant their legs deep in the earth and turn the whirling millstone. They sing together, Fenja and Menja:

"We'll grind sun and moon for you, a riot of stars around the earth. Day and night will come and go in flashes of white and black, and the heavens will turn like a wheel. Summer and winter we'll grind like a fever—warmth will flow over you and then give way to the cold.

"But at the end we'll grind winter for you. We'll toil for thousands of years, but an ice age will come last.

"Northern lights over our heads! We'll grind endless ice for you, and storms from the north and drifting snow all year long. We'll grind the hope out of you, and we'll sing out reckonings where the figures for cold are always growing. We'll grind eternal night for you, we'll sling the sun out in far-off orbits.

We'll grind crackling icebergs, with broken rock coming down from the north and out over the earth's rich plains, and cities will be crushed by our glaciers. We'll shatter everything that bears fruit.

"And we will turn your head to stone, we will spew out desolation, we will sing with frost-filled hearts until the mill bursts."

# 42. The Fiddler's Farewell

One morning in March when the king went to see how he was, Mikkel Thøgersen lay dead. The king had expected this for a long time, but even so he was inconsolable.

It was so sorrowful for him to look at Mikkel's stiffened face. It disquieted him as much as it grieved him. He could not accept the fact that Mikkel's face no longer moved in the slightest. The king walked back and forth in the tower and wept. Each time he came over to look at Mikkel, he was lying there utterly still, no longer pale, but white. The king felt a strange panic in his heart and he gasped for breath. He could simply not understand it.

Never had the king seen such a forlorn expression as that on Mikkel's face as he lay there. Now that the features had become motionless in death, the blighted hope could be seen so clearly. The high, desolate forehead was like a cupola over perpetual silence. The eyes lay deep under the abrupt, expansive brow. They were closed, but they seemed to be gazing with an all-embracing, languorous gaze. The long, capricious nose was completely white—Mikkel was quite sober now. The four facets at the tip, which had given him an air of wisdom while he was alive, looked like a signet or a little cartilage cross. Mikkel's white moustache hung straight down from the corners of his mouth, which was clenched in bitterness. This dead mouth was a whole world of stifled torment. As a consummation the mouth had fallen silent over grief. It was like a mystic cipher, holding the key to sorrow's secret.

There lay Mikkel, keeping his silence about what he knew, but the mute features were full of reproach. Just as I thought!—this could be read on his face. What difference did it make! Now it was finished with his delusions—completely finished—and he was just lying there, submissive. The cheeks were sunken between the strong jaws. It was the hard and somber mask of a man. It was the silent confession of a dead man, one who had fought back futilely for a lifetime and stood his ground staunchly but in vain, in the midst of his own fateful misapprehensions. There lay Mikkel. On his lips were silence, the fine humility of death, and defiance, now snuffed out forever.

Mikkel's poor head was like a cast object that had squandered seventy years in the mold before it could be cooled and completed. For seventy years his face had been molten, reflecting the thousand faces of life. His eyes were like flowing metal, capturing light until a film forms over it and it becomes solid and cold, hardening, as it is meant to do. Now Mikkel was finished— the casting had come to an end.

He was laid on straw down in the castle armory, and in the days before he was buried there was great solemnity, touching everyone at the castle. The servants, fearful of the dark, did not dare go down into the courtyard in the evening. They were afraid of looking by chance at the closed gate behind which the body lay. The smallest strange sound in the dark frightened them out of their wits.

But Mikkel lay harmless in the hushed armory. Weapons and banners covered the walls, and empty suits of armor stood in gloomy rows along the walls around the bier.

The king went in to look at Mikkel every day, and he wept bitterly. Mikkel's position was unchanged. Mold was beginning to form on his forehead. The king stood shaking his head over him and crying. He was old now, the king—and this could be seen when he grieved. His mouth sagged and he was bent. The earth would soon claim him too.

Mikkel was buried in the churchyard in Sønderborg. The king was only allowed to follow him to the drawbridge. Afterward there was a great burial feast at the castle in Mikkel's honor. The king had two barrels of German beer placed in the courtyard, at the disposition of all. By evening every man was drunk. Jakob the Fiddler, brokenhearted over Mikkel's death, was carried to bed stupefied.

The days passed, and then spring came. The young soldiers drilled inside the wall surrounding the castle and the bugle calls rang out.

Early in May it was noticed that Jakob the Fiddler was behaving strangely. It started—to everyone's astonishment—when he began to kick out at something right while he was playing. Then he took to staring into corners and screwing up his face in disgust. When they asked him what was wrong, he complained about the great number of rats everywhere. The others could not see any rats.

In order to regain control, Jakob drank, but it wasn't long before he was seeing rabbits. He chased after rabbits which only he could see, and the people in the castle made great fun of him. One day to his horror Jakob met in the portal a gigantic rabbit, big as a cow. He had a violent struggle with it, calling the watchman for help, screaming, beating the air, and wrestling with it. All the soldiers at the castle stood around him, writhing in laughter. For three days Jakob's wild struggles with invisible animals were the cause of great mirth. They let him stay in the castle courtyard, where he could do no damage. There he hunted by the hour, and they saw him piling the corners full of dead rats and rabbits. He killed so many that he had to stand on his toes to reach the top of the imaginary piles. Just as he was crushing rats flat against the wall at one end of the courtyard, rabbits began springing about at the other end, and Jakob dashed after them.

From time to time he would rush out undaunted into the middle of the courtyard and grapple with a beast. Judging by the range of his feints and the size of the holds he took, it must have been a very large and dangerous one.

When it grew dark there was no one who would remain in the deep castle courtyard, which might well be haunted by Mikkel Thøgersen. Jakob had no concerns about this, however, and he often stayed there all night if no one came to take him away.

One evening at dusk Jakob saw an animal coming into the courtyard through the portal. It was as big as a load of hay and was just about to squeeze through. This was more than a match for him. The watchman could hear that Jakob was in the greatest danger to life and limb, but he didn't dare go into the courtyard until he had gotten two fellow soldiers to go with him. They found Jakob on the cobblestones in the middle of the courtyard, where he lay screaming and frothing at the mouth. He was in convulsion, and they laid him in his bed.

After several days of fever and hysteria, Jakob got better and began to play a little again. He was calm and sober for some weeks, tottering about in his wooden shoes, pale green about the nose and with a wretched appearance. Then one fine evening in May he started drinking again, and from this time on he drank heavily every day.

And then it was St. Hans's Eve, the day of the summer solstice. Throughout Denmark the bonfires were burning for the return of the god Balder. The giantess Thøk sat alone out on the field with tearless eyes, the only one in all creation who refused to weep and thus win Balder's release from Hel.

For the celebration Jakob the Fiddler bought a barrel of fine wine, using all his money, and he invited the soldiers to carouse with him. He was in fine form that evening and he played

269

with all his heart. When it was growing late Jakob sang this
brand-new song that he had made:

And now to all, good night,
I'm weary of the fight;
Your threats and pleas can't hold me
To a world that's borne, then sold me.

In my grave I'll take my ease
Under sun and stars and breeze;
Once I saw—or was I dreaming? —
Our Lord and the heavens beaming.

On my bed in the earth I'll rest
With the worst as well as the best,
With the lonely, blissfully sleeping
Down there in the earth's safekeeping.

Farewell, my jolly jug,
My lively, foaming mug;
And thanks, my bow and fiddle,
For your help with rhyme and riddle.

I leave no debt behind,
For all's been paid in kind;
And blows to my foes and brother
They'll get, no doubt, from each other.

Farewell and thanks so much
To lords and louts and such;
You're welcome to trade your sorrow
For my joy today—tomorrow.

And so farewell to each
Whose heart I've tried to reach;
If the music's less than splendid,
No matter—now it's ended.


The next morning they found Jakob hanging high up in the big silver poplar in the rose garden. A crow was sitting on his head with its claws buried in his gray hair.

# A Note on the Translation

Several Danish analysts have drawn attention to the highly varied vocabulary found in *The Fall of the King,* a richness that includes occasional use of dialect words and of what are felt by speakers of the Scandinavian languages to be foreign words.

More distinctive, however, is Johannes V. Jensen's structuring of the prose itself. Toward the end of the novel we read that "Mikkel had a spare and direct way of telling his stories." No description of Jensen's own narrative style in this novel could be more accurate and succinct. Long and complex periods, with carefully devised and balanced sections of coordination and subordination are not often found in the story. The chapters and paragraphs are, as a whole, brief and concentrated, and sentences are often built by juxtaposing short clauses and phrases, frequently without supporting connectives. It is important to note these special features of the text before examining the technique used in producing the present translation.

A basic principle has been that any language formulation derives from a deeper, nonlinguistic structure, and that close analysis of this structure must precede transfer of the material into a new language. The content of each period—that is, its deeper meaning—is of course signaled by its realization in Danish.

As in all translation, however, and especially with the type of prose found in *The Fall of the King,* any attempt to turn Danish words directly into what may appear to be corresponding English words will give an unsatisfactory result. Some may feel that such lateral movement of lexical items will help "preserve the author's intention," and that a certain amount of discomfort is the price the new reader should willingly pay for a lack of ability to read the work in its original language. In fact, a translation made in this way will often effectively block the transfer of meaning at many critical points, and it will nearly always mar the work aesthetically, which can hardly be seen as preservation of the author's intention.

The goal of this translation has been to identify with the greatest possible accuracy Jensen's deeper structures, in sequence and in scope, and then to realize them faithfully and completely in a form that is convincing for an English-speaking reader. In the years that have passed since publication of the first version of the translation, it has been possible to reexamine the entire English text. A significant number of changes have been made, most of them for the purpose of reflecting even more precisely the author's thought as expressed at the deepest level of the Danish text.

Although exact realization in English of the original material has been the central concern, occasional deviation from this goal may be noted. Expansions of geographical items will serve to orient the non-Scandinavian reader, and in a few instances slight additions to the text, amounting to camouflaged footnotes, may also prove helpful. In a dozen or so places there are short formulations not found in the original text, and these can perhaps be seen as a sort of personal signature on the translation. Typically they grow out of the new English text, and they should be considered only as slight augmentations, certainly not as emendations. The four poems are, of course, somewhat independent in form, but they have been constructed in close accord with the thematic inventory of the original poems, the first two in German and the last two in Danish dialect.

Extensive work with this novel over a period of many years has led to ever increasing regard for it, and this may in some way reflect the remarkable influence it has exerted for most of the twentieth century on Scandinavians. It is hoped that this new translation will now open the work to a larger number of readers.

## Author Biography

**Johannes V. Jensen** (1873–1950) is widely considered the first great Danish writer of the twentieth century and the father of Danish modernism. Born in Farsø, a small town in northern Jutland, Denmark, he studied medicine at the University of Copenhagen before devoting himself to writing. He was awarded the Nobel Prize in Literature in 1944. *The Fall of the King* is regarded as his most important work and perhaps the finest historical novel from Scandinavia; it was twice voted the most important Danish novel of the twentieth century by Danish book reviewers, publishers, and readers.